PAYMENT IN BLOOD

Several of the men entered the vault and began removing the cylinders. When the vault was empty, the guard turned to the hawk-faced man, obviously relieved. "And now . . . my money?"

"There is no money," the leader replied coldly. "You will receive a traitor's pay."

Behind the guard, one of the other men drew a curved Japanese sword from a sheath he carried thrust into his belt. The sword swung in a wide, glittering arc, cutting clean through the guard's neck. The severed head seemed to leap from his shoulders. Then it fell, thudding soddenly onto the concrete floor.

"I do not trust men who sell their loyalties," the leader murmured contemptuously. "There is always the danger that they will do it again."

FREE AGENT

ROBERT STOKESBERRY

AVON BOOKS · NEW YORK

FREE AGENT is an original publication of Avon Books. This work has never before appeared in book form. This work is a novel. Any similarity to actual persons or events is purely coincidental.

AVON BOOKS
A division of
The Hearst Corporation
1350 Avenue of the Americas
New York, New York 10019

Copyright © 1992 by Robert Stokesberry
Published by arrangement with the author
Library of Congress Catalog Card Number: 91-93012
ISBN: 0-380-76703-1

First Avon Books Printing: March 1992

AVON TRADEMARK REG. U.S. PAT. OFF. AND IN OTHER COUNTRIES, MARCA REGISTRADA, HECHO EN U.S.A.

Printed in the U.S.A.

RA 10 9 8 7 6 5 4 3 2 1

Prologue

The guard had been watching the clock on the wall since midnight. Now the clock said that it was nearly time. Nervousness had been growing inside him for hours; he could not stand the room any longer. In a bid to escape, he picked up his machine pistol, slung it over one shoulder, and went outside.

It was dawn but not yet sunrise. Thick mists rose from tangled waterways, pushed into swirling eddies by the faint morning breeze. A damp smell of rotting vegetation assailed the guard's nostrils. All around him was a world of water, the Nile Delta, where the great river unraveled into a hundred sluggish streams, an isolated world of heat and silence and birds, an insubstantial world, where the ground trembled underfoot.

The guard shivered. He knew that later the day would grow hot, but now he was cold. He was originally from farther south, from upriver, where the mornings were bright and clear, where the dry desert air etched the palm trees sharply against the morning sky. He did not like this delta land, and he did not like the structures that covered

1

the land around him, the central metal dome and the squat concrete buildings surrounding it, and, a hundred yards away, invisible now in the mist, but humming and crackling against the dampness, the huge wire enclosure crammed with electrical gear.

The mist gave the buildings a menacing surrealistic air. The central dome swelled up out of the earth like an immense fungus. It was the things inside that dome that most unsettled the guard . . . this was not a good place to work, not a good place for a man to be. Well, after today, if all went well, he would have enough money to quit this job. If all went well. As he waited, his nervousness continued to mount.

A hundred yards away a file of dark-clad figures moved cautiously through the mist, silent except for the occasional clink of a weapon and the soft shuffle of their feet against the damp ground. But these small sounds were quickly swallowed up by the velvety fog.

The mist parted ahead, revealing the buildings. A hawk-faced man at the head of the file sank down into a crouch, waving the others down with him. He turned to the man behind him, whispering, "There it is. But I don't see the guard."

At that moment the guard came around the corner of the nearest building. He peered into the fog, his head swiveling back and forth anxiously. At a sign from their leader the file of men rose and noiselessly approached the guard. He shrank back, barely able to make them out in the mist. "Comrades?" he called hesitantly.

The black-clad men quickly surrounded him. "Where is it?" demanded their leader.

"In there," the guard whispered nervously, pointing toward one of the low concrete structures. "But . . . you are late. . . ."

His voice trailed away as he looked into the other man's eyes. He turned quickly, toward a metal door set into a thick wall. Opening the door, he led the way into the building. The room inside was packed with electronic equipment. There were radiation warning signs on the walls.

Propping his machine pistol against a cabinet, the guard took a key from a ring and unlocked another door set into an inner wall. The door was very heavy; the guard leaned into its weight, slowly swinging it open. Inside was a large concrete-lined vault. A number of stainless steel cylinders, each about four feet long and five inches thick, were spaced on racks along three of the walls. "There they are," the guard said, stepping back out of the doorway.

Several of the men entered the vault and began removing the cylinders, two men to a cylinder. It was not easy work; the cylinders weighed more than their appearance had at first indicated. The men grunted as they picked up each one. "Do not get them too close together," the guard warned.

Finally the vault was empty, the last of the cylinders on its way out of the building. The guard turned to the hawk-faced man, obviously relieved. "And now . . . my money?" he prompted.

"There is no money," the leader replied coldly.

"But . . . I was promised!"

"You will be paid . . . a traitor's pay," the leader replied.

The guard looked puzzled, then he understood, and his face filled with fear. "No . . . no, Comrade . . . forget the money," he said hastily. "I . . . I had expenses, but it was really for the sake of the cause that I . . ."

The guard's voice had risen to a whine. He backed away from the hawk-faced man, unaware that one of the others had moved around behind him and was drawing a curved Japanese sword from a sheath he carried thrust into his belt. The swordsman's flat oriental features were expressionless as he raised the blade high over his head, both hands wrapped lightly around the long grip.

"Tsunogi . . . shut him up before he wakes the entire installation," the leader said, nodding over the guard's shoulder to the swordsman.

"Yes, Hassim."

When he heard the voice behind him, the guard started to turn, but too late. The sword swung in a wide glittering arc, cutting cleanly through his neck. The severed head seemed to leap from the guard's shoulders, then it fell, thudding soddenly onto the concrete floor. The headless body continued to stand for a moment, blood jetting from the severed neck arteries, then it fell full-length next to the head, where it lay, legs twitching spasmodically.

His face still expressionless, the swordsman flicked the guard's blood from his blade and slid it back into its sheath. Hassim walked over to the guard's body and looked down contemptuously. "I do not trust men who sell their loyalties . . . even once," he murmured. "There is always the danger that they will do it again."

He watched the twitching legs for a moment, then abruptly turned and walked outside, where the men were waiting. "Now we must hurry," he said. He pointed to the bright polished surfaces of the cylinders. "We must get them back to the rendezvous point as quickly as possible."

The men turned, moving off into the fog. The room was silent now . . . except for the joyful buzzing of flies as they discovered the congealing pool of blood on the floor.

1

_____

The golden flickering glow of the old kerosene lantern turned the interior of the cabin into a warm wooden cave, softening sharp edges, pushing the corners back into obscurity.

The lamp cast shadows. Ryan could see his own on the wall next to the bed, so closely intertwined with Inge's that it was impossible to tell where his left off and hers began. He turned from the moving shadows and looked down at her, lying beneath him. Her skin was damp, glowing golden in the lamplight. Her long blond hair fanned out over the pillow, shimmering, subtly changing color as she slowly, sensuously twisted her head from side to side. Her entire body was moving rhythmically, and Ryan's with it, but when he pushed his torso up with his arms so that he could see her more easily, she thought he was going to leave her. "Oh, no, Austin . . . please," she murmured.

"Take it easy. I'm not going anywhere," he murmured back. He began moving his body more rapidly, more powerfully. Still looking down, he watched her face change as she grew more and more excited, watched her features soften, her skin flush, her tongue flicker helplessly over wet red lips, saw how her half-lowered eyelids veiled the smoky blue of her eyes. She was staring into nothingness, twisting, shuddering, uttering sharp whimpering little cries that told him she was getting close. For a moment her face looked like the face of someone dying; it radiated an orgasmic intensity, a glowing transcendent agony, a momentary juxtaposition of death and passion. Ryan shook off the image; he'd seen too damned much of death, perhaps not enough of passion. He put his arms around Inge, drew her close as his own orgasm neared. Their two bodies strained together . . . reaching . . .

The phone rang.

Ryan stopped moving and turned toward it. "Oh, come on," Inge gasped incredulously. "You're not going to *answer* it. Not *now*?"

"It'll just take a second," he muttered. It was not that he had lost interest in Inge, it was simply very difficult to resist picking up the phone. No one was supposed to know where he was. No one was even supposed to know this number.

It was a long reach. He tried to keep his body joined to Inge's, but it was impossible. She gave a sob of anger and frustration as he rolled free of her. He lay on his back and put the receiver to his ear. "Yes?" he grunted.

"Good evening, Ryan," a smooth but oddly grating voice purred into his ear, a voice he knew very well.

"What the hell do *you* want, Central?"

"I need to see you right away."

"Forget it. I'm busy."

Ryan heard a weird sound over the phone. It took him a moment to realize that it was Central, chuckling. "I can hear you panting, Ryan. Did I interrupt something private?"

"Fuck off."

"Ten bucks against a buffalo fart you were pronging that big-titted blond broad, Inge."

Ryan's eyes narrowed. "What brought that on, Central? Been drooling over your pornography collection lately?"

"My, my, Ryan, you're developing quite a wit. What's the matter? Running out of booze?"

"Like I said, Central. Get lost."

"There could be a lot of money in it for you, Ryan."

"I don't like your kind of money. It ... smells."

Several seconds of silence followed. Ryan was about to take the phone away from his ear and hang up when Central abruptly said, "Fifty thousand dollars."

Now it was Ryan's turn to fall silent. "Fifty thousand dollars," he finally replied. "That's a lot of money. What would I have to do to earn it? Win back Vietnam?"

"Quit clowning. You know I can't talk about it over the phone. You'll have to come to headquarters ... right away."

"I'll ... think about it."

"It's important, Ryan. Important to your country, important to the whole world."

"Louder, Central. I can barely hear the violins."

Icy silence, then Central snapped, "You've got exactly fifteen seconds to let me know whether or not you're coming in."

Ryan let most of the fifteen seconds go by. "Okay," he finally said. "I'll come on in, and I'll listen, but ... no commitments."

"Fair enough. Now ... get your goddamn ass into town."

"Tomorrow. Like I said, I'm ... currently occupied."

Ryan heard Central catch his breath, but as usual he did not quite lose control. "Is she that good a jump, Ryan?" he finally asked, his voice full of cool snicker. "Okay, tomorrow. But call in the moment you reach town."

The line went dead. Ryan thoughtfully put down the phone, automatically turning toward Inge, his hand reaching out to stroke one of her breasts, which Central had so accurately described as big, unaware of her stony silence.

"Hey! Forget it!" she said angrily, pushing his hand away.

Ryan looked at her in surprise. "What the hell's the matter with you?"

"What's ... the matter?" she burst out incredulously. "You can ask me that with a straight face after ... Why, you self-centered son of a ... you stop right in the middle of making love, to answer the goddamned telephone. I mean, that's bad enough, and then you call off the last half of our vacation without even asking how *I* feel about it. Do you know how many lies I had to tell to get this week off? God, I've had it up to here with your mysterious phone calls, with your running off whenever you feel like it, with you expecting me to be waiting patiently when you finally get around to coming back. If you think I've got nothing better to do than sit around and wait, like a sweet, faithful little—"

"I thought I made the situation clear from the start," he cut in. "You had choices, which you were free to either accept or reject."

She was up on her knees, her hands on her hips, very naked, very beautiful, very sexy. "Are you pretending you leveled with me?" she asked acidly. "Oh come on now ... do you really think I bought all that bullshit about you being some kind of hotshot insurance investigator, that that's the reason you're on call all the time, the reason for the guns and that other weird stuff? Give me some credit for intelligence."

Ryan said nothing, just stared straight into her eyes, concentrating on pinning her down with "The Look." He'd seen homicidal maniacs wilt under the impact of "The Look" and it seemed to be working once again. Inge's voice faltered. She stared back at him, eyes big. "What ... what the hell are you doing?"

And then she suddenly burst out laughing. "Oh, God, I think you're actually trying to *scare* me."

Her face grew more serious, and she poked him in the ribs with her finger, hard enough to hurt. "Ryan, I ... sometimes I ask myself ... sometimes I just have to wonder ... about the kind of games you played when you were a kid."

Ryan mumbled something unintelligible.

She poked a little harder. Ryan winced. "Uh-huh. Sometimes ..." But now he could see the beginnings of a smile tugging at her lips.

"Oh, shut up, woman," he muttered, pushing Inge down and rolling over on top of her.

2

Ryan was looking at himself in a mirror. Everyone does it now and then, just to make sure they're still there, still the same familiar but inscrutable them. In Ryan's case it was an occupational habit. He liked to keep track of what was happening behind him.

The mirror was behind the cashier's desk of his favorite Washington restaurant. Ryan studied his image as he paid. He was a big man, powerfully built but not fleshy, with thick longish hair that was either light brown or dark blond, depending on the light. His big tanned face was bisected by a bushy mustache that curled down the sides of his mouth, screening his teeth. They were good teeth, white and straight, the fruit of many miserable boyhood hours spent at the dentist's. He had light blue eyes, which were looking a little morose at the moment.

He was sucking a toothpick. He watched it shift up and down in his mouth, then he turned away from the mirror and walked out of the restaurant, still savoring the meal and the aftertaste of the wine. If Central did rope him into working for him again there was no telling where he might be sent, what kind of slop he might have to survive on. And Ryan loved to eat.

He stepped out into the warmth of a late spring day, blinking in the bright sunlight after the cool dimness of the restaurant. His mood was mixed. He kept thinking about Inge, remembering the feel of her body, the effervescence of her mind. Quite a woman. There was a possibility that he might miss her. But at the same time he felt free, light, unencumbered, ready to move, unattached to anything or anyone. He decided to hang on to this second feeling and miss Inge later.

There was no point in delaying any longer. Time to call in. He flicked away the toothpick and stepped into a phone booth. He dialed. There was an answer on the third ring. "Trans-Ocean Industries," a flat, bureaucratic male voice said.

"Austin Ryan, checking in."

There was a moment's silence, during which Ryan thought he could hear the soft flutter of pages being turned; to the man on the other end of the line, Ryan was only a set of written instructions. A moment later the man spoke again, directing Ryan to a street corner a few blocks away. "Ten minutes," the voice said without inflection. Then the line went dead.

Ryan checked his watch. He debated taking a cab, but decided a walk would do him good, clear his head—there had been quite a lot of wine with the meal. It was late afternoon, a fine time for walking. The sidewalks were crowded with people, and as he walked along, Ryan covertly studied his fellow pedestrians, automatically varying his pace, alert for anyone trying to stay even with him. No one stood out. Just pedestrians. Most of them were probably going home from work, perhaps some were going on night shift. Ryan smiled. Going nuts, that's what they were really doing, going nuts, pushing, rushing, racing toward insanity, a pack of scurrying rodents operating on someone else's time schedule, living by the clock, punching in, punching out.

Deadening. He shuddered. They were following a deadening routine. Poor bastards. Ryan shook his head. He had long ago decided that his life would not follow that particular path, he could never exist that way. No routines, no schedules. He wanted his time to be his own, full of change and excitement, a constant reminder that he was still alive. If life had taught him anything, it was one simple fact ... remaining alive was, in itself, a truly marvelous accomplishment.

The assigned intersection lay ahead. There was a newspaper stand on the corner and he was tempted, but he knew how conspicuous a person looks leaning against a wall pretending to read a newspaper. People only do that in the movies. He simply walked slowly, gauging the ten minutes, and by the time he reached the intersection he saw the car turning the far corner. It was the usual big black limousine. He stepped off the curb as the car pulled up next to him. When he reached for the rear door handle he heard the sharp click of an electronic lock. Before he stepped into the soft luxury of the car's interior he took one last look behind him at the sidewalk people. Some were looking at him enviously as he prepared to leave their midst in such style. Some looked bored. One little old lady actually looked happy for him. He smiled at her and closed the door. Another metallic click told him that he was locked in.

As the car pulled away from the curb, the windows began to darken. Ryan didn't understand the technology behind it, but within seconds he could no longer see out, and since the backseat was closed off from the driver's compartment, he was effectively locked inside a plush, moving black box.

Ryan settled back against the seat. He knew he had at least a half hour's drive ahead of him, which didn't necessarily mean he was going very far. Usually the driver zigzagged through the streets in apparent circles. The first time Ryan had made the trip he'd amused himself by trying to memorize each turn, but after the twentieth one he'd given up, and since then he'd no longer bothered. He was simply on his way to Central.

The first time he'd run across Central, Ryan had already been in his present line of work for several years. Originally he had worked for one of the big federal agencies. They called it an intelligence agency, which Ryan found amusing. The bungling stupidity, interdepartmental rivalry, career throat cutting, touchy egos, and political treachery were overshadowed only by a mountain of paperwork that threatened to bury the entire system.

Ryan was not really employee material. Because of his nonorganizational proclivities he didn't last long with that particular agency, but he did gain experience and training in the essentials of the trade: codes; weapons; memory training; shadowing techniques; fake identities—how to blend into a foreign scene, how to be another kind of person; all the basics. What he did not learn was how to take orders and follow them without question. Nor would he ever learn. He was a born loner, a free-lance, an anomaly in the intelligence world, where everything is supposed to be a team effort. He should have been destroyed early, but, paradoxically, his lone-wolf approach acted as a kind of camouflage. Everyone was so busy looking for the rest of his team that they missed Ryan himself.

When he'd first branched out on his own as a free-lance it had been hard going, but he'd slowly begun to build a reputation, because he got results, often under the most difficult conditions. But that kind of reputation also had its negative aspects. More and more frequently he found himself being called in only when the situation had become so dangerous that an agency hesitated to hazard its own people. So far, Ryan's special talents had always gotten him out alive, but he was beginning to wonder how long that kind of luck would hold.

His first job with Central's organization had been particularly messy. By the time he'd extricated himself, there were bodies everywhere, fortunately not including his own. The only good thing about the experience had been the money.

Good money. Central paid well. But was it worth the inevitable hassle, the bad feelings, the ugly memories that usually came wrapped up in a Central operation? Ryan wondered about his own greed, which had pushed him to work for Central too damned many times. Well, of course, he usually needed the money, he was always broke. After all, why risk your life if you don't intend to live well? Or was it the very fact of risking one's life that pushed him to spend money like it was water? That kind of money never seemed quite real. Maybe he had to spend big to prove to himself that it was all worthwhile. Maybe he wasn't as free an agent as he thought.

Nevertheless, he'd continued doing jobs for Central, but early in the relationship he'd decided to try to learn what he could about Central and his organization. He looked up an old friend who'd been in the business for a long time. He found him in a bar, drinking . . . the usual occupational hazard. When Ryan started probing his friend about Central's group, the man stared down at the bottom of his glass for a long time. "Rough bunch," he finally murmured. "Very, very heavy."

Ryan pumped his friend by the simple expedient of buying him lots of drinks. As the liquor flowed, so did the information. The man told him that few people even knew that Central's group existed. It had been formed by a particularly paranoid president as his personal intelligence agency. The normal funding channels were avoided; it was in essence a self-sustaining organism, answerable to none of the usual watchdog agencies, since officially it did not exist. From the beginning, it used its resources to gather information about anybody in government who mattered, anyone who could be used, intimidated, bribed, or rewarded, the usual things.

After that particular president left office, the new organization did not want to give up its existence, normal enough behavior for anyone feeding at the public trough.

Fortunately for them, they had enough dirt on enough people to ensure a grudging support. That kind of knowledge meant power. As Ryan's friend put it, "They grew like a mushroom in horseshit." With the people who should have done something about it prudently looking the other way, Central's group was very close to being accountable to no one.

So there they were, waxing fat and healthy on the rich meat of unlimited funding, by now both public and hidden, snug in their warm cocoon of national security, so secret, so tightly run, that they could work close to the edge, which was perhaps why they paid their agents so well. But despite the high pay, Ryan did not like working for Central. He always felt uncomfortably expendable.

Ryan sat up straighter as he felt the car slow down, turn, bump over a sill, then go down an incline. A moment later he heard the sound of a powerful electric motor. Something heavy and metallic clanged shut. The limousine's door clicked and Ryan knew that it was no longer locked. He was at Central's headquarters.

3

Ryan opened the car door and stepped out into the brightly lit glare of a large underground garage. One of the driver's windows rolled partway down. Ryan caught a shadowy glimpse of the driver's face. The driver started to say something, but Ryan was already turning away, heading toward an elevator door set into a wall about thirty yards away. When he reached the elevator, he punched the call button. A second later the door slid open smoothly. He stepped inside and thumbed the single control button. The door shut and the elevator began to drop, nudging Ryan's stomach up toward his throat.

It was a fast elevator. Ryan was wondering how deep into the earth he was when the elevator braked to a stop. The door opened onto a long concrete corridor, with a massive metal door at its far end. Ryan left the elevator and headed down the hallway, which was about forty yards long. Other, less impressive doors were spaced along the hallway, but Ryan headed straight toward the metal door, idly speculating on the cost of constructing all this high-tech secrecy. Probably equal to the annual budgets of some of the smaller countries. But then, genuine paranoia tends to be expensive.

There was a shiny black plate set into the wall next to the big metal door. Ryan pressed his palm against the plate. There was a moment's wait, and then the door slid open slowly and smoothly. Ryan shrugged. He'd always wondered what would happen if someday somebody showed up with just his hand and pressed it against the plate.

When the door had opened far enough, Ryan quickly moved in through the opening; he hated to stand framed in a doorway. The room he stepped into was big, or at least he thought it was big; he couldn't see all of it, most of the lighting was directed toward him, not blindingly, but with enough brightness so that he could not easily see past the front of the room. There was a big raised desk, not unlike a judge's courtroom bench, situated about fifteen feet inside the room. A figure was seated at the desk, but with the light coming from above and behind the desk, Ryan saw only an outline. He assumed that the figure was Central. Assumed, because he had never actually seen Central's face.

A chair had been placed in front of the desk, just inside the doorway. Ryan sat down in the chair, aware of the sound of the door sliding shut behind him. The chair was not particularly comfortable, nor, Ryan suspected, was it meant to be.

He had a considerable wait. There was no sound from the desk except for an occasional rustle of papers. Finally the figure behind the desk spoke. "I suppose you're wondering why I plucked you from Inge's sweet body."

Yes, it was Central. No mistaking the odd grating quality underneath the surface smoothness of the voice, as if a cleverly made but not quite perfect machine was trying to speak.

"I'm here. . . . I'm listening."

Uncharacteristically, Central got right to the point. "A

group of terrorists just hijacked a large amount of pluto-nium."

Ryan's eyebrows rose. "Weapons grade?"

"Not quite. It'll take some processing. But there's more than enough to build a bomb. They lifted it from an Egyptian nuclear power plant. They killed a guard, but we suspect that he may have been in on it, initially."

"And so you figure . . ."

"That they're going to build a bomb? Probably. It would be naive to suppose otherwise, especially with the additional information we have. A nuclear physicist is missing. He's from one of the Warsaw Pact countries, Hungary. His name is Ernst Kranek. He has a rather messy background; drinks too much, and is supposed to be in poor health, but despite all that he has a reputation as a competent enough nuclear physicist. I suppose you could say *glasnost,* or *perestroika* did him in. No more sinecures in the good old Eastern ex-Bloc. He lost his job in the shuffle, then drifted to the West. He was last seen in France, where he disappeared under . . . interesting circumstances that might tie him to this particular terrorist group. The one we think stole the plutonium. Our guess is that Kranek is the man who's actually going to build the bomb."

Ryan shrugged. "Lot's of suppositions. And even if a bomb is actually built . . . which may not be as easy as you make it sound . . ."

"We have to assume that they'll succeed," Central said dryly. "And assuming they succeed, if they actually do build a workable bomb, we doubt they'll use it for humanitarian purposes."

"Well, one man's terrorism might be another man's humanitarianism."

"I see you're still dabbling in sophomoric philosophical speculations."

"Sure. I'm speculating right now on why you called me in here."

"That should be obvious. We'd like you to get the plutonium back, or failing that, see that the bomb is never actually built."

"Oh, really? Just like that?" Ryan asked, amused.

"Don't be snide. We have leads, of course, or you wouldn't be here. One of our Mediterranean operatives thinks he's spotted Kranek on the Spanish island of Majorca. If you find him, I suspect that you will have found the terrorists."

"You must have plenty of people working in the Mediterranean. Why not just have some of them follow Kranek?"

Central gave an exasperated snort. "Our people can't move. The whole area's crawling with operatives: the KGB, the Chinese, the British, the CIA. Even the goddamn Cubans. This is a hot issue, Ryan. Nobody, East or West, is particularly happy about the possibility of anything as potentially destructive as an atomic bomb ending up in the hands of a bunch of nuts. With all the instability in Eastern Europe and the Middle East, no one can afford any wild cards. That's why all the traffic. Our local people are known. If they go after Kranek, they'll simply lead the rest of the pack straight to him."

"So what? If it's of such international concern . . . Oh, of course. It matters *who* gets the plutonium back."

Central chuckled. "I didn't know you were so politically conscious, Ryan. Of course it matters. You hear a lot of nattering about the end of the Cold War. As far as I'm concerned, it's just entered a much more subtle phase. We're way ahead on points now, especially after the Gulf War."

A moment's silence, then, with intensity: "We want to stay ahead, Ryan. We want to make certain we're in control. All the way. Most important of all . . . if the other side breaks this thing, they'll simply hush it up. After all, terrorists used to be, in general, *their* boys and girls. Now, if we break it, we could end up with even more leverage. That is, as long as it's kept out of the fumbling hands of the CIA, or—"

"You disgust me, Central." Ryan slowly shook his head. "Here we have a bunch of nuts with a potential atomic bomb, and all you can think about is scoring points . . . even if it gives these idiots a greater opportunity to build their bomb."

"Oh, it needn't come to that. You'll be able to—"

"Give me a break, Central, or do you really think one man's going to be able to take a fascinating toy like a potential atomic bomb away from a terrorist group sharp enough to steal it in the first place? What you're talking about is clearly a team operation, and you know damn well I work alone."

"You don't have to take the plutonium away from them, Ryan. Just take away Kranek. No physicist, no bomb. You simply have to make certain that he's . . . no longer around."

"Damn it, Central! I'm no hit man!"

"Oh? If I got the wrong idea, I got it from your record."

Ryan stared up at Central's silhouette. "Have you ever killed anybody?" he asked in an icy voice. "I mean, personally?"

Central seemed amused. "With my own hands? Don't be absurd. I don't need to, not when I can use other people. Like you, Ryan. You're such a fine tool, such a strong right arm. . . ."

Central's voice trailed off into a weird laugh. Ryan sat quietly for a few seconds, still looking up at the desk. "You can shove this one," he finally said. "I'm not going to do it."

"You don't actually have to kill Kranek, you know. You can just take him out of the area."

"Not even that way."

"Not even for fifty thousand dollars?"

"Not even if you promise to kiss my ass."

"Oh . . . you'll do it. You'll take the assignment," Central replied, his voice still showing signs of amusement.

Ryan abruptly stood up. "Your money doesn't mean a fucking thing to me, Central. Time is what counts. Time. Not money, not power, but time. That's all we really ever have. It's something money can never buy back. My time belongs to me, and I decide who I rent it to. Rent it, Central, not sell it. I'm a free man, a free agent, and as a free man, I think your proposition sucks."

Central chuckled. "Ah, yes ... the ever-recurring illusion of personal freedom. You're in the wrong century for that, Ryan ... if there ever really was a time when personal choice existed. Did you ever read George Orwell? He may have been a little overdramatic when he wrote *Animal Farm* and *1984,* but he pegged our century pretty clearly. Everything has its price ... particularly freedom."

"I'm ready to pay it. Now open the fucking door. I want some fresh air."

"You'll take the assignment, Ryan."

"The hell I will. Now open the door or I'm coming over the top of your desk."

"I forgot to tell you who stole the uranium," Central said silkily.

Ryan looked up warily. "I don't think I want to know."

Central ignored him. "A splinter group of Palestinian terrorists ..."

"So, what's new?"

"... allied with some Japanese terrorists."

Ryan turned pale. Central chuckled. "Yes ... the Red Dragon Brigade, Ryan. I think you know them ... the group run by that woman."

"That's not possible! She's dead. She's got to be dead. It's been so long ..."

Central chuckled again. "She's not dead, Ryan. She's alive ... and obviously in business again."

"You bastard," Ryan half whispered.

"She's still running it, Ryan. She's resurrected it. She's right in the middle of this plutonium thing. Now ... do you still want out?"

Ryan sank back down into his chair. "I . . . don't know. I . . ."

"Make up your goddamn mind!"

"I . . . yes. . . . Okay, I'll go, damn you."

"Good. You'll have to leave at once. We can't waste time. Are you armed?"

"Of course."

"You'll have to leave your weapons here. You can't take them on the plane, not the way you'll be traveling. I'll make sure you get them back when you reach the other side of the pond. Drop them on the floor next to your chair."

Ryan reached back toward the right side of his belt, under his jacket, pulled out an automatic pistol, and placed it on the floor.

"The knife, too."

Ryan swore under his breath, but leaned forward and quickly unstrapped a sheathed knife from his lower leg. It joined the pistol on the floor. "Try not to smear your fingerprints all over them," he said. "They'll rust."

For the first time Central lost a little of his mocking cool. "I know how to handle weapons," he snapped. "Now, get your ass in gear. There are briefing instructions in the upstairs office. Read them, destroy them, and go. Try not to miss your plane."

Ryan smiled as he stood up. "Handy with knife and gun, is that it, Central?"

The big steel door slid open behind Ryan, a wordless invitation to leave. Ryan stepped out into the corridor, then turned and faced Central again. "Ever go out on a job yourself?" Ryan asked.

"That's for me to know, you to guess," Central replied stiffly.

Ryan laughed. "It'd do you good, Central. You spend too much time in this claustrophobic gopher hole. You're rotting. Why not get out with the troops once in a while? Build morale. See how the peasants live."

"God save us from amateur comedians," Central grated.

He must have pressed a button then, because the massive door slid shut with a heavy metallic clang. Ryan looked at its blank surface for a moment, then turned and headed toward the elevator, laughing loudly, hoping Central could hear.

4

The charter terminal was separate from the main airline terminal. It was a big drafty building, with open iron beams spiderwebbing the metal ceiling. There wasn't much luxury inside, just a couple of washrooms and a stand selling coffee.

It was part of Central's plan that Ryan travel by charter flight. Central claimed that he would be less easily spotted than on a regular scheduled flight. The plutonium theft had generated so much international heat that all main airport terminals were under close surveillance.

So there Ryan was, standing in a long line, inching up toward the check-in counter, using his feet to push a small battered suitcase over the gritty floor each time the line shuffled forward another yard or two. Like most of his fellow passengers, Ryan was dressed casually, in his case, deck shoes, jeans, a pullover shirt, and a short blue denim jacket. It was a no-frills crowd.

He finally reached the window. The clerk looked very tired. He took the ticket and passport Central had provided Ryan. Central's people had done their usual fine job. The passport was two years old, with a goodly collection of entry stamps and visas already decorating its pages. It gave his name as John Stevens.

The clerk worked swiftly, stamping papers and tearing out tickets. "The flight'll be delayed a little while, Mr. Stevens. About an hour. We'll be loading at gate two. Please listen for the boarding call."

The clerk was already reaching for the next person's ticket before Ryan had fully turned away. His luggage tagged and gone, Ryan wandered over to the waiting section and sat down in one of the plastic chairs. It was not a particularly lovely chair; it was bucket-shaped and was colored a hideous shade of orange, but it fit Ryan's ass in a comfortable and soothing manner, so he wondered why he kept shifting his weight around . . . until he realized that he was missing the familiar weight of his weapons. He felt vulnerable.

He covertly studied the people around him. Most seemed to be students, a harmless-looking bunch, nothing to worry about, so he diverted his mind onto the mission. Which immediately made him think about the woman. At last. He was finally on her trail, and with the weight of Central's organization behind him, there was now a chance of evening the score. How many years had it been since she'd destroyed Yoshiro? Ten? Twelve?

When he was in his early twenties, Ryan had spent two years in Japan. The move was a natural one; since his teens he had been studying the Japanese martial arts. His principal instructor in the States was one of the greatest of the Japanese karate masters, a martial arts missionary, who had come to America twenty years before to teach the barbarians. He had advanced Ryan to the rank of *san-dan,* or third-degree black belt, a considerable accomplishment in the master's strict school. Then the master had urged Ryan to go to Japan to study with his own former teacher, Master Nakashima, not necessarily because Nakashima was a better teacher but because in Japan Ryan would be totally immersed in the martial arts tradition.

Once in Japan, Ryan lived at the old master's house. The training was rigorous, beginning every morning at dawn. In wintertime it was necessary to break the ice in the water pitcher before washing in the stinging cold water, and he ran barefoot over icy ground until his feet bled. In the summertime he endured heat, went with little sleep. Sometimes, when the day's training was over, he was so exhausted that he simply lay down on the tatami mats that covered the dojo floor and fell asleep, too tired to go to bed. In such a manner, with such training, Ryan slowly began to learn the parameters of his own endurance.

He studied karate; judo; aikido; kenjitsu, which is the art of the sword; and Japanese knife-fighting, including the use of the *shiruken,* the razor-sharp little slivers of steel that are meant to be thrown. For more than two years he immersed himself in Bushido, the Way of the Warrior. Naturally his body toughened and became highly disciplined, but this was not the main benefit of the training. Little by little he realized why his master had sent him to Japan. It was principally to develop his mind, or as the Japanese would put it, his "spirit," a concept not easily translated into English.

There was no magic involved, none of the hype that permeates what a true martial artist thinks of as television karate, none of the circus atmosphere or emotional mysticism one sees in a Kung Fu film. It was all very practical, designed to make Ryan's mind steady yet flexible. He learned to be more fully conscious, to have an enhanced awareness of the world around him. It was a concept that he could not have put into words, nor was it ever meant to be put into words. Ryan had heard some instructors say that the body becomes an extension of the mind. Others said that the two become the same thing. Master Nakashima told him that all such viewpoints are only talk. It is the feeling that matters.

Ryan did not gain great wisdom. He did not become a saint; he did not become all-knowing. He had already noticed that many martial artists of great skill remain brutal bullies. What Ryan gained, in addition to the physical skills, was the ability to pay total attention. "Mind like still water, reflecting everything," was the way Master Nakashima phrased it.

The master had another student living with him, his grandson, Yoshiro. Yoshiro was a few years younger than Ryan, but he shared the same unyielding discipline, and despite the difference in their ages, Ryan and Yoshiro grew close. It was a special closeness growing out of shared stress. The two young martial artists spent most of their time together.

Near the end of Ryan's stay with Master Nakashima, Yoshiro became interested in politics, and due to the peculiarities of his particular nature, he turned in the direction of radical politics. First he joined the leftist student group Zengakuren. For a while he was a member of its Sampa Rengo faction, which considered itself the cream of the radical left. Later, dissatisfied with what he considered an overabundance of talk, Yoshiro joined the Yoyogi, the Communists, taking part in several pitched street battles against Tokyo's riot police.

Eventually he became dissatisfied with this too. "All we're doing is providing a circus for the newspapers," he told Ryan disgustedly, using the queer singsong speech of the revolutionary left. "The greedy capitalist swine who feed off the people's labor laugh while they watch the show from their penthouse windows. We should be striking directly at them, not at their underpaid stooges, the police."

Ryan was both amused and puzzled by Yoshiro's fascination with radical causes. He would have expected Nakashima's rigorous training to slant Yoshiro instead toward the old conservative samurai values. Ryan himself had, even at that early stage in his life, already developed a deep contempt for politics, politicians, and government in general. It didn't matter to him whether the rhetoric was from the left or from the right, the ultimate result was always the same—unlimited power for those individuals who made it to the top.

For a while he wrote off Yoshiro's enthusiasms as an outburst of late-adolescent energies. In his own youthful cynicism, Ryan was not yet wise enough to consider that it was possible to be motivated by genuinely held principles. All he himself cared about at the time was the martial arts; politics was a futile exercise designed for natural thieves. None of that mattered to Yoshiro. He was looking for that most illusive and dangerous of all commodities—certainty.

One day, Ryan, the quintessential lone wolf, asked Yoshiro what he was trying to accomplish. "Do you really believe that all this garbage is going to change the world?" he taunted. That was the closest he ever came to losing Yoshiro's friendship. The younger man shouted something about Ryan's lack of political awareness, then stalked out of the room. They never again talked politics together.

A short time later Ryan returned to the United States, having acquired during his stay in Japan those "special skills," that "special training," that were later to help make him so effective in his work. He did not see Yoshiro for years. They wrote often; their friendship was still strong. Master Nakashima never wrote, but Ryan communicated with him through Yoshiro.

Ryan didn't let Yoshiro know when he entered intelligence work. Yoshiro would never have approved. Ryan could imagine, could actually hear the words in his head, Yoshiro calling him "a tool of the Big Bosses, an Enemy of the People."

Two years later, yes, it had been two years, Ryan had accepted an assignment that took him to Japan. It was a fairly simple operation, one that would provide him with spare time to look up old friends. Ryan visited Master Nakashima. Yoshiro no longer lived in the house, and at first the old man was curiously hesitant to talk about his grandson. Although the old master never had been one to let his feelings show, Ryan could sense that he was worried about Yoshiro. Eventually, in a typically roundabout Japanese way, he got it across to Ryan that he would appreciate it if Ryan would look into it himself.

Ryan arranged a meeting with Yoshiro for the next day. The two men were delighted to see one another. "Let's go out and get drunk!" Yoshiro shouted.

Ryan thought that was a fine idea, so he invited Yoshiro to a geisha house, normally a ruinous extravagance, but he was on an expense account. He and Yoshiro laughed, joked, ate sushi, and drank sake. Yoshiro drank an enormous amount. It seemed to Ryan that he drank almost feverishly. The old man was right. Something was wrong.

Ryan didn't push, and finally, when Yoshiro was drunker than Ryan had ever seen him, he burst out, "I've finally found the right political group . . . people dedicated to direct action." Then he laughed. "Would you believe it? They're led by a woman!"

That was the first Ryan heard of Yoshiro's involvement with the Red Dragon Brigade. At the time, he wondered why Yoshiro was telling him so much. It wasn't just the sake. Ryan sensed an enormous pressure inside his friend. Bit by bit, the story came gushing out. Yoshiro told him how he and the other members of the group, mostly young men, considered themselves true samurai, like the warriors of previous centuries, pledged to obey their leader without hesitation. Their lives were at her disposal.

Ryan was amazed. In Japan it was not customary for women, other than one's own mother, to exert direct influence over a man. As Yoshiro became even drunker, and talked more and more freely, Ryan began to understand the source of the pressure inside him. He was in love with the woman. He didn't say so directly, but Ryan gathered that she slept with Yoshiro, and what was bothering Yoshiro was the suspicion that she slept with some of her other followers too. The more sake he drank, the more Yoshiro's jealous anger emerged. "She'll see . . . she'll see," he muttered. "She doesn't think I have the courage to do it, but I'll show her. And all the rest of them."

"Do what?" Ryan asked, but Yoshiro finally caught himself. "I've already talked too much," he mumbled. After that he barely spoke at all, just sat and looked stolidly down at his sake cup.

Ryan had to half carry Yoshiro home. He didn't have a chance to see him over the next few days, his work took him to the far north of Japan, but he was determined to have it out with Yoshiro when he returned to Tokyo.

He never got the chance. Ryan was in his hotel room in a northern city, reading the *Mainichi Shimbun,* Japan's biggest newspaper, when he discovered what Yoshiro's cryptic words had meant.

Front-page coverage with photographs. According to the accompanying text, Yoshiro had burst from the crowd at a right-wing political rally, with a *wakazashi,* a short curved sword about eighteen inches long, gripped tightly in both hands. He'd pursued the terrified main speaker across the stage, stabbing him repeatedly, killing him with the last thrust. Ryan stared at one of the pictures. There was Yoshiro, wearing the *Hachimaki,* the white headband of the samurai, arms pulled back for the final thrust, the curved blade covered with blood, his victim in front of him, stupefied, already mortally wounded, glasses tipped sideways on his fat round face as he ineffectually tried to ward off the blow.

The article stated that immediately after the murder Yoshiro had run backstage. There was no chance of escape, the police had him boxed in, so Yoshiro knelt on the floor and committed *sepuku,* cutting open his lower belly with the *wakazashi.* The police found him still kneeling, his hands full of his own guts. He died on the way to the hospital.

Ryan rushed back to Tokyo. There was a letter waiting for him . . . from Yoshiro. "Dear friend," the letter began. "I know the shame I will bring my family because of what I am about to do, but honor demands that I carry it out. I have sworn. And the woman will have nothing to do with me if I fail. What would life be worth then? You cannot know what she means to me. Speak to Grandfather. Don't tell him about the woman, tell him only that I did what I saw as my duty. Forgive me for the embarrassment I cause you."

How Japanese, Ryan thought, to end with an apology. But he did as the letter requested, bearing the news to Master Nakashima. When he saw how rigidly the old man held his face, when he sensed the pain within him, an enormous rage built up inside Ryan. He wanted the head of the bitch who had sent Yoshiro to his death. The way she had done it was particularly offensive. Sexually, Yoshiro had been curiously innocent. She'd cold-bloodedly manipulated him with her body. Ryan would make her body pay.

He neglected his work and spent the next two weeks trying to track her down. He got nowhere. Eventually, the fact that he had a contract to complete took him out of Japan. But he did not forget. He began to research the woman's organization, eventually amassing a considerable store of information. As he had earlier noted, it was a curious anomaly in male-dominated Japanese culture that the fanatic Red Dragons were led by a woman. Her name was Tetsuo Hidaka, a former bar girl turned revolutionary. She bound her followers to her by playing on their emotions, using not only sex but also the hypnotic, repetitive rhetoric of the radical left. She was very effective. As Ryan had seen in the case of Yoshiro, her followers would do absolutely anything she ordered.

She provided the Red Dragon Brigade with a quasi philosophy, a meandering mishmash of Marxism stirred in with the old medieval Japanese values, Bushido, Shinto, and most of all Gunjin Sheishin, the evocation of the warrior spirit. Her young men played samurai games with real swords, cutting up real people in banzai attacks against "Enemies of the People," which, Ryan suspected, translated to enemies of Tetsuo Hidaka.

The only observable aim of the Red Dragons was to create as much chaos as possible. They apparently hoped in this way to destroy the current world order. What was to happen afterward was very vague, a mumbling incantation about a bright, shining future never clearly defined, but apparently a world worth killing and sowing terror for. And undoubtedly a world with Tetsuo Hidaka at the top.

Neither Tetsuo nor her group had been heard of for years. It had been thought that she was dead, her group disbanded. Or perhaps they had simply grown tired of their games, had, in other words, grown up. But now it appeared that they were back. Once again, Ryan asked himself why. Had to ask himself about the woman. Was there a purpose, or was she merely playing games, tilting against boredom, laughing all the while as she moved people around like chess pieces, sacrificing a pawn here, wiping out an enemy there? Yes, perhaps to her it was only a game of power. But that would end now. With Central's group behind him, Ryan was going to call checkmate.

5

Ryan was still sitting in the molded airport chair, silently savoring the prospect of revenge, when something caught his attention. It was nothing overt, perhaps only too quick a movement, or an aura of tension out of keeping with the heavy sense of boredom prevailing in the waiting room. Suddenly he was aware of someone standing in the entranceway. He turned his head and saw a short, baggy-suited man staring at him. When their eyes met, the man darted back through the doorway.

Ryan cursed inwardly. The worst of luck. He'd recognized the man; he was an informer, a small-time hanger-on named Heller who sold information to anyone who would pay. Ryan knew that Heller had recognized him. Heller would now make sure that certain organizations got the news that Ryan was slipping out of the country on a charter flight. Unfriendly organizations. Ryan would be followed from the moment he stepped off the plane at the other end of his journey. If that happened, there was really no point even getting on the plane. They'd have to abort this flight; Central would have to set up new travel arrangements, provide him with another phony passport, arrange new connections, critical timing would get screwed up. . . .

Unless he stopped Heller.

Ryan leaped up from his chair, ready to race after the man, then had second thoughts. If he followed too closely, Heller would simply seek the protection of the crowd. He'd be able to telephone the information right in front of Ryan. Might as well lend him the quarter.

Fortunately, Ryan had already reconnoitered the terminal area, memorizing the layout of the buildings. He always liked to know what lay around him, and he knew that the corridor down which Heller had headed bent to the left, toward the main terminal and its banks of telephones. It was up to Ryan to make certain that Heller never got that far.

Ryan left the waiting area by a side door and headed along the outside wall of the corridor. He stopped for a second to peer in through a small window. There was Heller, puffing along the corridor, glancing nervously back over his shoulder to see if he was being followed.

There was a door in the corridor wall about thirty yards ahead. Ryan put on a burst of speed, wanting to reach that door ahead of Heller. It was only then that he began to realize that his intentions toward Heller were somewhat confused. What, exactly, did he intend doing with the man? He noticed a stack of chairs and supplies nearby. He was in a storage area, cut off from any access to the flight area, of course, or airport security would have made it impossible for him to be here. It was a real backwater, a perfect place to hide a body until his plane was safely airborne. But did he really have to kill Heller? He remembered the way Central had casually pegged him as an assassin. Why not simply clobber Heller, tie him up, and dump him alive behind that stack of chairs? A quick phone call to Central, and a cleanup squad would baby-sit Heller until Ryan's plane had reached its destination and he was safely out of sight again. Or was he kidding himself? Baby-sit, hell . . . they'd kill him.

Ryan was still pondering these alternatives when he reached the door. He eased it open a fraction of an inch. Heller was coming down the corridor toward him, walking more slowly now, apparently convinced that he was not being followed. Ryan quickly sized up the situation. There was no one else in sight. A perfect setup. Heller was not particularly big, so Ryan foresaw little difficulty in handling him. In another few seconds he'd be opposite the door. . . .

Heller suddenly veered aside, into a small alcove, a little waiting area just off the corridor, containing about a dozen seats . . . and a wall phone. Heller was heading straight for the telephone.

Ryan ducked back as Heller cast another nervous glance around him before picking up the receiver. He was obviously about to phone in his information. Shit!

Still no one in sight. If Ryan wanted to get on his flight it was now or never. It suddenly occurred to him that Central might even abort his part in the mission if it was even *suspected* that he'd been compromised. He'd lose his chance at the woman.

He waited until Heller was absorbed in dialing, then slipped quietly into the corridor and padded toward him. He probably wasted a second trying to decide how to take the other man—Heller was short and thick and didn't offer many targets. Ryan was still ambivalent as to exactly what to do, which slowed him. Heller suddenly spun around, having sensed movement behind him.

Ryan watched Heller's eyes widen with fear, and Ryan was suddenly very angry, mostly with himself. He struck hard with the heel of his hand, aiming straight at the point where Heller's thick neck joined his skull, directly beneath his left ear, which should have rendered Heller unconscious or dead, but in his anger Ryan miscalculated the timing, and when Heller instinctively flinched away, the blow hit his collarbone instead.

Ryan heard the sharp clean sound of the collarbone breaking. Heller fell back against the wall. "You son of a bitch!" he snarled. His face was twisted into a mixture of pain, fear, and anger. And a desire to survive.

Ryan realized he was bungling it. Any moment now Heller would begin screaming. Ryan sank his fist deep into the other man's belly. Heller grunted and bent forward, barely able to breathe, but he still had the strength to turn away, ready to run, ready to call for help.

Which might not be far away. Ryan was suddenly aware of the sound of voices from farther down the corridor. Someone was coming!

There was now no chance of simply immobilizing Heller, there just wasn't enough time; the luxury of making choices was past. If Ryan wanted to continue the mission, Heller would have to die. Immediately.

Ryan still carried one weapon that Central had not known about. He reached into the side pocket of his jacket and pulled out a length of strong nylon cord, his ace in the hole. Leaping after the staggering Heller, he whipped the cord around the other man's neck from behind and pulled back hard with both hands. Heller's feet ran right out from beneath him. He would have fallen, except for the cord around his neck, but he was sagging badly, sagging so low that Ryan could not turn his back on Heller and loop the cord over his shoulder, which was the way it should have been done.

It became a wrestling match. Ryan twisted the cord tighter. Heller bucked and jerked, his breath wheezing past the tightening cord. His breath finally shut off with a rattle, then somehow he worked a finger under the nylon and tugged it away from his windpipe. He managed another gasping breath or two before Ryan, cursing the other man's unexpected strength, shut off his air again.

Ryan twisted the cord tighter and tighter. The sour smell of Heller's fear was sickening. Ryan found himself staring at a boil on the back of his victim's neck, right above where the cord cut into the flesh. Ryan's own flesh crawled. He wanted it to be over with, it had to be over with, because the voices down the corridor were closer now. He had only seconds left. "Die, you bastard," he pleaded. But Heller continued to struggle.

Ryan suddenly loosened the cord. Heller was so relieved that he relaxed for a moment, gratefully sucking in air. Ryan immediately wrapped his right arm around Heller's neck in a headlock, then kicked both of his own feet out to the side. As Ryan fell, Heller had to go down with him ... with Heller's neck bearing the combined weight of both men. The neck stayed bent at a grotesque angle for a moment, then broke with a loud snap. Heller's legs jerked two or three times, then he was still.

The people coming down the hall were quite close now. Ryan got to his feet. He had to get rid of Heller's body. But how? Where? If he dragged it across the corridor to the outside door, he'd be seen.

There was nothing in the little alcove large enough to conceal a body, only chairs and the wall phone. A chair would have to do. Ryan shoved the cord back into his pocket and began wrestling Heller's inert body into a chair next to the wall. God, he was heavy. Ryan was covered with sweat by the time he got Heller into the chair. He tried to prop the dead man's head against the back of the chair to make it look as if he were sleeping, but because of the broken neck, Heller's head kept lolling into impossible positions. Nor could Ryan get Heller's eyes closed. He finally propped the head against the wall, then swept up a newspaper someone had left, using it to cover Heller's face.

Ryan sat down next to the body. The people coming down the hall were only a few yards away when he noticed that one of Heller's hands was twitching spasmodically; the severed spinal cord was still sending out confused messages. Ryan mashed down on the hand with all his weight. Bones crunched. The hand stopped moving. A moment later three people entered the alcove, a man and a woman, with a boy about seven. "I'm tired," the boy whined crossly. "When are we gonna get on the plane?"

The woman sighed. "Johnny ... if you ask me that one

more time ..." She was in her late thirties, worn-looking. The man, fat and in his forties, sat in one of the chairs and began reading a magazine, obviously tuning out. The woman sank down next to him. The boy sat opposite Ryan ... and Heller's body. He glanced around for a moment, then looked straight into Ryan's eyes. It was a sly, arrogant look. A mean, spoiled little brat, Ryan decided, one of the twentieth century's legion of hyperactive, neurotic little monsters. Ryan hoped the boy would stay quietly in his seat, but he doubted it. He definitely was not going to wait around to find out.

Ryan stood up. Keeping his face averted as much as possible, without making it too obvious, he walked out of the alcove. With luck he'd be airborne before the body was discovered. But he began to sweat again when he heard the woman's low spiritless voice saying, from behind him, "Johnny ... for God's sake, leave the man alone. Can't you see he's sleeping?"

6

There was no alarm, no cry of "Murder!" Ryan got on the flight without incident, but he did not relax until the plane had reached thirty thousand feet.

He was disgusted. He'd let himself lose control. "Stewardess," he called, and ordered a drink. The alcohol helped, but he still seethed internally, his mind alive with a succession of disconnected images—the boil on the back of Heller's neck, the sour smell of the man's fear, the sharper odor when Heller had died and lost control of his bladder. It had been ugly.

It was not exactly guilt that he felt. Heller had known the rules of the game, he'd taken his chances. Death was always a possibility. The trouble with this particular action was that it had been . . . how could he put it? Had been so lacking in honor. That was the way Nakashima would probably have described it.

Damn it! If he hadn't been so obsessed with Tetsuo Hidaka, Heller might still be alive. What was that crap he'd given Central about being a free agent? Bullshit. He was becoming so obsessed by revenge that he was beginning to lose his ability to act rationally. It was bad enough having Central manipulate him, but when he began to manipulate himself . . . Well, another reason to take out that bitch, Hidaka. Try to relax, he warned himself. Stop blowing it.

He ordered another drink. When he had finished it he was relaxed enough to fall asleep.

When Ryan awakened, the plane was over Ireland, beginning its descent toward Gatwick. He leaned over and looked out the window at the green land below. The miles and the hours had detached him from Central, from Heller; all of that was behind him now. He must think of nothing but his immediate surroundings, the descending plane, the people on that plane, what he might expect when he was on the ground.

The landing was uneventful. When the plane reached the terminal, and while the walkway was being positioned and the door opened, Ryan remained in his seat, letting the others, most of them first-time travelers, crowd into the aisle and wait. He was last off the plane, having had the opportunity to examine each of his fellow passengers as they filed past his seat. There was no one he knew, no familiar faces, although that did not necessarily mean that none of the other passengers knew him.

Inside the terminal he recovered his suitcase and headed for the train that would take him into London. He had barely settled into a seat when he felt the jolt of the train starting. He spent the next hour watching the green countryside pass by outside the train window. Lovely. Very lovely. It was raining, of course, the price for all that green.

Suburbs began to appear, then industrial areas. Finally the train was moving through the vast dingy sprawl of London. Ryan liked London. There was something honest about its dowdiness. A century before, it had been the seat of the largest empire the world had ever known, the greatest city in the world, the center of unquestioned power. Power taken for granted. Maybe that was why the English, unlike the more insecure French, had never felt the need to make a great display of their power. A little of that homely grandeur still remained.

The train pulled into Victoria Station, a vast, sooty place, with concrete floors stained a sticky black-brown. Big iron girders spiderwebbed the opaque expanse of dirty glass that made up most of its arched ceiling. The station was as crowded as if the automobile had never been invented. Ryan picked up his small suitcase and moved along with the other passengers, out of the train and down the long platform, past the ticket barrier and out into the immense waiting room, which looked a little like the inside of a factory. His shoes gritted against the dirty floor as he worked his way through the dense pack of people. Eventually he reached the exit and stepped out into the London afternoon.

It was difficult to tell if the sun was shining or not; the sky was the usual London dirty gray, with few distinguishing characteristics. Ryan walked straight across the bus park, past the taxi stands, then crossed the road, heading in the general direction of Buckingham Palace. He walked past a pub, and looked longingly inside. He was hungry and thirsty, but he wanted to lose himself in the city before he ate.

He saw a cab farther down the street letting out a family of Pakistanis. A good cab for him to take. Finding it this far from the station, and so loaded down with miscellaneous humanity, there was very little chance that it had been planted there just for him. He ran down the street and entered the cab through one rear door while the Pakistani wife was still exiting from the other. The driver gave him an annoyed look, then slid open the little window that separated the passenger's compartment from the front. "Where to, Guv?"

"The King's Road," Ryan replied curtly.

The window slammed shut, the flag went down, and Ryan settled back into his seat as the cab got under way. Ryan liked London cabs; he liked the large boxy passenger compartment, liked having the driver shut away from him by the glass partition. No annoying New York–style chatter, no instant amateur psychology. The driver's function was simply to drive.

Ryan descended from the cab about halfway down the King's Road, in an area of trendy shops. He paid the driver, but kept him in sight until he'd seen him pick up another, very normal-looking fare. Only then did Ryan begin walking down the road, lugging his little suitcase. He strolled along for about a hundred yards, observing the bizarre Chelsea street life. Skinheads swaggered past in their heavy boots, tight trousers, and metal-studded jackets. There were consumptive-looking punks with vari-colored hair dyed bright oranges, greens, and pinks. The faces of both the male and female punks were grotesquely made up. All around him moved the inevitable decay of the modern welfare state: the confused, the spoiled, the opportunists.

Ryan diverted his attention to the girls, the "birds." There was one in particular who was quite pretty, and unusually healthy-looking for a member of England's poorly fed working class. She was wearing a short skirt and a gauzy blouse, walking with as much bounce as possible, consciously making her breasts jiggle and her buttocks sway, looking sideways at the passersby to see if they were noticing. Most of the men were, including Ryan, who was enjoying the pinkish outlines of the girl's nipples through the thin material of her blouse. She gave Ryan a hard little urban smile, but her expression grew somewhat uncertain as she looked more closely into his eyes. Then they had passed one another forever. Ryan turned to take a parting look at her neatly swaying little ass.

Next to him a big red London bus slowed for traffic. Ryan jumped onto the rear deck, then moved quickly up the stairs to the top level. The bus was not crowded; he took a seat right at the front, and since the upper deck overhung the front of the driver's compartment, he had an excellent view as the bus slowly wound its way through London's narrow streets.

There were a great many people on the sidewalk, an incredible mix of races and classes, a much different mix than when, as a student, Ryan had made his first visit to London. There were fewer native English now, and many, many more foreign imports: Pakistanis, West Indians, Arabs, Greeks—the human rubble of a collapsed empire. Most of the people on the sidewalk seemed rather sullen, eyeing their polyglot neighbors warily, all of them caught in the midst of a multiple culture clash, which was intensified by the idiocy of the British class system. Fascinated, Ryan watched these refugees, these reminders of faded imperial glory, stream by him. It was vaguely reminiscent of something in a film he had seen, *Star Wars*. The scene in the alien bar.

He got off the bus near Paddington Station, in an area that had once been fashionable but had long ago gone to seed. Yesterday's elegant homes were now decrepit little hotels, their new status announced by small metal plaques over their front porches. Ryan picked one that looked reasonably clean. The clerk was Indian or Pakistani, Ryan had never learned to tell the difference. Demonstrating neither friendliness nor hostility, but rather a kind of surly boredom, the clerk took Ryan's money and handed him a large key. The cost was reasonable but not that reasonable. Despite its low wages England was expensive . . . the class system at work again. Well, that was a problem for the English to work out. At the moment, anonymity was what Ryan was after. Not wanting others to anticipate where he might go, he himself had not known his destination until he'd passed by this particular hotel, a random choice.

Climbing narrow rickety stairs smelling of age, he eventually ended up in front of a door that had been painted so many times that it was much thicker than when it had been made. He unlocked the door and went inside. The room itself was small, dark, and damp, with a narrow single bed. A patch of sooty gray sky glowed dimly through the one small window. But wonder of wonders, the room had its own bathroom, a rarity in London. A primitive shower had been rigged in one corner, an even greater rarity in a land where the population preferred to soak in its own dirt ... although Ryan had to admit, hot baths might be a necessity for the British, one way of coping with the lack of heating.

Ryan quickly showered, then dressed, picking clothing that was a little warmer, a little more European than the clothing in which he'd arrived. He divided his money, a considerable wad, between his wallet and a money belt. He carried cash rather than traveler's checks. He might be forced to change his identity from time to time. With each new identity, traveler's checks made out to another name would be both useless and incriminating.

When Ryan passed through the tiny lobby, the clerk was busy with another customer. That was fine with Ryan. He did not want to leave his room key at the desk, as was the custom; he wanted to retain as much control over his environment as possible.

Outside, there was still some daylight left. It was the last week in June, and in these far northern latitudes darkness came quite late at this time of year. However, it was still difficult to tell just where the sun was; the light was murky and weak, filtering down through a heavy cloud cover mixed with diesel fumes.

Ryan began walking, looking for a place to eat. He passed several kabob houses, run by Cypriots or Greeks, but he was not in the mood for what they had to offer. He was looking for a pub, an old-fashioned English pub, if real pubs still existed. He turned down a side street. Perhaps, away from the main thoroughfare, with its non-English mix ...

He noticed a group of young men lounging on a street corner. Four skinheads, unusually large skinheads, unusually well-fed, posing languidly, hip-shot, all of them dressed in the regulation tight-fitting blue jeans, metal-studded leather jackets, and heavy stomping boots. Their heads sprouted a quarter inch of ugly bristle, their eyes were full of the dull glare of ignorance. They stood, practicing their own version of insolence, lazily scanning the sidewalk around them. One of them looked at Ryan, leered, said something in an accent so atrocious that Ryan could not make out the words, undoubtedly an insult, but Ryan looked the punk straight in the eyes, and the man faltered. Ryan walked past, not bothering to look back. Normally, skinheads were a danger only to the helpless.

Halfway down the street he saw a pub, an appealing one with small leaded windows set into dark wood. A sign over the door said "Hot Food." He stepped inside and immediately felt comfortable. The interior was paneled in more dark wood, with low-beamed ceilings overhead. Big brass beer pumps gleamed behind a long mahogany bar, real pumps, not pressurized valves. The easy familiarity among the patrons suggested to Ryan that he had found a "local," a pub that catered to the inhabitants of the neighborhood. The bartender and customers all appeared to be native English. The patrons looked at him—a stranger—somewhat askance, but there was nothing hostile about their demeanor. The bartender greeted Ryan with that old traditional English politeness and friendliness that he remembered from long ago.

To Ryan's delight he saw that the pub featured a selection of what was called "real ale," rather than the usual commercial swill. Ryan had the bartender draw half-pint glasses of each type, then line them up on the bar in front of him. Ryan tasted each, then ordered a pint of the one he liked best, an English pint, twenty glorious ounces of a marvelous reddish brown brew. Ryan watched the bartender work the brass pump. At each stroke the polished brass nozzle spouted a stream of frothy but not fizzy beer. When the big glass was full to the top, Ryan picked it up and quaffed a deep draft, a real mouthful—beer is not a sipping drink. His nose filled with a yeasty, wet aroma, his mouth with the rich flavor of malted barley, the sharp bite of hops. There was no sour chemical aftertaste whatsoever. The beer was cool but not icy. It did not need to be icy. Only thin, foul-tasting beer, such as American beer, which Ryan considered the worst in the world, needed to be chilled to the point where the bad taste is no longer quite so noticeable.

Ah . . . delicious. An old-timer had once told Ryan that long ago all the beer in England had tasted like this, then a few large breweries had bought up the hundreds of little independent breweries and hired scientists . . . *scientists,* not brewmasters, not artists . . . to mix foul potions, a disgusting chemical swill. Only recently had pressure from beer purists enticed the breweries to once again begin making a few brews in the old style. "Thank God for real ale," Ryan muttered under his breath, then once again buried his nose in his glass.

He ordered a large portion of homemade steak-and-kidney pie. Taking his beer and his food to a small table well back in a corner, he began eating. This was the only English food that he considered palatable. The pie's crust was a crisp golden brown, the meat inside swimming in rich gravy. He washed down each mouthful with the yeasty wetness of the ale. This goddamn poor-man's mission was finally shaping up.

Ryan stayed in the pub for over an hour, drinking two more pints of ale. He watched a small group of people playing darts. They seemed to be having a very good time. Ryan liked British pubs. They were well lighted, places to laugh and to talk and to meet people, very different from the usual Stateside dim, dark cave, inhabited by solitary drinkers staring at themselves in a mirror on the far side of a bar that was more barrier than invitation.

Ryan left the pub satisfied. It was dark out now, or more correctly, nighttime. A glaring indirect light imparted a ghostly glow to the street, the reflection of the city's lights bouncing off the low murky cloud cover. Ryan didn't mind. His stomach was warm, and he was beginning to grow sleepy, perhaps he was even tired enough for his body to welcome the uninviting cot in the hotel room. Time to start moving in that direction.

He had walked only a short way when he noticed a small knot of people farther down the street. He crossed to the other side, intending to avoid them. He was about thirty yards from the group when he recognized the four skinheads he'd seen earlier. They had stopped a young man and woman and would not let them pass. As Ryan drew closer he could hear the skinheads speaking in their hideous East London accents. "Fine great knobs she got, ain't she, Alfie?" one of them said, reaching out to fondle the girl's breasts. She gasped and tried to push his hands away, but he laughed and squeezed harder. The girl squealed in pain, and her escort moved toward her tormentor, but two of the other skinheads pressed in on him from either side, twisting his arms behind his back.

There were other people on the street, but none offered to help; rather, they averted their eyes and attempted to slip by unnoticed. Noninvolvement, a sure symptom of a disintegrating society. Ryan did not want to become involved either, it was important that he not draw attention to himself, but something made him move forward, something from within. Perhaps it was an instinctive loathing for the bullying skinheads, perhaps a vestigial touch of the obligation that the strong should feel toward the weak. In any case he found himself crossing the street, approaching the skinheads and their victims.

By now the skinhead in front of the girl had pulled up her sweater, baring a pair of large and well-shaped breasts, which he began pinching wickedly, leaving ugly red welts on the soft skin. The girl struggled wildly, trying to break free, but another of the punks grasped her by the buttocks, holding her in place. "Christopher!" she shrieked.

Her escort tried to jerk free, to help her, but one of the punks hit him in the stomach. Christopher doubled over and began to sag, held up by the men on each side of him. All four of the skinheads were giggling crazily.

Ryan was only a yard or two away when one of them noticed him approaching. "H'it's that big 'un again," he said, leering. "Come to get yers too, mate?"

This particular punk was standing behind Christopher, twisting the boy's arm, looking back over his shoulder at

Ryan, both legs braced stiffly so that he could more easily hold his prisoner. He started to say more, looking challengingly at Ryan, but his voice turned into a hoarse scream when Ryan kicked him in the knee from the side, driving the edge of his right foot, with all his weight behind it, against the joint. The knee swiveled inward, dislocating with a loud snap. As the skinhead went down, screaming, eyes wide open in amazement, his mouth a small round circle of pain, Ryan changed stance, and kicked him full in the face with his left foot, crushing his nose.

The others were only slowly beginning to realize they had a problem. The one on the far side of Christopher released his hold on his victim, letting the young man fall onto his hands and knees. The skinhead started to move to the side, since Christopher was between him and Ryan, but Ryan kicked again before the skinhead had taken his second step. Ryan's bent leg swung in a wide arc, parallel to the ground, passing over Christopher's bent back, the foot snapping out at the last moment with great speed, the toe of Ryan's shoe smashing into the skinhead's jaw. Bits of broken teeth, blood, and pink tissue sprayed from the skinhead's mouth, and he went down hard, his jaw broken.

The one who had been holding the girl from behind spun toward Ryan, snarling. Ryan's leg was just snapping back from the kick, his weight on one leg, his groin apparently open. Nakashima had always told him that kicking left one vulnerable, and the skinhead was quick to take advantage of the opening, aiming a kick at Ryan's crotch. But the weight of the skinhead's heavy stomping boot slowed the kick. Ryan simply slid backwards and grasped the skinhead's boot in both hands. He twisted the skinhead's foot, torquing with his hips, using the weight of his entire body. His opponent's lower leg bones splintered, a multiple-torsion break. The skinhead screamed in agony and began to fall, his face white with shock. Ryan stepped in quickly, hammering the bottom of his right fist against one side of the gaping mouth, breaking the jawbone, then followed with the other fist from the other side, compounding the damage.

Only a few seconds had passed and three of the skinheads were down. That left the one who had been mauling the girl's breasts. He pushed the girl aside, and reaching into his jacket pocket, pulled out a short leather sap. Snarling with a combination of rage and fear—he had seldom had the experience of people fighting back—he sprang at Ryan, swinging the sap down toward Ryan's skull. It was a vicious blow and would probably have fractured Ryan's skull had it landed, but Ryan spoiled the attack by suddenly stepping in, rather than back, inside the descending arc, jamming the blow, his crossed forearms trapping the skinhead's arm. The rest was easy. Ryan simply stepped past the skinhead, forcing his arm back and over his shoulder, then he pulled down hard, hanging all his weight on the arm until the shoulder joint separated with a grinding crunch.

As the skinhead fell, screaming, Ryan maintained a light hold on the ruined arm while driving the heel of his right hand against the man's nose, smearing it across one side of his face. When the skinhead's body hit the ground, Ryan's grip on the arm tightened, pulling up hard, while he drove his foot deep into the skinhead's armpit. Ribs broke, and the arm separated from the shoulder in a new direction.

There was little more to do. The skinhead who'd been kicked in the jaw was trying to get up on all fours, blood bubbling from his mouth. Ryan kicked him in the elbow, breaking the joint. The skinhead fell, floundering. The man with the ruined knee joint was still writhing on the ground, moaning. The one with the torsion break and the smashed jaw was unconscious, and the one whose shoulder joint had been ruined was lying on one side, his arm completely behind his back, trying to find a way to breathe.

Farther down the street, people were staring in Ryan's direction. Christopher was struggling to his feet. The girl, her sweater still pulled up above her breasts, was staring down at the bodies sprawled all around her. She was taking in huge gulps of air. Ryan knew that she would begin screaming very soon.

He turned and began walking down the street toward the pub. There was a narrow opening, an alley, branching off just before the pub, and he entered it. A maze of narrow branching passageways lay ahead. He took them randomly, wanting to put as much distance as possible between himself and the scene of the fight. He'd just made himself extremely visible.

Traveling in a large circle, he made his way back toward the hotel. The hotel was quite close to the scene of the fight, and as he walked up the hotel steps he could see a pair of policemen running in that direction. Little knots of people were forming.

The desk clerk looked up as Ryan passed through the lobby. "What is going on out there?" he asked.

"I'm not sure. A fight, I think."

Once in his room Ryan debated packing his suitcase and leaving, but realized that would be a stupid move. Even stupider than getting involved in someone else's trouble. The clerk might connect his sudden flight to the violence farther down the street. He might call the police.

Ryan closed his suitcase, put it on the floor, then lay down on the bed. Definitely a foolish move, the fight. But satisfying. Skinheads. Shitheads. Central had intimated that he was a man of violence. Perhaps so, but sometimes violence . . .

His mind went back to Heller. An unnecessary killing. One that had made him feel . . . dirty. He thought back to the fight that had just taken place, to the terror on the young woman's face, to the skinheads lying on the ground, bleeding. That had been different. That . . . was justice. Simply justice. "Heller," he muttered. "That one was for you."

7

Ryan left the hotel before dawn. The streets were deserted; he was a little surprised when he found a cruising taxi. He took the taxi to the nearest Underground entrance, paid off the driver, then descended into the dark maw of the subway. Hot, fetid air rushed out of the stairwell at him, pushed upwards by the movement of a train deep underground. He could hear its muted thunder far below. He reached the track. The air smelled of burning rubber, old dirt. At that time of the morning trains were few, but eventually the one he was looking for came along and he boarded, settling himself into one of the hard contoured plastic seats. The train began moving, gathered speed. Its clacking roar bounced off the circular concrete tunnel walls and back into the passenger compartment, dinning into Ryan's ears.

He got off at the British Rail terminal serving points north. Within another few minutes he was aboard a regular surface train heading for Luton, about a forty-five-minute trip north of London.

It was growing light by the time he reached Luton. Here, the dawn was cleaner and softer than in London.

The little city was only just waking up, people were beginning to move about, but as yet there was very little traffic.

Ryan took a taxi out to Luton's small charter airport. Once inside the terminal, there was nothing to do but wait. Since he had arrived early, the terminal was at first empty, but as departure time neared, more and more people began to arrive, until the waiting room was packed. Most of those waiting seemed a little confused; there was the problem of flogging one's brain awake at this early hour, but most were also rather excited. They were principally working-class people—shop girls, hourly laborers, office help—off on their annual vacations. The plane they were all waiting for, Ryan included, was part of a package tour—flight, hotel accommodations, and meals all included in one ridiculously low price, the only way England's poorly paid working class could afford to travel.

The plane left more or less on time. Ryan, still traveling as John Stevens, boarded without incident. This was the second phase of Central's rather elaborate plan for getting Ryan on the ground in Majorca without being spotted. This leg of the journey would take him to the Spanish island of Ibiza, which lay about fifty miles from his final goal, Majorca.

Ryan took a window seat. He watched the clouds and fog of England drop away behind them. Soon they were flying over western France, wine country, the land of claret. The terrain was gradually becoming drier, the soft greens of the north fading into a harder olive green. An hour and a half after leaving England, they had reached the Mediterranean. Ryan watched the coast slip away behind him, fade, disappear, and then they were flying over a vast expanse of water of the most intense blue, stretching from horizon to horizon, unmarred by waves, a flat azure sheet, glinting metallically under the bright hard light of the southern sun.

A quarter of an hour later a smudge appeared on the horizon. Ibiza. The island rose slowly from the sea, indistinct at first, then the plane banked for its approach, turning toward Ryan's side, so that most of the island was visible below him. The terrain was ocher-red, streaked at the higher elevations with the dark green of pines, and, lower down, with the lighter, silvery sheen of olive trees. The mass of the island rose out of the intense blue of the sea quite abruptly, ringed by sheer cliffs, which gave the island an edge, a shape, an appearance very much like a twisted piece of old bronze set into a vast sheet of turquoise.

The landing was British smooth. As the passengers stepped out onto the tarmac they were welcomed by a blast of heat, and by bright sunlight. Most looked much happier than when they had boarded. This heat, this wonderful light, was why they were here.

The airport was quite small, a single building surrounded by a profusion of flowers. Customs was almost nonexistent. Spain lived by tourism. Foreigners with money to spend, while if not exactly welcomed with warmth, were certainly not harassed.

Ryan left the terminal building along with the pack. Huge motor coaches waited outside. Guides, both male and female, all of them young, most of them dressed in semiuniforms, usually a blazer with a hotel or travel agency crest on the left breast, called out the names of various hotels. Most of the people around Ryan were herded into one bus or another, but he quickly walked over to a taxi rank. *"A la ciudad,"* he said to the driver.

It was a two-mile trip into town. The road ran relatively straight, past rocky fields bordered by crumbling stone walls. The land looked dry, tired, worn out, but wonderfully beautiful, ancient, lived in, real. The wind blowing in through the open taxi window was warm, with a slight perfume that was difficult to classify. It was all quite wonderful.

The Old City, called simply Ibiza, was situated on a small bay at the foot of steep hills. Most of the town was crammed into a narrow strip along the waterfront, with the hills pressing right down into the back streets. One long avenue ran along the harbor, backed by a facade of ancient, weatherbeaten buildings, most of them built of faded, pastel stone. Small windows, bordered by green louvered shutters, were set deep into yard-thick walls.

When Ryan paid off his taxi, it was still an hour or two short of siesta. The local inhabitants, the Ibizencos, bustled all around him, going about their various businesses of buying, selling, carrying, all performed amidst the cacophony of their strange, harsh language, Ibizenco, a dialect of Catalan, a language so utterly different from Spanish that Ryan found it incomprehensible.

In contrast to the busy activities of the Ibizencos, dozens of long-haired, vacant-eyed youths of both sexes sprawled lazily in the shade of arches and doorways. Most of them were tall and quite thin, none of them showing much energy. "Heepees," as the locals called them, they were part of the hordes of lost youths who swarmed down from the north each summer in search of sunshine and drugs.

Ryan walked to a small outdoor café, put down his bag, and took a seat. He caught a waiter flying by, ordered a beer, then sat quietly, drinking the beer, looking out over the harbor, at the sunlight on the water, at the tiny, ancient fishing boats, at fishermen bent over nets they had spread out over the pavement so that they could mend them. He liked it all.

"Pretty fucking nice, isn't it?" a voice said in English from behind and to one side. Ryan turned. A tall young man with long blond hair, but with a little more light in his eyes than most of the others, was smiling at him. "I c'n see you like it. I mean, really like it. Not in the same way as those tour dorks running off to their hotels on the other side of the island. I mean, this is the real Ibiza. This is the place where the Carthaginians lived. It's old, man. Really old."

"Yes. I can see that."

Ryan took another sip of his beer, turning away from the young man, who nevertheless continued talking.

"Those hotels . . . they're something else. I mean, they're broken up by nationality; one for the English, one for Germans, one for Swedes. Weird. But nothing like over on Majorca. I mean, they've got whole hotel *complexes* there, like little cities ten stories high and a block long, where a tourist is surrounded by signs in his own language, where he can't buy hardly any food but home food, where he'll meet nobody but people from his own country. Hard to figure why the poor bastards ever bother to leave home at all. For the sun, I guess."

Ryan turned back toward the young man, his eyes questioning. Had this kid been planted on him? He did his best to hide his suspicions, but the young man picked them up nevertheless. "Look," he said, flushing. "I don't normally bug strangers, but sometimes it's nice to have someone to speak American to. I mean, talking to the English isn't quite the same thing."

"No . . . it's not," Ryan admitted.

"I wasn't completely sure you were American," the young man continued. "It was kind of a guess. But you're too big and healthy-looking to be English. German or Dutch, maybe. Yeah, you could pass for Dutch easy. I wasn't sure, but I just thought I'd give it a try."

"You guessed right."

The young man hesitated, then held out a hand. "The name's Glen," he said, smiling.

Ryan's own hesitation was so slight he hoped that it was not noticeable. "John," he replied, extending his own hand.

They shook hands. "Staying long?" Glen asked.

"No . . . just passing through."

For a minute or two neither Glen nor Ryan had anything to say, although Ryan was studying the other man carefully. Glen interested him. Despite the initial grubby impression, the long hair, the rather shabby clothing, the natural comparison to the bums hanging around the harbor, there was a certain air about this young man, something hard to define. Ryan finally settled for the word *entrepreneurial*. A sharp kid.

Ryan restarted the conversation by buying both himself and Glen another round of drinks. The alcohol oiled the way to an easier flow of words. Encouraged, Glen began to talk about himself. He told Ryan that he had been living in the Mediterranean for several years. "The place kinda gets to you. Maybe it's the light ... or the way of life. The rest of the world, that big world up there in the north, or back home, gets to seem kinda ... well, weird. Home especially ... the States. It hasn't got any real history. But ... I guess I'll probably go home someday. Home is ... home."

Is it? Ryan wondered. He had no real home. And speaking of home ... "What's the hotel scene like around here?" he asked.

"At this time of year, real bad. People are practically hanging out of windows. But," he added, holding up the drink Ryan had bought for him, which was now nearly empty, "one good turn deserves another, and I know for sure that a room just came vacant today in a little pensione at the back of town. Costs maybe twenty-five hundred pesetas a day. That's twenty, thirty bucks."

Glen told him about the pensione, that it had been in one family for over a hundred years, that the people who ran it were very nice. Normally, Ryan would not have considered a place recommended by someone else. That took away control. But he suspected that Glen was right, that lodgings were hard to come by, and he had things to do here in Ibiza City, and very little time. He thanked Glen, who gave him directions to the pensione, pointing toward the opening of a narrow passageway. "Just follow that street until it gets so narrow you can't go any further. Then you'll be there."

Ryan nodded. He got up, paid for the drinks, then headed in the direction Glen had indicated. The street angled away from the harbor. The higher it climbed, the narrower it became, until the roofs on either side seemed to close in over Ryan's head. The street seemed very old; it was paved with small round stones. Since there was only foot traffic here, the stones were shiny, and very clean. He passed a woman who was down on her hands and knees, actually washing the paving stones in front of her house.

He found the pensione with very little difficulty, there was a sign over the front door. The door was old and very large, set into a massive wall. He swung a big brass door knocker against the old wood. He could hear the sound reverberating off stone somewhere inside. A moment later he heard slow footsteps approaching. The door swung open, revealing an old woman dressed in black. She was very thin, but erect. Her hair was white and thick, tied back behind her head in a bun. The smooth lines of her face indicated that she must have been very beautiful at one time. Hell, she was still beautiful. She looked at Ryan questioningly. *"Busco habitación,"* he said.

His Spanish seemed to be working. The old woman nodded, then stepped aside so that he could enter. He watched her swing the big outer door shut again. It thudded into place quite solidly. Saying not a word, she turned, and preceded him into a dark entranceway. There was just enough light for him to make out the pattern of the floor tiles. Like the old woman, they were lovely with age.

As he went deeper into the building, Ryan saw that it was of three stories, with a small enclosed patio in the center. Orange trees clustered around a tiny fountain. Two benches were crowded into the little patio. Balconies overhung the patio and fountain. It was all very Moorish, very Mediterranean.

The old lady led the way up steep stone steps. Stopping outside a door, she took a ring of keys from her belt. The keys were old and very large, made of black iron, some of them eight or nine inches long. She fitted one of the keys into the lock, then turned it. There was a grating sound as the ancient bolt slid back. The old woman pushed the door open and motioned for Ryan to enter. He stepped into a room about fifteen feet square. It was cool inside. The interior walls were coated with whitewashed plaster; it was their thickness that kept the room, the entire house, cool.

Ryan quickly inventoried the room. The furniture was of wood: old, heavy, dark and solid. There was a huge armoire, a table and two chairs, and an immense sagging double bed. Small bars of light streamed in through the closed, slatted shutters. It was a room from another century. Ryan liked it very much. He nodded his acceptance. The old woman smiled. Ryan smiled back. He liked her as much as he liked the room.

He gave her his passport; he would be able to pick it up later. She left him with the big key, then made her careful way downstairs. He wondered how old she was. He shut the door, slid an inside bolt into place, threw his bag up onto the bed. The bed bounced and jiggled. He was tempted to lie down, but he knew that he had a lot to do before it would be time to rest.

He stripped to his underwear, then opened his bag and took out lighter clothing, more suited to Ibiza's climate. He went over to the washbasin and splashed cold water on his face. Dressing, he left the pensione and once again headed for the waterfront. When he passed the café he noticed that Glen was no longer there. Good. No point in making too many local connections . . . people who might remember him.

8

The streets were practically empty; it was now more than halfway through the afternoon siesta, four hours of sleeping, eating, and drinking. The stores and shops would not open again until four o'clock. It had been a long time since Ryan had been in Spain; he'd forgotten about the siesta. With everything shut down there was little point in doing anything but eating ... which easily fit in with his mood.

Most of the restaurants were packed. In a back street Ryan finally found a restaurant with an empty table. It was very small, located in a half-basement across from a row of little vegetable stands. The food was all he had hoped for, simple but delicious, beginning with a wonderful *potaje,* a rich garbanzo soup full of greens, and chunks of locally made *buteferano* sausages. The main course was *calamares rellenos,* tender baby squid stuffed with pork, vegetables, and spices, accompanied by a fresh salad. The wine was abundant, good, and inexpensive. The entire meal came to a little more than ten dollars.

When Ryan finally wandered back out into the street, he was possessed of a fuller appreciation of the four-hour siesta break. After such a meal he didn't feel like doing much of anything except sleeping, or perhaps taking a nice slow, aimless walk.

But duty called, and some of the shops were now beginning to reopen. Ryan walked back toward the port, searching in his head for the directions that had been included in the briefing notes he'd studied before leaving Washington. After asking a few questions, he eventually found himself in front of a small building about forty yards from the water, with a sign over the door reading "Ibiza Marine." When he knocked, no one answered. Then he saw a small handwritten sign in the window: "I'm at the Bar España across the street."

Ryan looked in that direction. All he could see of the Bar España was a small sign over a dark open doorway. He crossed the street and pushed his way through a beaded string curtain designed to keep out flies but not customers. It was a very small place, with a short wooden bar in one corner and four tables standing on a dirty tile floor. There was hardly a straight line in the place: the whitewashed walls curved haphazardly; heavy dark beams sagged overhead.

There was only one customer inside, a slender, dark-haired man who did not look Spanish. "Are you Ken Rowell?" Ryan asked.

The man had been staring down at a half-empty glass. Now his eyes jerked up toward Ryan, nervously appraising him. "Uh-huh . . . that's me," he finally said.

Ryan sat down at Rowell's table. "My name's Stevens. From Washington. I understand you sell boats."

Rowell licked his lips, took a quick sip of his drink, licked his lips again. "Yeah. I sell boats."

Ryan looked quizzically at Rowell. This was not going the way it was supposed to go. "I'm looking for a boat," he prompted. "Something big enough to live on but small enough for one man to handle. I asked around before I left Washington. Your name came up."

Rowell was still holding his glass, which was empty

now. There were many other empty glasses on the table-top. Apparently this bar still used the old system of accounting: when you were finished drinking, you paid for the number of empty glasses on your table. Rowell didn't seem to think there were enough glasses. He looked over at the bar. The bartender was sitting on a chair, half asleep, paying no attention. "I was told you'd have what I'm looking for," Ryan prompted again.

Rowell's eyes jerked back toward him. "Yeah. Sure. I've got a boat you'd probably like."

He stood up, headed toward the door. The bartender finally came awake, started to get to his feet. "Put the drinks on my bill," Rowell said in Spanish. The bartender gratefully sank back down onto his chair.

After the dimness inside the bar, the light out in the street was blinding. Rowell led Ryan onto a small dock. He stopped beside a lovely little sloop. "Thirty-four feet," he said curtly. "Sleeps four in a pinch, two comfortably. It's a fast sailer, but steady enough in rough weather."

Rowell jumped aboard. Ryan followed him. Once his feet hit the deck, Rowell became more animated; he obviously loved boats. "It's got all stainless steel rigging," he said, twanging a stay. "That's worth as much as the rest of the boat put together. Now . . . let's take a look below."

Rowell led the way from the cockpit into a small cabin. There was a good-sized bunk on each side, with a small galley set aft of one bunk. Forward, through a small hatch, Ryan caught sight of a cramped but adequate head.

He studied the sloop's interior with appreciation, but when he turned, he saw that Rowell was staring at him with hostility. "Okay, 'Stevens,' " Rowell said acidly. "This is the boat I was instructed to sell you. But I don't like any part of this cloak-and-dagger shit, I want to get it over with as fast as possible, so I'll show you the special built-in features before some inquisitive bastard shoves his nose down here."

He was fumbling under a countertop. There was a sharp click, and the countertop swung up. Inside was a small radio transmitter plus several other pieces of electronic equipment.

"This is a high-speed sender," Rowell said, pointing. "You encode the message first, then record it on tape. You pop the cassette in here and push this button. It's capable of sending a fairly long message in seconds, too quickly for anybody to get a fix on where it's coming from. It's already locked onto the frequency you'll be using."

"Thanks for the tutorial," Ryan said coolly. "But I've seen this kind of thing before."

"I'll bet you have."

Ryan met Rowell's hostile glare and held it. Rowell turned his gaze away. Ryan turned, and calmly ran his hands over the equipment. He spied a small cabinet farther down inside the counter. Rowell saw where he was looking. "That stuff came in by special courier yesterday," he said, his voice jerky.

Ryan opened the cabinet. Inside, held in place by elastic straps, were his weapons, the pistol and the knife, plus another pistol. Ryan pulled out his pistol, checked to see whether it was loaded. It was. "Jesus!" Rowell snapped. "Put that damned thing away. If we get busted with this shit . . . I'd rather sink the fucking boat than have the Guardia find this stuff."

Ryan put the pistol back into its plush-lined cabinet, then shut the countertop.

"Let's get back to the office," Rowell said. "I'll fill out the papers transferring the boat to you, and then you can get the hell out here."

"You seem awfully anxious to get rid of me, Rowell," Ryan said icily. "And you seem a little nervous for this kind of work."

"I am, damn it. And I don't like doing it."

"Then . . . why do you?"

Rowell looked at Ryan, didn't like what he saw, and looked away. When he answered, there was less hostility in his voice. "I wish the hell I knew. Greed, I guess. They fronted me the money to start this business. It was all done over the phone, I never saw any of them, but the guy who talked to me had a really weird voice. Hell, at the time I didn't have a pot to piss in, and I really love the Mediterranean, I love boats, and I wanted to find a way to stay. Me and my family. And up until now it hasn't been too bad, just passing along information now and then. But this . . . shit! If I'm caught, I'll go to prison!"

Ryan studied Rowell, vacillating between contempt and pity. Here was another of Central's tools—one with a very dull edge, another typical alcoholic expatriate, holed up in a warm place with cheap booze. Rowell would break at the first application of real pressure, then he'd be casually discarded. For a moment the pity won out over the contempt. "Then get the hell out!" Ryan said abruptly.

"What? What do you mean?"

"Just get out of here. Leave. Go back home . . . wherever that is. Take your family and find someplace else where you can start over again."

"But . . . I can't," Rowell whined. "I'd be wiped out. Nothing's really in my name."

Ryan's pity drowned under a wave of contempt. "So stay, then."

He moved closer to Rowell, so that their faces were only inches apart. He pinned the other man's eyes with his own. "I'll tell you this once, Rowell, and only once. If you get nervous and screw anything up while I'm here, I'll cut your fucking heart out."

Rowell started to say something, but seemed to choke on the words. His face was very white. He stayed frozen in place, unable to look away.

"Now that we understand one another," Ryan finally said, "let's go take care of that paperwork."

By the middle of the next afternoon all the necessary papers had been signed. The boat now belonged to Ryan, or rather, to John Stevens. He checked out of his room and carried his bag down to the dock. He stood on the dock for a few minutes, admiring the sloop. A damned sweet little boat. He went below and stowed his gear, prowling around the galley and cabin, getting the feel of it. Satisfied, he went up on deck, then jumped over onto the dock and headed toward a bar, where he bought a bottle of Ciento Tres, a rough, cheap, but drinkable local brandy. Returning to the boat, he made himself comfortable in the cockpit, where he poured brandy into a glass he'd brought up from below.

The boat was the last piece of Central's elaborate plot to get him to Majorca. Overelaborate, Ryan suspected, but then, maybe Central was right, maybe it really was that tight getting in and out of Majorca. No matter, he had the boat, and he liked having it. Sitting here in the cockpit, sipping Ciento Tres, with the ancient town in front of him and the promise of the sea only a day away, he had almost forgotten why he was here, which maybe was a good thing. At least for a little while.

By sundown the level in the bottle had lowered about four inches, and Ryan was glowing nearly as much as the western sky. Suddenly he sensed someone on the dock next to the boat. Looking up, he saw Glen. "Hey . . . I thought I found you a hotel," Glen said, smiling.

"I decided to buy my own," Ryan replied amiably. "Come aboard."

Glen jumped into the cockpit. His eyes were darting everywhere. "Go ahead . . . take a look below," Ryan said.

Glen slid down the ladder and began poking around inside the cabin. Ryan wanted to see if he'd notice anything strange about the countertop. He didn't.

"Bring another glass," Ryan said as Glen started back up the ladder. Glen picked a glass out of a wooden rack, then sat in the cockpit, across from Ryan. Ryan poured him a drink.

"How'd you swing this?" Glen asked.

"With money."

"Of course. Stupid question. But it must have cost a lot."

"Enough. Now I'll just cruise around the Mediterranean until the rest of my money runs out."

Glen looked appraisingly at Ryan. "It doesn't *have* to run out. Not with a fine little boat like this."

"How do you figure that?" Ryan asked idly.

"Hell. A boat is capital. You use capital to make money. You can hire the boat out for charters."

"It's kind of small for that."

'Then you can carry things. From point A to point B. Especially when the value of the goods is a lot higher at point B."

Ryan was still only half listening. "What kind of things?"

"Small things. Valuable things."

It was the intensity of the expression on Glen's face that finally alerted Ryan to what he was talking about. "Dope?" he asked sharply.

"Well, hey . . . don't say it like it was a dirty word. It's money, man. Dope's dirt cheap in Tangiers. Sells for maybe ten times as much here. I'm not talking about smack or coke. I'm talking about hash, grass, Moroccan kef."

"You're also talking about a mountain of grief. Spanish dungeons."

"Well, yeah, there's always that possibility. But sometimes a guy has to take chances."

Ryan's annoyance quickly turned to amusement. Take chances? Which reminded him why he was here. Tetsuo Hidaka. Yoshiro. Terrorists. Plutonium. And possible trouble from talking to this kid about smuggling dope. "The subject is closed," he said firmly.

Glen looked disappointedly at Ryan, as if he were somehow lacking. The conversation lagged, and when Glen had finished his drink he thanked his host, then left the boat. Ryan watched him walking back into town, a slight, alert figure.

He'd been right about the entrepreneurial streak in the kid. A nice clean-cut American boy, a budding capitalist.

Ryan chuckled as he poured himself another drink. He looked out over the ancient town. It was growing dark now. A few stars were rising above the horizon, brilliant in the clear air. Take away the electric lights and the cars, and the town would look pretty much like it must have looked centuries ago. Centuries? Longer. This place must have been old when the Romans first dropped by. It had class. Glen did have a point. The boat could be a passport to a newer, freer kind of life. It would be wonderful to simply ramble around the Mediterranean, visiting other places like this, with no duties, no gut-wrenching assignments.

"Hola . . . señor!"

Ryan looked up. Two members of the Guardia Civil, Spain's national police, were standing in the dim glow of the dock light. Slowed by the brandy, he stared stupidly up at their olive-green uniforms, at the jackboots, at the shiny patent-leather hats turned up in the back, at their Sam Brown belts, and the heavy machine pistols slung over their shoulders.

The larger of the two Guardia called out again. When Ryan didn't answer, he switched to a heavily accented English. "We are coming aboard, señor."

The two men clumped aboard in their heavy boots. Ryan winced, thinking of the planking. Fortunately, it was protected by fiberglass. *"Sergente* Ferrer," the larger one said, introducing himself. "We have a few questions to ask you, señor. First of all, your name."

"John Stevens," Ryan replied, quickly producing his passport, trying to appear the flustered tourist. Sergeant Ferrer looked at Ryan's picture in the passport, then up at Ryan's face, then back down at the passport. He did not hand the passport back. "Why was that young American aboard?" Ferrer abruptly asked.

"Just . . . visiting."

"Do you know him well?"

"Not really. I met him yesterday. He offered to help me find a hotel room."

"But why do you want a hotel, señor, when you have a boat?"

"I just bought the boat. Yesterday."

Ferrer looked around. "A very beautiful boat. If you want to keep it, you should be careful whom you let aboard."

"Glen?" Ryan asked innocently.

"Yes, señor. He has too much to do with drugs. You do not use drugs, do you? You do not have any aboard?"

"Absolutely not."

"Good. Then you will not mind if we look below."

Ferrer was already motioning the other Guardia toward the cabin. The transmitter! The weapons! Ryan wondered if the hidden compartment would withstand a thorough search.

But the search was not very thorough. After poking around inside cabinets and under mattresses, the Guardia shook his head and started back up the ladder. "Pardon our intrusion, señor," Ferrer said. "For a long time we have been trying to catch this young man, but with no luck so far. It is the new laws. In the old days, when the *Caudillo* ... when Franco was still alive, we would have simply ... But never mind. We will get him someday."

Neither of the two policemen refused when Ryan offered them a drink. The atmosphere immediately became friendlier. The bottle was nearly empty by the time they left the boat. Ryan watched them go, outwardly calm, but inwardly seething ... at himself. "You stupid bastard," he muttered once they were out of sight. What an idiot he'd been ... acting like an amateur.

It was the boat that had done it. The boat, and the ancient harbor, and the sunset, and the brandy. The promise of freedom—or the illusion of freedom, if you listened to Central. A fragile kind of freedom, because he'd almost gotten himself nailed with a boatload of the worst kind of contraband imaginable in an uptight place like Spain. Weapons. Transmitters.

Ferrer had finally given him back the passport. Of

course, that didn't necessarily mean that they wouldn't check him out, maybe spread his name around to other ports. He hoped that they wouldn't. He hoped the brandy had mellowed them sufficiently. He hoped that they were as inefficient as they looked.

Whether they were or not, he wasn't taking any more chances. He'd make sail first thing in the morning.

9

Ryan cast off the mooring lines at first light. The morning breeze wasn't up yet, so he motored out of the harbor on the auxiliary. The town grew small behind him, a pastel jumble at the base of rugged slopes. Ryan was well out to sea when the sun came up, rising from behind a sharply etched horizon, its blinding disk gilding a bright path over the quiet water. He headed straight into the sunrise, a little east of northeast, toward Majorca. The water glinted red beneath the bow.

Ryan hoisted the two sails while there was still no wind, then returned to the cockpit with the boat still under power. Fastening the tiller, he went below to make himself a cup of coffee. He was above decks, drinking the coffee, when the first gentle puffs began to fill the main and jib. Killing the engine, he freed the tiller. The boat yawed aimlessly until the wind began to blow more strongly. Crack! The sails tautened, and the little sloop heeled over. The rudder bit, giving life to the tiller. Water gurgled past the counter. Glancing down at the compass, Ryan set his course.

The live feel of the boat exhilarated him. The sun began

to grow hot. Ryan took off his shirt and lay back in the cockpit, one hand looped lazily over the tiller. The vibration of the rigging hummed through the hull and into his hands. He listened to the water rushing past. The sun and the wind felt very sensuous against his skin. He began to toy with the idea of putting the helm over and sailing past Majorca, sailing on and on.

Ryan had been sailing for a couple of hours when he noticed a growing darkness on the horizon, behind him. At first he didn't pay much attention, but the next time he looked over his shoulder, the darkness had grown. What had at first seemed only a thickening of the atmosphere had coalesced into a solid mass of threatening black clouds. They seemed to be heading in his direction.

Ryan had no experience sailing the landlocked Mediterranean, he was a blue-water sailor, but he knew an approaching squall when he saw one. He kept glancing back over his shoulder as the black mass behind him grew larger and drew nearer. He was suddenly aware that it was racing toward him with a terrifying velocity.

Leaping to his feet, Ryan quickly took in sail, leaving only a tiny triangle of jib showing forward. He returned to the cockpit just in time; a moment later the squall struck. The wind hit first, like a solid wall, nearly knocking him off his feet, gusting wildly, ripping the tops off rapidly building waves, hurling water at the boat. Needle-sharp spray rattled against the deck. Seas began to pour aboard. Almost blinded by the fury of wind and water, Ryan slammed the hatch shut, latching it tightly, to keep water out of the cabin. He stumbled back to the tiller, clutching it for support. Picking up a piece of line, he quickly lashed himself to a stay.

Large seas were building, but in an unsteady pattern. Each wave crest was broken by a cross-chop that was difficult to decipher. Several times Ryan was surprised by water breaking over the transom. There was only one consistent pattern to the waves—they were growing larger.

What should he do? His mind raced. The boat would be

a lot more stable if he headed it into the wind; the high, sharp bow would protect the rest of the craft from the full fury of the waves. If, in addition, he rigged a sea anchor aft, he should have no real trouble.

But it was probably too late. Ryan doubted he could now bring the boat around in the madly churning seas. One big wave over the side and he might be swamped. The hell with it anyhow. The storm was blowing him in the direction of Majorca; he might as well take advantage of its power.

A few minutes later Ryan was having second thoughts. The waves were building more quickly than he'd expected. So far the cross-chop had kept down the height of the waves, but now, about a quarter mile astern, he saw a succession of huge rollers approaching. My God, but the boat seemed small. Christ! If he judged wrong and let the boat broach, he'd be rolled under by one of those huge mothers, and it would be all over. He was grateful for that small piece of jib showing forward; it gave him steerage way . . . as long as the canvas held.

Gripping the tiller tightly, Ryan looked back over his shoulder and watched the first roller bear down on him. It towered over the boat, threatening to bury him under its immense volume. Spray blew off the wave's ragged top in a steady stream; it looked as if it were going to break at any moment and crash down on top of the boat. Ryan braced himself for disaster.

But the boat responded beautifully. The slender sloping stern rose gracefully out of the water and began to climb up the face of the wave, higher and higher, until the hull was balanced on its crest. Then the bow shot up as the wave rushed past, and a moment later the boat was siding down into the trough.

Ryan realized that he was laughing. He shouted loudly, triumphantly. He was winning! The boat felt as alive as a bucking horse. He rode it gleefully.

The little sloop took the next wave in the same manner, and the next. Ryan laughed again, the sound of his voice snatched away by the wind. How clean, how real this was, battling against the sea, just himself and the boat against the uncaring, primeval power of the Mediterranean.

The sea ground on remorselessly, oblivious to his presence. Then Ryan stopped laughing. The waves he had so easily passed over had been only outriders. One hundred yards behind, a much larger wave was bearing down on him, headed straight toward the stern, a huge green mountain of water, building in height as it raced into the trough of the wave ahead. Towering as high as the mast, the wave promised to destroy him—it was clearly going to break just as it reached the boat.

Now it was right overhead, a vertical wall, glassy near the bottom where its bulk protected it from the wind. Ryan stared straight into the wave, into the murky green coldness that was about to swallow him. Instinctively he shrank away as the crest toppled over onto the boat.

Ryan felt the boat shudder, pounded under by the wave's terrible weight. He knew that his sloop was broaching, but he could do nothing about it, he was buried under the wave too, holding his breath, his lungs feeling as if they were going to burst.

And then the boat struggled free. Tons of frothy water cascaded from the rising stern. The wave raced by, and Ryan was in the open again, gratefully gulping air.

But the sloop had swung around dangerously; it was lying half-sideways in the path of the next wave. Ryan struggled with the tiller, fighting to bring the bow around, certain he wasn't going to make it. At the last moment the stern bobbed up and the wave passed harmlessly underneath.

Fortunately, none of the waves now building were anywhere near the size of the one that had almost swamped him. Shortly afterward, the squall began to die, almost as quickly as it had blown up. Within another hour Ryan was once again sailing over a nearly smooth sea, his wet clothing steaming in the hot sun. A small amount of water had leaked into the main cabin, but that was the only reminder of the immense power that had nearly destroyed both him and the boat.

An unaccustomed sense of peace now took possession of Ryan. He began to seriously consider Glen's suggestion ... not necessarily running dope, but of somehow using the boat to make money. Well, what the hell, why not run a little grass? He liked the idea of making a living by shoving his thumb in bureaucracy's eye. What he did not want was any more Hellers.

Pipe dreams! He was, at the moment, committed. Central had absolutely no sense of humor about agents who copped out on a mission. He'd never live to enjoy a future if he backed out now. And then there was the woman. Always the woman.

Ryan sailed on. Night fell. He slept a little, but stayed above decks, keeping himself half alert. He was in heavily traveled waters, in the route of the big ferries that traveled to Majorca from the mainland and the other islands. They'd run him over in the dark and never even realize they'd hit him.

Just after dawn, he saw land ahead. Majorca. He had come in a little too far to the north. High, sheer cliffs rose straight up out of the sea, with rugged mountains inland. He turned to starboard, heading southeast. An hour later, breaks began to appear in the cliffs. There were coves where the cliffs dipped to sea level. High-rise hotels and apartments crammed the coves and beaches ... probably the tourist cities Glen had told him about. The building density increased as he neared a jutting headland. Rounding the headland, Ryan saw Palma spread out ahead of him. Palma de Mallorca, the ancient capital of Roman governors, of sultans, of crusaders and kings.

The city was beautiful from the sea. It curved in a crescent around a large, very blue bay. Low hills rose at the western end. A plain lay behind the city, and at the far end of the plain, perhaps ten miles distant, a jagged wall of mountains thrust up through the morning mist.

The city itself was the lovely, faded buff color of most

old Mediterranean cities . . . except for the garish smear of new hotels that lined the northwestern end of the waterfront. The southeastern end was dominated by a massive gothic cathedral, and next to the cathedral, a crenelated Moorish palace. Spires, arches, towers, and fortifications stood out against the bright blue of the sky. Halfway between the hotels and the cathedral, set slightly behind the city on a hilltop, a round, buff-colored castle stood outlined against the sky.

A breakwater and mole reached out into the bay, creating a smaller artificial harbor. Ryan had once read a book on harbor design. He recognized the mole as nearly identical to the layout used by the Romans in other Mediterranean harbors two thousand years earlier. He wondered if the Romans might have built the original breakwater here; their designs were hard to improve on.

He sailed into the harbor under the shadow of the mole, heading for the boat basin. For a little while he could not see the newer part of the town, could see only the old part, and below it, the remnants of the huge city wall, with its moats and guard towers and water gates. The great mass of the cathedral rose high above the wall. Farther in, past the cathedral and palace, he could see ancient, cream-colored buildings, a scene right out of a Renaissance painting. For a few minutes, eight centuries rolled away, and Palma was once again the city of the Crusaders.

Ryan tied up at the Royal Yacht Club. It took a couple of hours to clear customs. The customs officers made no effort to search the boat, so once again the hidden cabinet was not put to the test. Ryan spent another hour swabbing salt water out of the cabin. Visiting the yacht club's showers, reserved for boat owners, he scrubbed salt off himself. Then, tired, he returned to the boat, lay down on a bunk, and slept.

It was growing dark when he awoke. He lay quietly for a few minutes, clearing his mind, letting his body wake up thoroughly. Then he got up and dressed in shore clothes. Next, he pried apart the false bottom of his small suitcase and took out another passport, in the name of Martin Peters. The John Stevens passport went back into the false suitcase bottom. He wanted nothing ashore to connect hm to the boat.

Then he armed himself. He took out the knife first. It was very old, and Japanese, of the type known as a *tanto*. The blade was fairly heavy, a little over six inches long, single edged, and slightly curved, with a broad, almost chisel-shaped tip. It had been made by hand by a master sword maker, three hundred years before. Hand-forged iron had been folded over onto itself again and again, forming thousands of layers of incredibly tough steel. The knife's edge was extremely hard, but the body was flexible enough to keep it from breaking under stress. Wavy temper lines zigzagged along the razor edge. Ryan handled the knife with respect. No one but the Japanese had ever made blades of such quality. Although the knife had not been polished in over twenty years, it was still bright and sharp.

The knife went into a sheath strapped to Ryan's calf. Its flat handle made it easy to conceal. He took out the pistols next. One was his regular Colt .45 lightweight Commander, a cut-down version of the old Army .45. No James Bond popguns for Ryan. He preferred cartridges that would stop a fight by knocking an opponent off his feet.

He picked up the other pistol, the new one, something that either Central or one of his minions had thoughtfully provided. It was a Rogak P-18 nine-millimeter automatic. Ryan hefted the Rogak thoughtfully. It was big, it was double-action, and it held eighteen rounds, with another in the chamber. But the caliber was nine-millimeter, not as much of a man-stopper as the .45. Still, nineteen rounds was a lot of firepower. The .45 only held eight.

The Rogak was awfully large, hard to conceal in a warm climate where clothing was necessarily light, so Ryan picked up his little .45, slammed a magazine into the butt, and jacked a shell into the chamber. He then took the magazine back out and stuffed in another round before ramming the magazine back into place. Now he had his eight rounds.

He slipped a small holster in between his pants and his skin, then filled the holster with the Colt. With the tail of his light jacket over the pistol butt, nothing showed. That was one of the things he liked about automatics: their flat grips made them easy to conceal.

Ryan searched his memory for the address where he was to meet his Palma contact, his key to finding Ernst Kranek. Then he shut the countertop, went on deck, locked the hatch, and set off on foot toward the center of town.

10

The Nordic Bar was located in a small street in the old part of Palma; it was more alley than street, too narrow for cars, open only to pedestrians. The bar was in a semi-cellar, reached by walking down a half dozen concrete steps. According to a sign on the wall, the Nordic Bar, and all the other establishments in this area that were below street level, had at one time been enormous underground wine vats. It appeared to be the truth. The rough concrete walls curved overhead like the interior of a huge barrel.

Even though it catered mostly to foreigners, the Nordic was not a tourist bar, but rather, one of Palma's many dim little places where expatriate northerners congregated to grow drunk and reminisce about "home." The decor inside the Nordic was mock Scandinavian with a dash of England. Tin Viking helmets with plastic horns hung haphazardly on the grimy walls. Most of the posted notices were either Swedish or English.

Ryan sat at a small table half lost in a shadowy alcove, sipping a beer and observing the other customers, the majority of whom were clustered around the small bar, drinking hard. He knew the type . . . expatriates who probably called themselves "artists" or "writers," which boiled down to "no visible means of support." When they were too broke to buy the cheap Spanish booze, they daubed paint onto canvases and sold them to tourists, or spent a few days working frantically on pornographic novels.

All the customers were men, with the exception of one young blond woman in her early twenties. Ryan was impressed by her looks . . . until his eyes became used to the dim lighting. Then he noticed the haggard look on her face, the tense features, the quick jerky movements, the way her teeth worked nervously at a bloodless lower lip. A speed freak. Methedrine Mary.

In a tiny kitchen behind the bar, a seedy-looking Englishman in his mid-thirties was swigging belts of gin out of a bottle with one hand while stirring an enormous pot of curry with the other. His dirty T-shirt was plastered to his body with sweat. Not a prepossessing man, yet he interested Ryan a great deal. According to his briefing instructions, this grubby Englishman was his Palma contact, the man who would tell him where to find Ernst Kranek. So far, Ryan had not been able to approach the Englishman. The bar was too crowded.

A half-drunk, middle-aged American tourist came down the steps into the room. No one paid any attention as he bellied up to the bar, except for the blond speed freak. As he bellowed for beer, she slid close, smiling her ghastly amphetamine smile. The man was either too drunk or too stupid to know how much trouble was hiding inside that still-sexy young body. They went to work on each other: he, to prove that he could still make it with young chicks; she, to find a meal and a place to sleep for the night. And maybe a wallet left out in the open near her twitching fingers.

"A'right, mates . . . 'ere it is," the cook suddenly called out in a heavily slurred voice. "Getcher curry while it's 'ot. O'ny five hunnert pesetas a plate."

Ryan raised his hand. "Over here," he said. None of the

others in the bar paid much attention; they were watching the blonde stalk the tourist.

"Cor ... but you're a big 'un," the cook said as he approached Ryan's table with a steaming plate of rice and curry. "Too 'eavy to be a Swede. You must be a bloody Yank." He thumped the plate down on the table. A little juice slopped over the side.

"Thanks, Cory," Ryan said evenly. The cook's eyes immediately narrowed. Ryan suspected he was not nearly as drunk as he appeared.

Cory hesitated. "'Ow'd yer know me name?" he asked in a low intense voice. "I'm goddamn sure I never seen you before."

"A little bird named Central whispered it into my ear. Now ... where's Kranek?"

"Jesus!" Cory hissed, quickly sitting down. "You got your brass, comin' in 'ere big as life, just poppin' out with it like that. ..."

"The quicker you give me the information, the safer we'll both be. Just tell me where he is and I'll leave."

"Okay. He's ..."

The cook's voice trailed away as two men came down the steps into the bar. He glanced quickly away from them, then stood up and began industriously mopping the spilled juice from Ryan's table. "See that curtain over there?" he mumbled. "It leads out back. I'll head that way in a few minutes. The loo's back there. Pretend the beer's got to yer, an' you gotter take a quick slash. Then follow me out.

"Five hunnert pesetas, mate," he said more loudly. Ryan paid him the money. Cory took it back to the cash register, then started serving the other customers. Ryan noticed that he was glancing nervously at the two newcomers.

Ryan began to eat. The curry was very good. While he ate, he covertly studied the two men who were making Cory so nervous. At first he had taken them for Spaniards; they were rather dark-complected. Then he changed his mind. In the first place, Spaniards would rarely come into a place like the Nordic. And, after another look, they didn't resemble Spaniards after all. Their features were too lean, too sharp.

The two men sat at the bar and ordered brandy. One of them glanced in Ryan's direction, which forced Ryan to look back down at his plate. He didn't want them to know he was interested in them, so he made himself pay attention to his meal for a full minute. When he looked up again, he received a jolt. The men were gone, and so was Cory. The beaded curtain hanging over the rear exit Cory had mentioned was gently swinging.

Ryan quickly got to his feet and pushed through the curtain. There was a narrow corridor on the other side, with a short flight of stairs at the far end, leading up toward a closed door. There was no one in sight. Ryan headed toward the stairs. There was another door off to one side, half open. As he passed it, he peered inside, into a tiny, empty, very dirty bathroom. Turning away, he cautiously mounted the stairs and slowly opened the door at the top.

It led outside, into a small enclosed courtyard formed by the back walls of other buildings. The courtyard was littered with junk, and brightly illuminated by an overhead light set on top of a high pole. In the harsh glare, Ryan saw the cook standing in the middle of a cleared space, facing one of the dark strangers. His hands were raised defensively in front of his body, while the man circled him, leaning forward, balanced on the balls of his feet. The man's right hand held a long, thin-bladed knife.

Cory had obviously been trying to ward off the knife with his bare hands. His forearms were streaked with blood. Ryan started to reach for his .45, but then realized that the roar of the shot, magnified within this enclosed area, would bring half the town running. And there appeared to be no way out of the courtyard except back through the bar. Silence was imperative.

Ryan was just beginning to move toward Cory and his attacker when it occurred to him to wonder where the other man was. He was answered a second later by a slight sound behind him. Turning his head, he saw the second stranger rushing at him from the shadows, one arm held high, ready to plunge a knife into Ryan's unprotected back.

Instead of trying to move farther away, Ryan suddenly stepped back into his assailant, so that the descending knife cut harmlessly through the air in front of him. As the man's arm thudded down onto his shoulder, Ryan, still facing away, gripped the knife arm in both hands, then, bending low, he effortlessly threw the man forward over his shoulder, keeping a tight grip on the arm, using its leverage to slam the man down hard against the stone paving.

Shaken, the man nevertheless attempted to twist free and renew his attack. Ryan scooped the Japanese knife from its sheath near his ankle, and struck down hard, burying all six inches of the blade deep into his opponent's chest. The man's eyes opened wide with shock. For a moment he clung tightly to Ryan's arm, staring incredulously at the knife handle protruding from his chest. Then his eyes clouded over and he sank back, dead.

Ryan looked up from the corpse just in time to see the other man make a lunge at Cory. The Englishman danced away backwards, but his foot caught on a piece of junk, causing him to lose his balance. The knife slipped in underneath Cory's guard, burying itself in his stomach. He gave a grunt of surprise, then a sharp scream as his attacker suddenly ripped the knife sideways, opening up his belly. A huge gout of blood shot from the wound, and Cory slowly sank downward, his bloody hands desperately gripping his attacker's knife arm.

Cory's attacker spun around quickly, tearing away from Cory. He saw Ryan crouching over his fallen companion. He swore in what sounded like Arabic, then started toward Ryan.

Ryan was in trouble. His knife, driven down so hard, had buried itself in his opponent's breastbone, and he couldn't get it back out. He tugged upward with all his strength, but only succeeded in lifting the corpse several inches off the ground. Then the other man was on top of him, and he had no choice but to surrender the knife and leap back.

The two men faced each other over the corpse, both of them panting. Unarmed, still unwilling to use the .45, Ryan continued moving backward, trying to lure his opponent into sacrificing his balance by stepping over the corpse. But the man edged around the obstruction, his footing steady on the uneven pavement. He held his knife well out in front of him, the point aimed at Ryan's face.

The man's steady advance forced Ryan to retreat farther, until his back came up against a stone wall. The man lunged, but Ryan sidestepped and spun away, the knife striking sparks from the wall.

Now their positions were reversed, the attacker's back against the wall, and Ryan in the clear, facing him. Ryan made his move before the other man could attack again, but instead of moving away, Ryan feinted forward, bringing his body within knife range. The man took the bait, slashing viciously at Ryan's stomach. With perfect timing, Ryan stepped inside the glittering arc of the knife blade. The man's forearm thumped against Ryan's ribs. Ryan immediately pinned the man's arm to his body with his elbow. The knife now jutted harmlessly behind him.

The man tried to jerk his arm free, but Ryan was already moving, driving a knee into his groin. As his opponent gasped with pain and started to crumple, Ryan slammed the heel of his hand up underneath the man's chin, then drove upward and back, his whole body lifting. The man rose a few inches off the ground, his head smashing back against the stone wall with a hollow crack, like a coconut splitting. His entire body stiffened for a moment, his eyes rolled in opposite directions, then he fell at Ryan's feet, dead, his skull fractured.

Untangling his feet from the corpse, Ryan ran to Cory, who was trying to struggle up onto one elbow. The front of his clothing was soaked in blood.

"Lie back!" Ryan ordered. Cory groaned and flopped back down, but immediately started to curl up into a ball, both hands pressed against his stomach. Ryan pulled Cory's shirt aside. He winced. Cory's lower abdomen was cut wide open. "Oh Christ . . . it hurts!" Cory whimpered. One of his hands fell away from his body. His fingers scrabbled hard against the cobbles.

"Where's Kranek?" Ryan demanded.

"Help me. . . . Help me!"

"I can't. It's too late. Just tell me where Kranek is."

Cory's eyes cleared for a moment. "I'm gonna die?"

Ryan nodded. "There isn't much time."

"Oh, shit. That bastard, Central."

Cory's body spasmed again, doubling him up. "Hurts! God . . . it hurts!"

"Kranek. Where is he?" Ryan demanded again. He was sure Cory would die any moment. His guts were spilling out into his hands, and the knife stroke must have severed the main abdominal artery. A huge amount of blood had already spilled out onto the ground.

Then, to his surprise, Cory began speaking rapidly, although not very clearly. "Little . . . little village called Son Feliu . . . mountains. The girl with the telephone . . . Kranek. He's hiding. . . . Oh . . . God!"

Cory's body spasmed again. More blood poured out through the wound. "Jesus . . . I'm dyin'. . . ."

"What girl? Who are you talking about? Give me her name!"

"Son Feliu . . . in the mountains. The girl. The telephone . . ."

Cory's eyes opened wide, full of astonishment. He seemed to be staring at something over Ryan's shoulder. Suddenly blood gushed from his mouth and his body went limp. For another second or two a last spark of life remained in his eyes, then it slowly died away.

Ryan let the body slump back down onto the ground. Rotten luck. Worse for Cory, of course. What a miserable way to die. And now his informant was dead and he had precious little to go on, just some disconnected references to a place called Son Feliu, a girl, and a telephone.

Ryan stood up and went over to the two men he'd killed. There was nothing in their pockets but a little money, nothing to identify them. Their sharp olive features probably belonged to the eastern Mediterranean. Arabs, perhaps, maybe some of the men who'd stolen the uranium.

He had to clean things up, he had to hide what had happened here, so the opposition would not know that another player had entered the game. To get his knife back, Ryan had to pound down on his first victim's chest with his foot while tugging on the knife handle. It finally came free. He carefully wiped the blade clean on the dead man's shirt before putting the knife back into its sheath.

The bodies were easy to dispose of. Ryan dragged the three corpses behind a pile of rubbish and covered them with more rubbish. He dragged junk over the bloodstains Cory had left. When Ryan was satisfied that it would take a little time to find the bodies, he went back inside, stopping in the grimy washroom to check for bloodstains on his clothing. There were none, although his hands were smeared. He washed them, then flushed the toilet and headed back toward the bar, the rush of water loud behind him.

Nothing much had changed inside the bar; no one seemed to have missed Cory, and probably wouldn't until they wanted another drink. The American had taken a long second look at the blonde, and was growing uneasy, but she was sticking to him like a leach. Ryan sat down and finished his curry, then left quietly. Out in the street an American sailor was crouched against the side of the building, retching up cheap Spanish brandy. Ryan detoured around him.

He took a roundabout route back to the boat. Only when he was certain that no one was following did he head toward the marina. On his first pass he walked right past the boat, glancing out of the corner of his eye to see if there was a welcoming party waiting there for him. Finally satisfied, he stepped aboard. He checked to see if the tiny piece of paper he'd wedged in the crack between the hatch and the deck coaming was still in place. It was. Satisfied, he unlocked the hatch and descended into the cabin.

Inside, he lay down on one of the bunks and tried to puzzle out the situation. One thing was clear—Central had been right, the heat was really on. The men he'd killed . . . he wondered if they'd already known where Kranek was, or if they'd merely intended to shut Cory up. They'd certainly made no attempt to question him. His death had been more like an execution.

Ryan's cover was apparently still good. The men in the bar had paid no attention to him at all . . . until he had forced them to.

He was tempted to go looking for Kranek immediately. But it was now late at night, he didn't know where the hell Son Feliu was, he didn't have a car, and if he remembered Spain correctly, he knew that he was unlikely to find transportation at this time of night. Besides, a good way to attract attention would be to go poking around a Spanish village in the middle of the night. If the terrorists already had Kranek, starting now would make no difference. If they didn't, but knew where he was, maybe they'd wait until the two men who'd killed Cory came back. That would be a long wait. The bodies might not be discovered until they began to stink.

Best to get some sleep, then start out first thing in the morning. Go prepared. Ryan undressed and lay down on the bunk again, his .45 near his hand. But before he fell asleep he reflected that the mission had hardly gotten under way and already four men were dead. Counting Heller.

11

Ryan was up at first light. He packed a small bag with a charge of clothing, and was about to shove the .45 into its holster when he had second thoughts. Opening the hidden cabinet, he picked up the Rogak. It was large and heavy. Nevertheless, it had all that firepower. In a village, in the countryside, the close-range heavy wallop of the .45 might not be as important as the firepower and longer range of the nine-millimeter Rogak.

He fitted the Rogak's holster to the inside of his waistband and slid the pistol into place. It made a sizable bulge, but as long as he wore a loose enough and long enough shirt, it shouldn't show.

As always, the knife was strapped to his lower leg. Armed, he picked up his bag and went on deck. It was a beautiful morning, the tourists would be happy today. The sun was just coming up over the cathedral, chasing the morning mists. The bright light gave color to the city, gently highlighting the rose-colored battlements of Bellver Castle, up on its mountaintop. The water in the bay was a deep blue, almost a purple, and everywhere, on every side, the wonderful, ancient stonework glowed with light.

Ryan locked the hatch, then walked into town. The trees along the Paseo Maritimo smelled sweet. The late spring leaves rustled softly in the first gentle morning breeze. It was still early, so it was peaceful; the day's mad rush had not yet begun. When he judged he was far enough from the boat, Ryan stopped at a bar and had a quick breakfast of coffee and *ensaimadas,* light, flaky rolls, unique to the island.

Afterward, walking north along the Paseo Maritimo, across from the various yacht basins, he found a car rental agency already open for the day's deluge of tourists. Along the way he had spent time noticing which car was the most common, the least likely to be noticed. He rented one of that make and model. It was a very small car, with barely enough room inside for Ryan to drive. After folding himself into the cramped little machine he had trouble getting his feet onto the pedals.

He'd studied a map of Majorca before leaving the boat. Son Feliu was about twenty miles from the city, in a mountainous part of the island. For the next ten minutes Ryan fought his way through quickly growing morning traffic. It was a highly competitive madhouse. The first time around, he missed the road he was looking for—there were few signs—but he made it on the second pass, and within another few minutes he was out of the city. It happened quite suddenly; one minute he was still surrounded by multi-story buildings, the next he was in open country. Behind him the edge of the city loomed up like a wall, rising quite abruptly from flat empty land.

Although the road was narrow, it was well surfaced. It ran relatively straight for about five miles, across a plain, toward a jagged wall of mountains. In the plain the road was bordered, as in Ibiza, by low stone walls, fencing off almond orchards and rocky fields. Shaggy sheep wandered in scattered flocks. Here and there, farmhouses lay within sight of the road, most of them made of the usual rough stone, topped with red tile roofs. Occasional large *fincas,* sometimes of several stories, dominated hilltops. Medieval strong points. Once again Ryan had the impression of a land relatively unchanged for centuries.

The mountains, which had seemed so far away, were suddenly straight ahead. The road narrowed and began to climb steeply. A shallow stream, nearly dry at this time of year, paralleled the pavement. Small pines and groves of olive trees were scattered over the steep mountain slopes. The mountains were even rockier than the plain. This was not a soft land.

About ten miles out from Palma, Ryan took the turnoff to Son Feliu, and now the road became even narrower, and much steeper, winding haphazardly over sheer drops. Many of the curves were so sharp, and the visibility ahead so limited, that he had to use his horn to warn approaching drivers that he was coming, although he only encountered two cars. Obviously, the area was relatively uninhabited. Once, he had to stop when a mule cart blocked the road. The driver stood, balancing easily on the flat bed of the cart, flicking his reins at his skinny mule, not deigning to pay any attention to Ryan. The cart blocked Ryan's way for five minutes, before the driver finally turned off onto a dirt path.

The road opened out onto the side of a mountain. Beautifully fitted stone retaining walls bordered the pavement, holding back tons of rock and thin soil. One final bend, and Son Feliu lay ahead, high above, perched on a hilltop, a pastel jumble of ancient buildings dominated by a massive lump of church. A squat, unattractive steeple topped the church.

Ryan drove into the village. There was a small parking lot near the church. He parked, then proceeded on foot up a short wide street into a small plaza. A large low building was located on one side of the plaza, across from the church. A sign high on one wall said "Pensione." It was an inn. The pensione's glass front door sported brandy advertisements, indicating the presence of a bar, and where there was a bar, there was often information. Ryan went inside.

It was quite cool inside the pensione; the huge mass of

stone easily resisted the rising heat of the sun. There was a small bar just inside the door. A short, thickset man with a broad face dominated by an enormous nose stood behind the bar. *"Cerveza, por favor,"* Ryan said. The man reached into a refrigerator, pulled out a frosty bottle of San Miguel beer, and thunked it down onto the bar, along with a thick glass. *"Tresciento pesetas, señor,"* he said, looking not at Ryan but at the wall behind him.

Ryan paid, poured the beer into the glass, then wandered around while he sipped. There wasn't much to see in this particular room, just a large table, perhaps for banquets, but he noticed bright sunlight coming in through windows toward the rear of the building. He looked questioningly at the bartender, who nodded, poker-faced, so Ryan headed toward the light. The room he entered took up most of the rear width of the building, a big glassed-in veranda. The ground fell away underneath; the pensione was situated on the edge of a precipice.

The room had a sweeping view of the countryside. Ryan carefully studied the terrain. The road he had come up lay below. On the far side of the road the ground dropped away into a green, lovely little valley. Beyond the valley, to the south, the land rose again, forming a dome-shaped mountain, its slopes bristly with scraggly pines. The mountain looked a little like the head of a giant who'd forgotten to shave.

Ryan was mostly interested in the road. He could see part of the route he'd taken, winding back down the mountainside to his left, then disappearing from view. To his right, the road continued on past the Son Feliu turnoff, heading down the western slope in a series of switchbacks. The land fell away steeply for the first two or three miles, then flattened out into a fertile-looking plain. From there, the road seemed to loop back to the left toward Palma. Ryan could see a glint of sea in the distance.

The view was stunning. Colors changed with distance, the greens and browns of the land eventually merging with the light blue of the sea, which lay perhaps seven or eight miles away. Perhaps. By now Ryan had begun to realize that distances were deceptive on Majorca. The landscape was so rugged, so vertical, so packed, that distant objects appeared larger than they actually were. A mountain that at first seemed to be thirty or forty miles away might be no more than ten.

Son Feliu was a quiet place; there was nothing to be heard but the sound of a rather steady wind, the buzz of insects, the rise and fall of an occasional distant voice. A nice place to escape to. Perhaps a nice bolt hole for a missing nuclear physicist.

Ryan walked back into the bar. The bartender was still leaning, poker-faced, against the wall. Ryan knew that the man was not being unfriendly, he was merely being Spanish: quiet, dignified, aloof. Ryan had little trouble striking up a conversation, once the bartender realized he spoke Spanish. Ryan quickly learned that the man was not merely a bartender, he was also the owner of the pensione and the mayor of the town. "Do you rent out rooms?" Ryan asked.

The owner, his name was Bendet, shrugged his shoulders. "Not for the last twenty years. First, my own family filled up this place, then the family of my wife's brother." At the mention of his wife's brother he spat into a corner. "And now it's full of the families of our children. These days, we only keep the bar and the restaurant open. But a hundred years ago . . ."

Ryan nodded. The Spanish sense of time, one of the things he loved about the place. A hundred years, ten years . . . it was all the same. The future was never imminent. In the old days a man might begin building a hillside terrace on which he would eventually plant one olive tree. If he was not a young man, he realized that the olive tree would not begin producing a good return during his own lifetime. But that was not a primary consideration. He was building for future lifetimes, he was building for the land and the people, he was building for that which went on and on, for the endless turning of the seasons, for the birth of new generations. Some of the olive trees that lined the terraces around the town were over a thousand years old—Ryan could tell by their immense gnarled bulk—and they were still producing. The men who had built those terraces had simply been building as their fathers had done, and their fathers' fathers, and their fathers' fathers' fathers, generation after generation, back through the centuries, since before the time of the Romans.

While he was talking to Bendet, Ryan was casually glancing around the room. He did not see a telephone, and Cory had said something about a telephone.

"Señor," he finally asked, "I remember that I have to call someone in Palma. Do you have a telephone?"

"Alas, señor . . . there is only one telephone in Son Feliu . . . at the *telefonica*. We're still a little primitive this far out. If you want to make a call, you must go further up into the village, to the shop that holds the instrument. There is a girl there, Petra, who will help you make the call."

Jackpot. A telephone and a girl. A girl with a name, now. Petra. This might be what Cory had meant, although Ryan wondered if it was all going too easily. He paid for his beer, thanked Bendet, and, following his directions, left the bar and headed for the *telefonica*.

The village was situated on a steep slope. It was a fair hike up the single narrow street, but the shop was easy to find, it was located in a portion of the lower floor of a massive old stone house. The family probably lived in the rest of the house. A sign outside, in the colors of Spain, red and gold, indicated that the shop was also the town's official *estanco*, the only place where postage stamps and tobacco could be legally sold. With the shop holding the town's only telephone, along with the *estanco*, it formed a neat little rural monopoly.

A small bell over the door jingled when Ryan entered. He stepped into a large room. It was quite cool inside, and rather dark. The walls were covered with shelves of canned food and bottles of wine and olive oil. Some of the wine bottles were extremely dusty. Ryan wondered how many years, perhaps even decades, they had been sitting there, a gourmet's dream. Big sacks of grain, potatoes, fruits, and vegetables were stacked on the floor. The rear wall was lined with wine barrels. It was rather difficult to see what was actually there; the dim light and the dust made the whole place look slightly out of focus.

At first there was no one in sight, then Ryan saw movement from behind a curtain near the back. A moment later a girl came through the curtain into the room. She turned on a light, but the bulb was of such low wattage that it made little difference.

But when the girl moved behind the counter, which was near the light from the front door, Ryan saw that she was quite beautiful, rather tall for a Spaniard, full-bodied, and wonderfully graceful in her movements. Her eyes were large and brown, dominating the strong planes of her face. Her thick reddish brown hair was pulled to the back of her head in a severe knot, which only served to draw attention to the lushness of the rest of her. She appeared to be in her middle or late twenties.

"Buenos dias, señor," she said. Her voice was flat, emotionless, wary.

"Buenos dias ..." A slight hesitation. Ryan saw that she was not wearing a ring, although that might not mean much here. *"... Señorita,"* he finished. She did not react, so perhaps she wasn't married, although she didn't seem to react to much of anything. "I would like to make a telephone call," Ryan continued. "Would you help me?" He handed her a slip of paper with a telephone number written on it.

She nodded, then pointed across the shop. Ryan saw it then, an ancient wooden telephone booth buried way back in a corner, near boxes of bananas. Its faded dun color melded in so well with the rest of the shop that it had, until now, been invisible to him. He headed toward the phone booth, while the girl moved to a handset bolted to the rear wall, one of the old hand-cranked models. The girl began to turn the crank briskly. It took her half a minute to get the operator, and another half minute for the operator to connect to the number Ryan had provided. The girl motioned, and Ryan went inside the booth and picked up the receiver. He heard the measured buzzing of a phone ringing. After several rings a woman answered, whom Ryan completely confused by talking in English, a language she obviously didn't understand. He had made up the number just before coming into the shop; he had no idea to whom he was speaking.

He talked for another few seconds, then hung up. The girl was waiting for him at the counter. *"Cien pesetas,"* she said. He paid her the money, then began wandering around the store, looking at goods on the shelves. On impulse, he bought a couple of those dusty bottles of wine. The price was extremely low, about fifty cents a bottle. They had probably been on the shelves since the girl had been a child. He also bought a *cesta,* a hand-made fiber basket, into which he put the bottles.

He tried to engage the girl in conversation, but she kept her answers to a polite minimum; obviously his attentions were making her uneasy. Or perhaps men in general made her uneasy. She exhibited a bitterness, an inner tension, that contradicted the promise of her face and body.

Suddenly there was the roar of a motor outside, followed by the repeated blaring of a horn. The girl's face tensed. *"Mi tío,"* she murmured, and immediately started for the front door. Ryan followed her outside. An old flatbed truck loaded with supplies had pulled up in front of the door. The driver was still leaning on the horn. "Petra!" the man shouted. "If you keep me waiting any longer . . ."

As soon as the driver saw the girl he jumped down from the cab, then climbed up onto the truck bed and began pushing sacks and boxes toward the edge. Petra lugged them into the store one by one. Ryan, standing just inside the shop door, noticed that the man was not doing any more work than he absolutely had to, leaving most of the real labor to the girl.

The man was short, and very broad, with a bloated belly

thrusting its way out from beneath an undersized gray sweater. His face was remarkably ugly and brutal, with a broad nose capped by a wart, a knife-thin mouth, mean little eyes, and a two-or three-day growth of beard. He was watching the girl with an unpleasant intensity, his eyes boring into her whenever she turned her back. He kept up a running stream of insults, ordering her to work faster, but Petra was not, at least not openly, paying any attention to what he was saying. She simply kept working, her face as expressionless as when Ryan had first come into the shop.

Apparently believing that he was not adequately tormenting the girl, the man on the truck, probably her uncle, as she'd murmured to Ryan before going outside, began sliding a heavy sack of flour toward the edge of the truck bed. When the girl came back out of the store, he pushed it off the edge. She automatically reached up for it, wrapping her arms around its bulk, taking its full weight. She was actually able to take several tottering steps toward the shop door before she began to lose her balance; the sack was simply too heavy.

Her uncle screamed abuse at her as the sack began to fall, although he was apparently delighted that she was going to drop it. Ryan quickly stepped out of the shop's doorway and caught the sack before it hit the ground. Apparently without effort, although his tendons were straining, he slung the sack over one shoulder and took it into the store.

Petra followed him inside. Her expression, as she faced him, was a mixture of gratitude and apprehension. *"Gracias, señor,"* she said softly. She might have said more, but a barrage of curses came blasting in through the door. "There is more to unload," she said to Ryan, then went back outside.

Ryan followed her out. Her uncle was squatting on the truck bed, glaring down at her as she walked over to the truck for her next load. The glare transferred to Ryan. Ryan walked over to the truck and looked straight up at the man, his face lower, but not by much. The two men locked eyes for several seconds, Ryan staring steadily at the other man. It was Uncle's eyes that dropped first. Ryan walked away, heading back toward the plaza and the pensione. Behind him, he heard the man snarling at the girl again, but in a lower voice than before. *"Puta,"* he hissed. "Whore. You and your foreign men. . . ."

Which interested Ryan greatly. What foreign men?

When he reached the bar he bought another beer, and took it outside, to a small table near one edge of the plaza. The plaza was situated on high ground. Probably at one time, centuries before, this part of the town had been a citadel, a place of defense, dominating the rest of the town and the valley below. From his table, nursing one beer, and then another, Ryan had a good view of the shop where the girl worked. It was only about two hundred yards away.

Half an hour later, Uncle drove off in the truck. He did not come back. Just a few minutes after that, the girl left the shop door and started walking up the slope, toward the upper end of town. Having already paid his tab, Ryan let her get a good lead, then got up and followed.

It was easy enough to follow the girl fairly closely and still stay out of sight while she was still in the village, but it was a small village, and within five minutes she was walking through open fields, and he had to drop farther back.

She took a path that led up onto the steep mountain slopes surrounding the town. Now the ground was rougher, and the path winding, so he was able to close the gap a little. At one point he got too close, and, walking around an outcropping of rock, realized she was only about fifty yards ahead, standing still, looking out over a valley. He ducked back out of sight and kept very still. About five minutes later he heard her footsteps begin again, crunching against the rocky surface of the path.

Ryan waited a while, spending the time studying the landscape. The terrain was quite rugged, made up of small but jagged mountains, steep rocky slopes, scattered pine forests, and spiky bushes. In a wild, romantic way, it was quite beautiful.

Over the centuries, most of the mountain slopes had been terraced. Close to town there were numerous beautifully built stone dry walls, creating small patches of level ground out of otherwise untillable slopes. At least, the old ones were beautifully built. In places some of the terracing had tumbled down, and the few repairs that had been made—most of the walls had been left in disrepair—showed a clumsiness of construction that contrasted sharply with the older work. Apparently the modern residents of the area had lost an ancestral skill. Not unusual in the twentieth century. Most of the people who had formerly tilled this land had probably run off to work at the tourist hotels, eager to earn the cash that would buy them radios, televisions, or other mechanical toys. The countryside was rotting away. Spain was becoming a nation of waiters and chambermaids.

Ryan waited perhaps a little longer than necessary, letting the beauty of the place soak into him. He tended to look at the world differently than the average person. His training, the martial arts, the meditation, Zen, had taught him the importance of, well ... seeing. Of having everything "out there" reflected "inside" his mind with as little distortion as possible, although what he had been taught suggested to him that there was really no "out there" as against "inside." They were both parts of the same whole. It was the daily living out of this knowledge that made Ryan so mentally and physically effective. He did not consciously think of this as he looked out over the landscape. By now it was all so ingrained that he was no longer aware of the actual mechanisms.

He began walking down the trail again, and soon became concerned when he did not catch sight of the girl. Where the hell had she gone? Tracking on this kind of ground would not be easy, it was too stony. He had little choice but to continue following the path, which led on around the side of the mountain.

He might have passed the girl completely had he not caught a glimpse of color and movement out of the corner of his eye. Ducking down out of sight he saw that the girl was now to his left, below the trail on which he was walking. She had obviously left the main trail, and now he could see where. About a hundred yards back, a faint track tipped downhill into a little valley. She was heading for a small house situated farther up the valley. It was obviously occupied: a thin plume of smoke rose from its chimney. He watched the girl go to the door, knock, then quickly push inside.

Ryan backtracked, then headed downhill on the path the girl had taken. He approached the house carefully, moving from tree to tree. He waited, studying the house. The main part of it was two stories high, a simple rectangular cube. To one side another roof branched off, much lower than the rest of the house. There were few windows, and what windows there were, were quite small, set deeply into thick walls.

The entire area was incredibly quiet; there was nothing to hear but the soft sound of the wind in the pines. He'd have to get closer. Using trees for cover, he moved next to one of the house's walls, one with no windows, then he carefully maneuvered around to the other side, where there was a window. Now he could hear the muffled sound of voices from inside. Keeping flat against the wall, using only one eye, he peered in through the glass.

Finally, satisfied, he moved straight to the door and pushed it open, stepping inside. The girl was standing in the center of a large room. Her eyes opened wide with surprise when she saw Ryan. Ryan nodded to her, then turned toward the room's only other occupant, a man seated in a chair in a far corner. An elderly man with longish gray hair and a lined, tired face, saved from being moribund by a pair of black, vibrantly alive eyes. Ryan walked up to him. "Dr. Kranek, I presume?"

The black eyes flooded with fear.

12

Neither Petra nor the old man moved, but continued to stare at Ryan as he crossed the room and sat in a chair by the rear wall, where he'd be able to see the door. He noticed that they were watching his hands. He remembered then that he was carrying the *cesta*. They were looking at the *cesta* as if it might contain a dozen cobras. He put the *cesta* down on the floor between his feet and took out the two bottles of wine he had earlier bought from Petra at the *tienda*. "Perhaps you could find some glasses," he said quietly to Petra.

It might have been the softness of his voice, or the familiarity of the wine bottles, but the tension in the room dropped a little, not much, just enough to slightly defuse the situation. The old man turned to the girl, asked her in heavily accented Spanish, "Do you know him?"

She nodded, never taking her eyes off Ryan. "Yes. He's the one I told you about, when my uncle—"

"You *are* Dr. Kranek," Ryan cut in, making it more of a statement than a question.

The old man nodded. "Yes," he replied in English. "And . . . you?"

"The name's Ryan."

Kranek's eyes were still wary, but now they showed a flicker of hope. "You . . . aren't from . . . them?"

"The people who stole the plutonium? No."

Kranek definitely reacted to the mention of the plutonium. "But you know about it?"

Ryan nodded. "Half the world seems to know. You're currently a very popular man, Dr. Kranek. Popular in a very dangerous way. People would literally kill to locate you."

"But I never meant for all this to happen!" Kranek burst out. "It was just a game, a simple mental exercise, something that I . . . then later I recognized that they had tricked me." He shrugged. "But then, you probably know all about it."

"Actually, I don't, and I would like to. But what happened to those glasses?"

Ryan turned toward Petra, held up a bottle. *"Vasos?"* he prompted in Spanish.

The low-key approach seemed to be working. Kranek was definitely relaxing. The old man turned to Petra, and, in his bad Spanish, asked her to get three glasses. The girl, who had been watching Ryan with a mixture of apprehension and hostility, obviously unable to understand what he and Kranek had been saying because it was in English, nodded, and left the room through a low door cut into a thick wall. Kranek turned back to face Ryan. "And," he said nervously, "who do *you* represent?"

"Friendly people. People who wish you well. Who want to get you out of this." Ryan flinched a little internally, trying to imagine Central and his organization as "friendly."

"I see. And," Kranek added with a wry smile, "I suppose I don't have much choice but to take you at your word."

"I suppose not."

"How did you find me?" Kranek asked.

"I followed the girl from town."

Kranek nodded. "She mentioned that a foreigner had been involved in some kind of incident involving her uncle. You're that man?"

"Yes. Her uncle is not very likable, is he?"

"Likable?" Kranek burst out. "The man's a pig. He . . ."

By then Petra had come back into the room, carrying three glasses and a corkscrew, which she set down on a tabletop. Ryan held up the bottles. She took them and placed them next to the glasses, then began the process of pulling the corks. While she was involved in the task, Kranek asked Ryan, "But how did you get onto the girl?"

"I was told by a man in Palma. One of my contacts. He was, incidentally, killed before he could tell me very much more."

"Killed?" Kranek asked, one hand coming up toward his mouth. "How? By whom?"

"With a knife. Probably by some of the men who stole the plutonium."

"My God! Did they also find out about the girl? Will they . . . ?"

"They're dead too."

"How?"

"I . . . interrupted them while they were killing my contact. They won't be coming after anyone."

Kranek's hand dug harder at his mouth. "You . . . killed them?"

"Yes. Or they would have killed me."

Ryan did not voice his suspicions that the men he had killed probably already knew more or less where Kranek was, or they would not have killed Cory before forcing the information out of him. Panic was the last thing he wanted.

Kranek nodded rather slowly. "This has been a terrible thing."

"It has. Now . . . you were going to tell me about it."

"You mean you don't know?"

"Not all of it. I, and the people I work with, suspect that there is a project to convert the stolen plutonium into a bomb, and that you are the instrument of that conversion. Am I right?"

Kranek suddenly became more animated. "Yes . . . yes, that's true, at least in that they want a bomb. And yes, they meant to have me design and build that bomb. Indeed, I have already designed it, but at first I didn't think they were serious, and when I finally found out . . ."

By now Petra had uncorked the bottles and poured the wine. She pressed a glass into Kranek's hand. Ryan noticed how the old man's fingers closed spasmodically around the glass, and how eagerly he drank, downing half the wine in one long gulp.

Petra gave Ryan a glass of the wine, keeping one for herself. Ryan let a period of silence grow as he held up his glass and studied it. It appeared quite old, apparently handmade, of a thick greenish glass that contained many small bubbles and other imperfections. The design was not particularly graceful, but the soft green glow of the glass itself, and the bubbles that appeared to float inside its imperfect contours, frozen in time, gave the entire glass an air of peasant antiquity.

The wine itself had an air of antiquity. It was of a deep golden color, almost amber. Ryan drank. The wine tasted the way it looked, rich and mellow. Most white wines deteriorate rather quickly with age, but this wine seemed to be an exception.

Kranek, who had by now finished his wine, held up his glass. Petra refilled it. The momentary silence, or perhaps the wine, seemed to start him talking. "As I said," he began, "when they first came to me, I thought of it as only a game. Two of them had been my students. They challenged me, in an academic sense, to prove to them that an atomic bomb could be built outside the normal channels, without huge laboratories or vast industrial facilities."

"They?" Ryan interrupted. "Who were 'they'?"

Kranek used the interruption to gulp another half glass of wine. "Why . . . students," he said. "And well . . . now that I think of it ... Palestinian students, studying at the university where I taught."

"Palestinians."

Kranek flushed a little. "Yes. I suppose that I should have guessed, but you have to understand, it all seemed so academic at first. We ... well, we considered ourselves somewhat of a radical group. We had been accustomed to holding informal meetings and discussions outside the regular academic environment. I do not like the system under which I had to teach, the stifling controls imposed from above by organs of the State. You people from the West, and I assume from your speech that you are an American, don't know how much some of us in the East Bloc longed for free discussion, how we grabbed at it every chance we got. And then, later, with *perestroika* and *glasnost,* we really did not know quite where we stood. Were we truly free at last? Or was it just another trick, another clever trap, an invitation to stick one's neck out, then get it chopped off. ..."

Kranek drank more wine, although a much smaller sip this time. "Well, I suppose they led me into it, read me correctly, played me along ... and that was how the plans for the bomb were begun."

"Did you complete those plans?"

Kranek nodded curtly. "Yes. But not right away. As I said, it was at first simply an academic exercise, at least for me, one that I never intended to let progress so far. But you see ..."—he rather wryly held up his glass—"I drink. They played on that, kept me drinking, and finally compromised me in a most serious way, in a way that might possibly have ended in a long prison sentence for me, something political, which the authorities would not have smiled upon. Even under *glasnost*. Then, after the stick, they held out the carrot. They would help me go to the West, to escape from our collapsing system. Yes, we in the East can travel now, but travel requires money, and if one wants to remain in the West, one must earn more money. They said they would help me find work. So I left with them, but once they had me alone they made certain that I stayed under their control. Or at least, they thought they did, by keeping me drunk and under guard, and during all that time they forced me to work on the design for their bomb, their do-it-yourself atomic bomb."

Kranek chuckled dryly. "What a fascination the atom has for those who wish to destroy. And why not, in our ruined world."

He looked up at Ryan, and smiled. It was not a happy smile. "The Bomb," he murmured. "Perhaps its initial discovery was no accident, but a natural defense . . . the planet's defense, nature's insecticide, against man the despoiler, against the parasite who is, in his uncontrollable numbers, in his invincible greed, destroying nature itself."

Kranek suddenly leaned forward and began to cough violently. Petra immediately came to his side, bent over the old man, one hand laid protectively against his back. Her concern was so evidently real that Ryan wondered if they were lovers. "Did you eat anything today?" she demanded of Kranek.

He waved dismissively. "Oh . . . a boiled egg."

"You cannot live off boiled eggs," she snapped. She turned and started toward the open interior doorway. Through the opening in the thick wall, Ryan could see a kitchen.

Kranek watched her go. "She takes very good care of me," he said to Ryan. There was pride, affection, in his voice.

Then he saw the way Ryan was looking after the girl. "Nothing like that!" he said sharply. "She . . . just takes care of me. The wounded helping the wounded."

When he saw the unspoken question in Ryan's eyes, he continued, a little haltingly. "You may have noticed her bitterness, her silence. She came by it the hard way. It was her uncle . . . that pig. When Petra was sixteen, he raped her. She made the mistake of running for help. Then everyone knew. Knew that she was no longer 'pure.' No longer marketable female meat. God, this miserable Mediterranean culture ... with its roots in repression, superstition, blood sacrifices. Petra is an outcast, has been an outcast ever since the rape. She is 'soiled' now, she can never marry a 'decent' man, never live the only honorable life open to Spanish women. In Spain, you know, there are traditionally only four kinds of women: virgins, wives, nuns ... or whores. And because she was ... used, Petra is one of the whores. She will bear that stigma for life, even if she never touches another man, which she has not, since the rape. And her uncle?" Kranek laughed dryly. "Nothing at all happened to him. Oh, certainly, he isn't liked. He's hated, even. But he's one of the richest men in the village, and that is enough to protect him."

Petra was coming back into the room with a platter of sliced bread, cheese, tomatoes, and onions. Kranek smiled at her fondly. "When I came here, I was ... very sick," he said to Ryan, with his eyes still on the girl. "I nearly died in this little house. She became aware of it, began coming here, helping me, bringing me food, making me slow down my drinking. I believe she saved my life."

They had been speaking in English. Petra could not understand the words, but she was aware of the look of affection on Kranek's face. She blushed a little, and for just a moment the tight twist of her lips softened.

At the girl's urging, Kranek placed a piece of cheese on some bread and took a bite. Not very enthusiastically, Ryan noticed. Kranek was indeed a sick-looking man. His face, his body, the lank gray hair, all reflected considerable physical weakness. "And you say that you finished the design?" Ryan prompted. "For the bomb?"

Petra frowned at Ryan's interruption, but Kranek nodded vigorously and put down the bread and cheese. "Yes, I'm afraid that I did. I probably could have faked it, designed something useless. But that old devil, pride, had me by the throat. In many ways it was a fascinating project ... to design the poor man's atomic bomb. A very successful design, really. I suppose in a way I'm proud of it. They were very pleased, too, and, of course, wanted me to build what I had designed. But, in their arrogance, they grew careless, and I escaped. I would never have built the bomb for them. After I got away, I used an old contact of mine, who helped me find this place to hide."

"And the plans for the bomb? Where are they now?" Ryan asked quietly, although he did not feel particularly quiet inside.

Kranek turned to one side. "Right over there," he said, pointing to a large briefcase that lay on a corner table. "I took them with me when I escaped."

Ryan looked over at the briefcase. It looked quite heavy. "But ... there must be other copies ... ones they could use to ..."

Kranek shook his head vehemently. "No. Only the ones in the briefcase. I made certain that I took everything with me, every scrap of paper."

Ryan nodded absently. He could not believe that it was all going so well. Too damned easy. Here he had the plans for the terrorists' bomb, the only plans, and he also had the man capable of making more plans for the terrorists. It might take them a long time to find another Kranek. He had only to get the man and the plans out of here. Or burn the plans and ...

Ryan remembered Central's veiled suggestion. Burn Kranek too? He instantly dismissed the idea. Kranek seemed to be reading his mind. "We ... must be taken care of, then. One way or the other."

Kranek was smiling. Ryan received a clear impression that it was all the same to Kranek whether he lived or died. Ryan leaned forward in his chair. "We have to get out of here. Now, before they come for you. And they will."

Kranek nodded. "Yes. Petra mentioned some strangers in the village the other day, asking questions."

They were so close, then. "I have a car. We can leave right away."

Kranek looked intently at Ryan. "And Petra? What of her? Do we leave her here to ... answer questions when they arrive? I know them pretty well by now, my old students. Those questions will be accompanied by a great deal of pain. And in the end, they will not allow her to live."

Ryan had been considering the same problem. His reason said to ignore the girl; she would have no knowledge of where he was taking Kranek. But he doubted Kranek would go willingly if Petra were left behind. And then there were those elements beyond reason to consider. To leave the girl to the kind of men who'd cut Cory open . . . To leave her to Tetsuo Hidaka, who was hidden somewhere in this whole mess, waiting, like a spider in a hole . . . Kranek had not mentioned her, probably did not know she existed. What would Tetsuo Hidaka do to a girl like Petra?

"Is she free to leave?" Ryan said. "Right now?"

Kranek appeared to be a little flustered by Ryan's easy acceptance of his proposal. He glanced at the girl. "Well, I suppose she would want to get a few things together. I—"

"No. We have to leave now. This minute. I have reason to believe that your former students are not far behind me."

Kranek looked startled. "Well, then. I suppose we must . . ."

But Ryan was no longer listening to Kranek. Marring the great silence outside, he had heard a disturbing sound . . . the sharp crack of a twig breaking. A moment later a man appeared just outside the doorway. A slender, dark-complected man. In his right hand the man held a pistol, and the muzzle of that pistol was just beginning to line up on Ryan's chest.

13

Ryan's reaction was immediate, no thought at all, no *time* to think. His pistol came out from beneath his shirt, the heavy weight of the Rogak filling his hand, his thumb slipping the safety off.

The man in the doorway did take time to think. Perhaps he had only expected to find Kranek and the girl. The sight of Ryan froze him for a moment, and by the time he was ready to press the trigger, Ryan had already done so. The big automatic bucked lightly in Ryan's hand. He shot the man directly in the center of the chest. But the man did not go down. He stood for a moment, staring in disbelief at the hole in his shirt, which was slowly welling with blood. But he was still standing, still had a gun in his hand.

Damned nine-millimeter popgun, Ryan thought, wishing he had his .45. He fired again, taking a little more time to aim, putting a bullet in the center of the man's forehead. The man uttered a wild, despairing cry, perhaps more instinct than anything else, staggered backward a few steps, then fell flat on his back.

Ryan saw more men outside, coming up the trail, toward the house. Some were carrying automatic weapons. He leaped forward, slammed the door, slid home the heavy iron bolt. A moment later, a cry of rage from outside; the other men had just seen Ryan kill one of their own. Ryan heard a burst of automatic fire, felt bullets slam into the door as he finished working the bolt into place. But the door was massive, made of thick slabs of wood. It easily absorbed the bullets.

Ryan quickly scanned the room. There were few openings: a staircase leading upwards at one end, the door into the kitchen, and a small window set about head-high in the wall, near the kitchen doorway, the window he'd looked through earlier, when he'd made his initial approach to the house.

There. A face in the window, the muzzle of an automatic rifle, breaking the glass, thrusting inside. Ryan fired quickly, three shots, two of them scattering plaster, one making a hit, because the man cried out and fell away from the window.

Petra, her face white, nevertheless ran to the window and closed the heavy inside shutters, locking them into place. Good girl, Ryan thought. The shutters were not as heavy as the door, but they would stop bullets for a while, and more importantly, no one would be able to see inside.

No worry about the walls. They were three feet thick, made of stone, rubble, and primitive cement, plastered over and whitewashed. It would take a small field gun to bring the walls down.

The kitchen. It was somewhat dark in there, but there was still a little light coming in, indicating on opening of some kind. But Petra had already slipped through the doorway, and a moment later Ryan heard the sound of more shutters slamming closed.

Ryan cursed. They were safe for the moment, but they were also trapped. There were few ways into the house, and conversely, few ways out. They might be able to stand off a siege for quite a while, but eventually the sound of firing would alert the local people. The police would be called. Ryan did not want the police, did not want their inevitable questions. Kranek would be taken away, giving the terrorists a better chance of getting him back later. Damn! If the men outside had shown up just twenty minutes later, they'd have been gone, Kranek, Petra, and himself.

Shut in a box. He had to see out. He went over to the window and eased the shutters open a crack. He could see two men close to the house, more coming along the trail. He raised the Rogak, got off ten shots, rapid fire, trying not so much for accuracy as for firepower. That was one thing the nine-millimeter was good for . . . firepower. Easy to control, too. The considerable weight of the pistol, plus the lightness of the nine-millimeter bullet, made for minimum recoil.

One of the men near the house grabbed his arm. The other sprinted to the side, disappearing from sight. The men coming along the trail turned and ran back around a corner. Within seconds there was no one in view. Maybe that would hold them for a while.

He had to get Kranek and the plans out of here. He thought quickly, remembering his impressions of the house as he'd approached it. A simple two-story rectangular structure, the entire first story of the back wall without doors or windows. If he tried dropping out of an upstairs window, he'd be a sitting duck against the blank, whitewashed side of the building. Nor would he ever be able to get a sick old man like Kranek to take the drop.

The kitchen. He glanced inside. There was a door there, heavily barred, but it was on the same side of the building as the front door. The men outside would have it under observation. In desperation he turned toward Petra. "Is there any way out of here except the doors?" he asked her in Spanish, knowing it was hopeless, that he was wishing for secret tunnels where none would exist.

Petra, her face white, had still not panicked. To Ryan's amazement, after a moment's thought, she eagerly nodded. *"Sí,"* she said. *"La bodega de le a."*

He did not understand at first, but she was already walking away toward the kitchen. Before following her, he fired three more shots through the window, ducking down just in time, as at least a dozen rounds from automatic weapons slammed into the house, splintering wood from the shutters and chipping plaster and stone from around the deep window embrasure.

Ryan slammed the shutters. At least they knew he was still dangerous, would perhaps keep their heads down for a while. He raced into the kitchen. Petra was already leaning down, opening what looked like a large cupboard door about three feet high and as many across.

Dropping down onto his knees, Ryan looked in through the small doorway. It was dimmer inside, but he could see scattered stacks of firewood, and beyond the last stacks, a glimmer of light. It was a little firewood storehouse, with wood shoved into it from an opening outside, and another opening inside the house so you didn't have to go out into the wet and cold to get wood. Most importantly, a possible way out of this miserable trap.

Ryan slipped into the little woodshed, worked past scattered chunks of what looked like olive wood, then, lying on his belly, he peered outside. Open ground for maybe thirty yards, then a trail disappearing into pine forest. If they could just make it to that trail unseen.

He backed out into the kitchen, then ran into the main room. Apparently Petra had already told Kranek what they intended to do. The old man was on his feet, but God, Ryan thought, does he look shaky.

Still, Kranek was moving. And looking determined. He walked over and picked up his briefcase. "I wish I had burned the plans," he said to Ryan. "But personal conceit . . . I was proud of how neatly I had worked it all out. I suppose I wanted to show it to someone . . . to someone who would understand. To a colleague. . . ."

Petra was urging him through into the kitchen. Ryan was about to follow when another storm of firing slammed into the house. He heard cursing outside in what sounded

like Japanese. Then the same voice called out in English,
"You fools! You will hit Kranek!"

A mixture of languages. Indicating Palestinians and the
Japanese Red Dragon Brigade working together, as Central
had said. Communicating via the world language. English.

Ryan heard a furious murmuring of several voices in at
least two languages. Then a new voice called out, in English again, hailing the house. "You in there! Whoever you
are. We have no fight with you. We only want the old
man."

A different accent this time, a very good accent, clean
and crisp, but probably coming from a man whose native
language was Arabic.

Ryan saw a chance to stall for time. He slipped next to
the living room window, not showing himself. "What if I
give him to you?" he shouted.

A quick glance into the kitchen, a glimpse of Kranek's
white, stricken face. Ryan shook his head, holding a finger
to his lips, trying to indicate that it was only a trick.
Kranek seemed to understand. He nodded, then he was
bending low, with Petra helping him into the woodshed
doorway.

After a moment, during which Ryan could hear more
murmuring from outside, the voice came back, "If you
come out without your weapons, we will take away the old
man. We wish him no harm. Then you will be free to go
wherever you want."

Sure, Ryan thought. As soon as you have Kranek, you'll
put a bullet in my head. You can't afford to let me live.
Same with Petra.

He stuck his head close to the window again. "Let me
talk it over with the old man. He doesn't want to see anyone else hurt. But I have to be sure you'll keep your
word."

He'd tried to inflect a little panic into his voice, to make
them think he'd do anything to get out of this alive. Mean-
while, there was the woodshed.

He ran silently into the kitchen, just in time to see

Petra's rear end disappearing through the little doorway. He was amused that he was still able to appreciate the view ... a damned nice rear end. The gonads never give up, he thought wryly.

Ryan took a moment to pop the nearly empty clip out of his pistol and slam home another. Then he wormed into the woodshed after the girl. Wood splinters stung his knees. It probably hurt Petra's knees a lot more; her dress would give her little protection. Then she was through, and a moment later Ryan was through, too, blinking in the bright light.

Unfortunately, Kranek had stopped to wait for them. Ryan gritted his teeth. Being the slowest, Kranek should have gone ahead. Waiting for the girl, no doubt. There he stood, with the heavy briefcase clutched to his thin chest, the damned thing practically slipping out of his hands. Petra saw, and tried to take it from him, but Kranek held on to it grimly. "Get moving," Ryan whispered, gesturing toward the trail into the woods.

Too late already. A sound from the side, a brief exclamation, and Ryan turned to see two men armed with Uzis coming around a corner of the house, to his left, not more than ten yards away. "Run!" Ryan shouted to Kranek and Petra.

His pistol was already coming up, toward the two men. They were apparently even more surprised than Ryan, or perhaps they were too poorly trained to react properly. Ryan opened up with the Rogak, rapid fire, feeling for his targets more than aiming. He stitched the two men with at least ten shots. One went down instantly, the other managed to get off a burst that whizzed by Ryan, then that man went down, too.

Ryan turned to run after Kranek and Petra; others would have heard the shots and the cries, they'd be here in moments. However, Petra and Kranek were not running. Kranek was down, with the girl bending over him. Blood showed on Kranek's right pants leg. Damn! That wild, unaimed burst from the Uzi, a dying man's last effort, had hit Kranek!

Petra was tugging Kranek to his feet. He barely made it, weaving badly. Kranek wasn't going anywhere, at least, not fast enough for them to get away. He bent down, to pick up his briefcase, but winced in pain. Petra picked it up for him, holding it tightly. Already there were shouts from both sides of the house, the sound of running feet. For one long second, Kranek looked at the girl, anguish on his face. *"Vaya!"* he said in Spanish. "Go! *Rápido!"*

"No . . . no!" she cried out, obviously unable to leave the old man.

He pointed at the briefcase. "They must not have it!" he hissed. "Go! Please . . . for me. . . . Go!"

She understood, then, understood that she would be doing this for the man who'd befriended her, the man who had given her empty life a little warmth. With one last anguished look, she turned and ran toward the trail.

She was still yards from safety when two men appeared around the side of the house to Ryan's right. They instantly saw the running girl. One screamed something in Arabic. They started to raise their machine pistols, to cut her down. A wild cry of rage and despair from Kranek made the men turn his way, and by then Ryan had the Rogak into position. He opened fire, hitting one man badly enough to make him drop his weapon, and driving the other man back around the corner of the house. The Rogak's slide locked open on an empty magazine, and while Ryan was releasing the magazine and driving another home, his last one, the wounded man crawled after his comrade, to safety.

Ryan looked toward the trail. No sign of Petra; she must have made it into the trees. Then, a sudden roar of gunfire from behind Ryan. He spun, bringing the Rogak up, knowing that he was way out in the open, a sitting duck. Then he saw that the firing had come from Kranek. The old man had picked up one of the Uzis dropped by the men Ryan had killed a minute ago. Another man had come around the building; he'd have shot Ryan in the back for certain if Kranek hadn't shot him first.

The trees. They still might make it to the trees. No. Wishful thinking. The men sheltered behind the house's right corner would simply shoot them in the back. And now more men were coming, the snouts of gun barrels were poking around both corners.

Kranek. He should kill him, shoot him now. As Central had said. In the hands of terrorists with access to plutonium, Kranek was a ticking time bomb. Shoot him and get back into the house.

His pistol was already half raised when Kranek turned back toward him. To his amazement, the old man was smiling. "I used to be in the army, you know. We all had to go into that damned Marxist army. They taught me to shoot."

Yes, he handled the Uzi like he knew, more or less, what he was doing. And because of that smile, Ryan knew he could never assassinate Kranek. Better to stand and fight and die together.

Which would be very soon. They'd been flanked. Men were fanning out behind cover, well beyond the edges of the house. Two men even raced toward the trail, obviously after Petra. "No you don't!" Kranek screamed. He fired a burst after them. Neither man seemed to be hit, but they instantly went to ground.

Kranek turned to the side, toward where there was movement behind the walls of a big garden. "You tricked me!" he cried out, waving the Uzi. "You tried to make me do something horrible. Something without honor."

"Back. Back to the house," Ryan hissed. But Kranek, standing, tottering on his wounded leg, remained in the open. Men were racing toward them now, guns in hand. Ryan wished he'd had the sense to pick up the other dropped Uzi, but to go for it now, where it lay out in the open, would be suicide.

He started toward Kranek, to pull him back toward the entrance into the woodshed. But the men running toward them were firing now, past Kranek, straight at Ryan. He dived for cover, half inside the woodshed. "Kranek!" he yelled.

But the old man had opened fire again, at the men running toward him. Not very effective fire, he was just spraying, but bullets are bullets, and one of the running men clutched his side and yelled a curse.

Perhaps they had not initially intended to kill Kranek, but now battle fever took over. Screaming curses, at least three men opened upon Kranek, on full automatic. Kranek stood for a moment, emptying the last of his magazine, standing with his legs spread wide, no longer looking old and weak. "You bastards!" he screamed once more. "You murdering bastards!"

Then the bullets took him, driving him backward into the side of an old stone oven. Ryan could only watch as bloody red blossoms flowered against Kranek's clothing, watch while bullets chipped stone dust from the oven's exterior.

More bullets hit Kranek even after he'd stopped moving; the only motion left in his body being that generated by the impact of bullets. How Arab, Ryan thought bitterly. Never able to control their fire. Images of exultant Arabs firing into the air to celebrate, celebrate anything, flashed through Ryan's mind. They couldn't seem to remember that what goes up must come down.

But he had other things to worry about. They'd seen him duck into the woodshed's low entrance. Bullets were seeking him out, and he had only a few rounds left. More than bullets were after him. He saw a man pulling the pin on a grenade. Ryan aimed and fired. The man, hit hard, dropped the grenade, then fell on it. The grenade went off with a load roar, lifting the man's body a foot or two off the ground. A vivid image, for Ryan, of the man's right arm flying into the air, all on its own, to make its own separate landing.

No matter. Two more men were pulling pins on grenades, from behind cover this time. Ryan shoved himself backwards, feeling wood splinters tearing at his flesh. Then he was in the kitchen, just as the grenades landed inside the woodshed. No time to make it into the living room. He dived beneath the kitchen table, tipping it over so that its thick wooden top faced the woodshed.

Blast, concussion, dust, disorientation. Then blackness, nothingness.

14

The sound of voices, and of something being moved. Ryan's eyes flew open. How long had he been unconscious? Dim light; he could barely see. Something hard and gritty was pressing against his cheek. He lifted his head, moved it only a few inches. Something was pressing against the back of his skull, restricting movement.

He could see better now. His face was inches from a floor made of rough red tiles. Then he remembered, it must be the kitchen floor; there had been red tiles.

The voices again. And the sound of something being shifted. "He must be dead," one voice was saying. Ryan recognized the voice. It was the voice that had called out for him to surrender. The voice with the slight Arab accent.

"We mus' be sure," another voice said. Heavy Japanese accent.

A quick exasperated breath. "We'll never move all of this. The whole ceiling came down. Even if he survived, he will never get out."

"If he's alive, and the police come . . ."

"Exactly," the Arab said. "The police will come . . . to

find us sifting through a bombed house, with dead bodies all over the place. We have to get out of here!"

Running feet. A voice, saying in Japanese, which Ryan spoke quite well. "We searched the whole house. We did not find him."

"We *have* to find him!" Once again, the Japanese who'd been arguing with the Arab.

More sounds of rubble being shifted. A shaft of light reached down to a point near Ryan's face. He tensed. If they found him, he'd get nothing but a quick bullet in the back of the neck. He tried to draw his legs up, so that he would at least be able to leap at them when they found him. But he could move his legs only a few inches, and that little movement was enough to move something else. Ryan froze as debris shifted above him. "What was that?" a voice called out.

The Arab replied, "Just some of the wreckage shifting. I tell you, we have to get—"

A new sound, a scream from some distance away. A woman's scream. Ryan could sense attention turning away from the wreckage. "What is that?" the Japanese voice asked.

The sounds of people moving away. A choked cry from a woman, closer now. "It's the girl!" The Arab voice, exultant now. "And look . . . they've found the briefcase, too!"

The Japanese voice, bitter. "And we would have had Kranek to go with it . . . if your men had been able to control their fire."

"What? Control their fire? But they are fighting men! Kranek was shooting at them. They shot back. What else would a fighting man do?"

"They might have captured the man who could build the bomb for us." Disgust evident in the voice.

Quick anger. "We have the plans. Isn't that enough? You always relied too much on that drunken old man. Why did we have to use him? There are plenty of men in the world of Islam just as intelligent, just as well trained.

Men who are not drunks. Our own people are perfectly capable of building this bomb for us!"

"What other choice do we have?" Sarcasm. "We must leave, then. We'll take the plans back to the boat. But first we have to clean everything up. Leave nothing behind that might lead the police to us. And the girl. We'll take her with us. It will be much easier to bring her along alive, on her own feet, than to carry her dead body."

The Arab again. "Tsunogi ... you are truly a compassionate man." Sarcasm to match that of the Japanese.

The voices moved away from Ryan. He heard quiet orders, something being moved. Ryan was tempted to move, too, perhaps try to find a more comfortable position; his legs were cramping badly. But he sensed menace nearby, and held perfectly still. His caution was rewarded a moment later when footsteps came near, and the Arab said, "Are you still here, staring at rubble? You're not convinced the man is dead? Two grenades ..."

A grunt. "Perhaps you are right. Nothing at all has moved in there. Not a sound. And even if they do find him alive, he will be so busy answering questions to save his own neck that he will not have time to think of us."

"Good. Let's go, then. We had better take the back way out ... we cannot go through the village with ... all we have to carry. How could we have expected to lose so many men, picking up one old man and a girl?"

"Because we were careless. One who does not prepare for trouble usually finds more of it than he expects. I wish I knew who that man was. He fought very well, like a professional. He must have been sent by someone, by some agency. How were they able to find Kranek before us?"

"What does it matter? We have most of what we want. Let's make the most of it."

Ryan, lying unmoving, listening to all these platitudes, was very aware of the friction between the terrorists. The careless, romantic world of the Arab versus the precision and sternness of the Japanese. He wondered how long they would be able to continue working together before the throat cutting began.

Sounds of departure. Within five minutes Ryan was able to hear nothing, except the ubiquitous wind in the pine trees, blowing over what had once been a house, once been a place where an old man had sheltered. Where he had imagined himself safe. A space the old man had shared with a lonely, bitter young woman.

Ryan remained motionless for another ten minutes. He had *felt* the Japanese before, standing, watching the rubble, alert for any sign of life. Perhaps he was there now, a little farther away, patiently waiting to finish what he knew had to be finished.

But Ryan did not feel the man. Nor was it likely that he would remain in the area, chancing the police. So Ryan finally began to move, to see if it would be possible at all for him to escape from the wrecked house.

He moved cautiously, first testing his body, alert for serious injury. Nothing apparent; his joints functioned well enough, a little stiff from lying motionless for so long. And there were no deep pains inside his chest or stomach. He was merely trapped.

Turning his head as much as he could, he determined that not only had the table saved him from the grenade fragments, when he'd turned it over, but it had also caught the ceiling beams when they came down on him. That was probably it . . . the blast had brought down the kitchen ceiling and roof . . . right on top of the table, partially breaking two of its legs, so that it made a sloping roof over him.

It took another five minutes for Ryan to draw his legs up beneath him. He was going to try to push the wreckage off himself. There was always the danger of bringing down more debris, but he doubted that would happen. The house's main walls were too thick to have been badly damaged by two grenades. The kitchen had been much more fragile. He remembered, then, that in former times Majorcan kitchens had usually been situated outside the house, covered over lightly, something like a lean-to. This was an old house. The outdoor kitchen had simply been enclosed.

Crouching, his legs directly beneath him, Ryan pushed upward. Nothing at first, only pain, splinters digging into his back, then a movement, a slight movement, but he could sense where the resistance was now, and instead of pushing directly against it, he drove his shoulder a little to the side. More movement. A beam, perhaps.

Halting a moment, gathering his strength, Ryan breathed in and out a few times, then drew in a deep breath. "Yaaaahhh!" he cried out, driving hard with his legs.

He felt the skin tearing on his back. Ignoring the pain, he drove upward harder. A grating sound, then a cascade of tiles, falling off the debris, shattering against the hard floor. Dust, pain, strain, but his head was in the open now, clear of the rubble.

After that, it was the work of only a few seconds to worm his way out of the debris. The kitchen had come apart, all right; the little woodshed through which he and the others had tried to escape was completely obliterated.

A glint of metal. Ryan caught sight of the Rogak lying beneath some rubble. He managed to work one arm beneath the wreckage, reaching the pistol. He wiped it off with his filthy, torn shirt, then quickly pulled out the magazine, jacked a shell free of the chamber, then made certain that the slide and hammer still worked smoothly. They did.

Six rounds. That was all that he had left. Against an unknown number of men armed with automatic weapons. Those six rounds would have to do. Because he was going after them, no matter what the odds. They had the plans for the bomb. He must get the plans back. Or destroy them.

And then there was the girl. Petra. They had her. And, in a way that he could not quite define, it seemed even more important that he get Petra back. Before they killed her.

15

Ryan checked the area. All the bodies had been removed, including Kranek's. Only bloodstains, already soaking into the dry earth, remained.

There was no doubt in which direction the terrorists had gone; the little path down which Ryan had wanted to escape was now well trodden. Ramming the Rogak back into its holster at the back of his belt, he set off down the path at a steady trot. Loaded down with bodies, the people he was following would have to move slowly.

The path led in a gentle curve to the right, around the back of a mountain. The terrain was very rugged, steep slopes dropping off to the left of the trail into a rocky little valley, steep mountainside rising above Ryan, to his right. The mountainside was studded with huge rocks and clumps of small pines. The ground itself was rocky, grainy, with a covering, in places, of years of fallen pine needles mixed with thin, spiky grass. Bad country for tracking.

So far, that was not a problem. The trail ran on, with no major paths branching off it. What branchings there were, were so small—probably trails made by sheep and goats—

that a large body of men passing by would have left a great deal of sign.

A quarter of a mile from the house the ground temporarily grew softer, where the trail dipped down into a depression, so that a little soil had collected. This soft soil now showed the marks of many feet. Ryan quickly checked the footprints. In several places he saw heel marks that were smaller, sharper than the marks around them. He thought back. Petra had been wearing low-cut shoes with a narrow heel. These must be her footprints. So, they had not shot her and tossed her off the trail. Why did they want her alive? To see if she knew anything about Ryan?

He did see a place where her heel marks had slewed sideways, as if she had fallen, then been dragged to her feet. Other footprints milled around. Yes, Petra must have fallen. Or been knocked down.

Ryan began to trot again. His footsteps crunched loudly against the path, except where there were pine needles. He imagined the sound carried a long way; it was very silent. Even the wind had died down. But he could hear nothing ahead. Apparently the terrorists had a big lead on him.

He was about to start trotting more briskly, when, just as he was passing some thick brush, he saw a glint of light flashing off something reflective about three hundred yards ahead.

Ryan immediately dived into the brush. The flash of light had come from some huge boulders that overlooked the trail. He watched the boulders intently. A moment later he saw a slight movement, thought he could make out part of a man's head.

A rear guard. They had left someone behind to watch the trail, to see that no one followed. Very professional.

Ryan studied the terrain. If he continued along the trail, he'd be in view of the rocks as soon as he left this brushy area. There was no way to leave the trail to the left and go around; the slope dropped off too sharply, and the bottom of the valley was not all that far below the rocks. The only possible way to bypass the man, or men, ahead was to climb higher. The mountainside bulged out, cutting the view of the higher slopes off from the boulders where he'd seen the movement.

Slipping back down the trail, Ryan found a place where he could start climbing. The going was not particularly difficult; stunted plants and clumps of trees had piled up soil that gave him almost level ground to walk on, particularly when he got to the top of the bulge. What was difficult was moving silently. Ryan had to proceed slowly, careful not to dislodge stones from the loose soil that would bounce down the mountainside, advertising his presence.

It took him half an hour to reach a point just above the boulders. Directly below him lay a flat area where a thin covering of earth and grass had been caught by the boulders. Two men were sprawled out on their bellies at the forward edge of this flat area, where it overlooked the trail. An Uzi lay next to one man, an automatic rifle next to the other. Both men were intently watching the trail. If Ryan had not seen the glint of sunlight reflecting off one of their weapons, they would have been able to kill him easily as he trotted past, just twenty yards below.

Being above them, and out of sight, it would be a simple enough matter to pass by without being seen. He'd join the trail farther along, follow the ones who had Petra and the plans. He started to turn away, then hesitated. A great deal of time had passed, first, getting out of the wrecked house, then, the half-hour climb up to where he now stood. The trail couldn't go on much longer. The others must have reached transportation by now. There'd be nothing there for Ryan to see, except perhaps a car remaining for the two men beneath him. And he would be even farther from his own car, which was parked in the little plaza by the pensione.

The two men below were the only connection he had to Tetsuo's group. To the whereabouts of the plutonium. To Petra. He would be foolish to pass them by.

Ryan began working his way down the slope, toward

the two men. It was not far, but he moved with infinite care. He was completely in the open now; if they heard him, all they would have to do was spin around and cut him to pieces with automatic weapons fire.

He was only ten feet away, directly above them, putting his feet onto a smaller boulder, when a small rock became dislodged, rolling noisily down the slope. One man did not move, the other started to turn, caught a glimpse of Ryan, then reached for the automatic rifle, his eyes wide with surprise.

Ryan jumped, straight down at the man. His heels slammed into the man's body with great force, knocking the wind out of him. The automatic rifle went clattering down onto the trail.

The other man, slower to react, was turning at last, his right hand clawing for his Uzi. Ryan bent low, scooping the *tanto* from its sheath on his leg. He did not dare use the Rogak; there must be no shooting, just in case the others were nearer than he thought. He kicked the man in the face. The man flopped backward, but he was not hurt badly. His hand was still on the Uzi, trying to bring it around.

No time for fancy games. The other man, the one Ryan had landed on, was beginning to recover. Ryan rammed one knee into the chest of the man with the Uzi. The *tanto* flashed forward, sinking into the man's throat, slicing through the jugular. The man let go of the Uzi, gurgled something around the rush of blood that was suddenly pouring from his throat and mouth. He clutched desperately at the hideous wound in his neck, his legs jerking wildly.

Ryan spun toward the other man, who, still gasping for air, was reaching for his companion's Uzi. Ryan launched himself at the man, striking with the knife again, but this time with its butt, slamming the pointed brass tip, which protruded past the end of his hand, hard against the man's skull.

The man stiffened, fell to the side, stunned, his hand

well away from the Uzi. Easy to kill him now, but that was not Ryan's intention. He wanted him alive. Reaching into his pocket, Ryan pulled out a length of thin, strong fishing line. It took him only a few seconds to whip the half-conscious man's arms behind his back, then tie his thumbs together with the fishing line. The only way he'd get loose now would be to tear at least one thumb off.

Ryan checked the man whose throat he had cut. He was dead, his brain starved of oxygen-carrying blood. He appeared to be an Arab. Ryan turned back to the other man. A Japanese. Perhaps the man who'd called out for him to surrender back at the house. On second thought, unlikely. That other man had been one of the leaders. Leaders do not stay behind on guard duty.

The man was coming to. His eyes remained glazed for a moment, then focused on Ryan. They were black eyes, very black, and they filled with hate and anger as the man stared at Ryan. He tried to bring his hands around, until he felt the sharp stab of pain in his bound thumbs. He looked over at the other man, saw him lying in a huge pool of blood. Just a moment's flicker of fear in those black eyes, then the hate was back, along with a fierce defiance.

Ryan cursed silently. He'd captured himself a fanatic. Too bad he hadn't killed the Japanese and spared the Arab. Arabs tended to be more practical. "What is your name?" Ryan suddenly asked in Japanese.

The man looked surprised. Westerners did not often speak his language. The surprise faded, replaced by a hooded alertness. "Where are your comrades taking the girl?" Ryan demanded.

The man's only answer was a look of scorn, accompanied by silence. Ryan picked up the bloody *tanto,* slowly wiped the blood from the blade. Then he moved the angled, razor-sharp tip close to the man's throat. The Japanese looked at him for several seconds, then actually smiled. Bending his head back, he bared his neck to the knife. "You cannot break me," he said, his voice filled with pride.

Bushido. The Way of the Warrior. The man was right. Whatever Ryan did to him, however great the pain, the man would revel in it, would swim in the sea of his own courage. Ryan would get nothing at all out of him. Probably better to kill him quickly, then run on down the trail with the slim hope that he would find some clue as to where the others were taking Petra and the plans.

A scurrying movement to one side of the Japanese caught Ryan's attention. Something small. Ryan turned quickly, saw a scorpion scooting crablike across the thin soil. The Japanese, following Ryan's gaze, saw the scorpion, too. A sudden look of fear and loathing twisted his features. He jerked his body away from the scorpion, an automatic reaction.

So, there *were* things that frightened this man. Or at least disgusted him. Not hard to understand. Scorpions were creatures straight out of most peoples' nightmares.

Damn. Another scorpion, moving along maybe ten yards away, heading in the same direction as the first one. Studying the ground in that general direction, Ryan thought he saw two more, despite the way they blended into the rocky soil. Strange. Why so many?

When Ryan had first seen the two men, he'd noticed the ruins of an old house about thirty yards from the boulders. Its fallen-in roof had convinced him no one was hiding inside, so he'd discounted it as a danger. But the scorpions did seem to be moving in the direction of the house. Perhaps some of them lived in the stones that made up the ruin's thick crumbling walls.

The Japanese had seen the other scorpions. His face still held that look of revulsion, of disgusted loathing. On a hunch, Ryan grabbed the man by his bound hands and jerked him to his feet. The man seemed so mesmerized by the scorpions that he put up little resistance ... until Ryan started to lead him toward the ruined house. The man stopped, tried to back up. Ryan rabbit-punched him on the side of the neck. The man started to sag. Ryan dragged him forward, toward the house.

It was quite a small building. Perhaps it had at one time been a shepherd's hut, now empty, with the shepherd probably bussing tables in a hotel restaurant. Once abandoned, these old houses deteriorated fast. The walls were essentially mud and rubble. Without constant plastering and whitewashing, and a roof to shield them from the rain, they more or less melted away; they were essentially neolithic in design. Hard to tell if this house had been abandoned for twenty years or only five.

Next to one crumbling wall, a squat cylindrical structure of cemented rock thrust up about three feet above the ground, the back of it anchored to the house. A frame and crossbeam rose several feet above the structure, with an old rope still hanging in place. The top of the structure itself was covered by a rotten wooden disk.

It looked like a well, but Ryan knew that it could not be a well, not on these rocky mountain slopes. It had to be one of the old *depositos*. Ryan looked up. Yes, rotten wooden troughs still led down from the roof into a spout at the rear of the *deposito*. During the winter rains runoff from the roof would have been guided, via the wooden troughs, into the *deposito*, to provide water during the long, dry summer.

A scorpion appeared from beneath the wooden lid and fell onto the ground. The Japanese was a little less stunned now. He was able, as Ryan flipped away the wooden cover, and as sunlight streamed into the ancient *deposito*, to see what had long ago replaced the water it used to hold.

A sea of scorpions. A nest of them. Dozens, perhaps hundreds, using the damp darkness of the *deposito* as a refuge against the fierce sun.

Although his own skin was crawling, Ryan pushed the Japanese forward, so that he could see more clearly down into the *deposito*. It was only about ten feet deep, belling out a little at the bottom. The intruding sunlight had obviously disturbed the scorpions; they were scurrying about madly, their long tails, each tipped with its deadly stinger, raised high. "So," Ryan hissed into his captive's ear, "are you going to tell me where your friends took the girl? Or do I throw you down there?"

The man shuddered so hard that he nearly broke loose from Ryan's grasp. "You would never do that," he said woodenly.

Well, no, I wouldn't, Ryan admitted to himself. Because then the man would never talk . . . he'd either be dead or too close to death to give any useful information. However, Ryan had by now discovered the man's private horror. Everyone has his secret demons, and to this Japanese, all that was horrifying to him, all of his worst imaginings, were embodied in those hundreds of scaly bodies below.

Before the man could resist, Ryan punched him in the back of the neck again, and as he sagged, swept his legs out from beneath him. The man fell heavily onto the ground. A scorpion that had left the *deposito* crawled toward the man's right arm. Ryan kicked it away. Then, while the Japanese was still groggy, Ryan pulled the old rope down from the crossbeam and made a loop of it beneath the man's arms, tying it around his chest. He flipped the free end of the rope over the crossbeam again, then pulled on it hard, jerking the man off his feet, so that he swung in the air over the *deposito*. Both the rope and the crossbeam creaked, but they held; the man was not particularly heavy.

Ryan began to lower the man slowly into the *deposito*. He was regaining his wits now, and slowly became aware of what was happening, but his legs were already below the stone rim, so he could not kick himself away. "No!" he cried out. "You can't do this to me!"

"The choice is yours," Ryan shouted back. "Tell me where they took the girl."

He was being careful to mention only the girl. Not the plans. The girl would not mean much to the man. The plans for the bomb, for his group's mission, would.

The man began to struggle. His struggles made the rope swing. Ryan was having a difficult time holding the weight. The rope slipped a little, and the man fell two feet lower into the pit, until Ryan was able to regain control. The man was now swaying on the rope. One leg brushed the *deposito*'s stone wall. A scorpion crawled onto his trousers. "Yaahh!" the man shouted. Kicking his leg wildly, he managed to shake the scorpion loose.

But now he was swinging again, dangerously close to the walls. To try to stop his motion, he held himself perfectly still, legs in tight, well away from the wall, with its crawling, rustling load of enraged scorpions.

Ryan, working the rope carefully, slowly lowered the man deeper into the *deposito,* until he was about a foot from the bottom. Dozens of scorpions milled about madly, just beneath his shoes. Ryan realized he should have taken off the man's shoes before lowering him into the pit. Too late now. "Where did they take the girl?" he called down to the man. "Tell me, and I'll haul you up."

Ryan was not certain the man heard him; he was making a strange, half-animal sound, a dull moaning. Ryan jerked the rope, called out more loudly, "The girl! Where did they take her?"

The moaning rose in pitch, mixed with words. "No. . . . Can't. . . . Can't tell you!"

Ryan decided to lower the rope another few inches. He miscalculated; the rope slipped a little in his hands, so that the man's feet slammed against the bottom. Screaming, the man pulled both feet up, but three scorpions had already gotten onto his trousers. Even from above, Ryan could see their stringers stabbing at the cloth, but since the trousers were loose, the venom did not seem to be penetrating through to the man's legs. "Please! Please!" the man babbled. "Get me out of here! Get me up!"

Ryan did haul him up, but only a few inches. The man was staring in horror at the scorpions, who were slowly working their way up his body. There was bare skin at his midriff, where his shirt had been pulled free of his pants.

"Where did they take the girl?" Ryan repeated, jerking on the rope.

By now the man was past defiance. "The boat!" he shrieked. "They took her to the boat!"

"What boat? Where?"

"A schooner. In a little cove two kilometers north of Valldemossa. There is a stone gate on the main highway. A sign. C'an Jordi. They'll sail soon, they'll take the girl. Get me out, get me out, get me *out*!"

Sensing that, in his terror, the man had told the truth, Ryan nodded, then began to haul him up. Much harder work than when he'd lowered him down into the hole. Ryan pulled hard; he wanted to get the man out before those scorpions reached his bare belly.

The Japanese seemed equally preoccupied with those three slowly ascending scorpions. As they neared his belly, he jerked his body up and down, hoping to shake them loose.

A terrible miscalculation. The rope, old and rotten in places, suddenly broke. The man seemed to hang in the air for an instant, then he was falling. "No!" he shrieked. But it was too late. His feet struck the bottom of the pit. With both hands tied behind his back, he fell heavily onto one side. And in an instant his body was covered by a sea of maddened scorpions.

Ryan did not know how the man managed to do it, but he got to his feet. Ryan stared down at him. There were several scorpions clinging to his face and hair, their stingers stabbing deep into flesh. A momentary image of agonized, terror-filled eyes, a gaping, screaming mouth. Ryan immediately pulled out the Rogak and put two bullets into the man's head. He fell like a sack of cement.

Sickened, Ryan backed away from the *deposito*. He knew he'd be seeing those eyes, that gaping mouth, remembering the man's horror for a long time. He would have had to die, of course, Ryan could not have left him alive. But to die in such a manner . . .

Tetsuo Hidaka. As usual, she was leaving a trail of horror behind her. First Yoshiro, with his hands full of his own guts. Kranek, torn apart by terrorist bullets. This man, a true believer, willing to die for the bitch. Many, many others. But so far, only isolated deaths. However, if she ever did manage to build an atomic bomb . . .

Ryan shook his head. Not while he was alive. She would never build that damned bomb while he had breath left in his body.

16

However, time was running out. If the plans, and the girl, had been taken to a boat. Ryan knew he would have to find that boat quickly. Before it sailed.

Which way to go? Perhaps if he continued along this trail he would find some kind of transportation left behind for the rear guard. Perhaps he would find the main body itself, waiting for them. And perhaps he would find nothing.

He did know that he had a car back in the village. That was a certainty. He would go for that certainty. He slid down the slope back onto the trail. The assault rifle the Japanese had dropped when Ryan leaped down on him lay right in the middle of the trail. Ryan picked it up, then threw it far down into the valley below. As for the bodies, with one lying on top of the boulders out of sight and the other in the *deposito*, it might be a long time before they were discovered.

Ryan loped back down the trail. It took only ten minutes to reach the house where Kranek had died. The area was deserted, no one had as yet shown up to investigate, although quite a few people had to have heard the shooting and grenading. Undoubtedly the police had been notified. Via the phone in Petra's *tienda*?

Ryan knew that it would be foolish to march right back into the village, coming from the direction of all the noise. He did follow the trail back for another quarter mile, until he had reached a high point where he could see for a considerable distance. The village lay below, still quiet.

There were many ways to reach the village. This land had been inhabited for centuries, perhaps for thousands of years. Well-beaten paths led off in every direction. Ryan chose a path that took him quite high, skirting the village. He crossed ancient terraces, passing between two ancient, gnarled olive trees; their trunks were at least five feet across. A fan of thin green shoots sprouted from the dense mass of wood, like feathers from a headdress. Suddenly Ryan heard the sound of several powerful engines. Sheltering behind one of the olive trees, he watched three light trucks pull off the main highway, then start up the village's main street. He caught a glimpse of armed men inside the rear of one of the trucks. Probably some kind of special antiterrorist police. The trucks halted. A few people came out of their houses and pointed uphill. Ryan could hear a distant gabble of voices, partially drowned out by the sound of the trucks' engines. A moment later the trucks started grinding slowly uphill again. Ryan watched them pass the plaza where he'd parked his car.

Good. Now all he had to do was reach the car. People were leaving their houses, moving slowly toward the upper part of the village. The plaza was at the bottom, near the Palma road. No way Ryan would be able to walk in on the village's main street, but, from where he was standing, he could see a rocky path leading down a steep hill to the base of the promontory on which the plaza was located.

Ryan took the path quickly, but not at a run. The climb up the side of the hill that held the plaza, the church, and the pensione was steep but manageable. Within five minutes Ryan was at the top, at a point just below the church and the pensione. Looking over the edge, he saw his car, fifty yards ahead, the only vehicle parked in the plaza.

No one in sight. Ryan stepped out into the open, began walking toward his car at a pace that did not waste time but, he hoped, did not indicate guilty haste. Ryan was just passing the door of the pensione when he realized that old Bendet, the proprietor, was standing just inside the doorway. In the interior gloom, all Ryan could make out was the man's face, a white blur, homely, marvelously impassive.

Ryan hesitated. Like everyone else in the village, Bendet must have heard the shooting. And Ryan's torn, dirty clothing might indicate some connection to all that noise. Would Bendet immediately call the police?

Perhaps not. There was the impassivity of Bendet's face to consider. He was an elderly man. He had lived through the Franco dictatorship, a time of terror, when a man who attracted too much attention could easily end up in the hands of the Guardia Civil, perhaps to be tortured, even shot, with his body thrown over one of the island's high cliffs into the sea. Bendet was of a generation that had been taught, with much painful instruction, to mind its own business.

Ryan walked on toward his car. He unlocked the door, got inside, started the engine. He looked back once, toward the pensione. Bendet was now standing just outside the doorway, looking in his direction. Did the old man have good enough eyes to make out the license number? Probably. And when he found out that one of the villagers, Petra, one of his own, was missing, he might even consider going to the police. Ryan hoped that by then he would have gotten rid of the car—and the ID with which he'd rented it.

Ryan drove out of the plaza, down to the main road. Decisions. He'd seen the police coming from the left; that was the main route from Palma. So he turned right. He'd go down the mountain by the back route.

The road almost immediately turned into a series of

steep switchbacks, which Ryan took as fast as he dared; he
wanted to put distance between himself and Son Feliu.
The switchbacks seemed to go on forever. He knew it was
only his impatience that made time move so slowly, the
frustration of the low speed the road imposed on his driving. Where the switchbacks approached the edge of cliffs,
he could see for a great distance. A flat plain lay below,
tantalizingly close, several miles of almond groves, dotted
with small villages and massive old farmhouses. Each
switchback promised to be the last but always led into another, until, finally, Ryan reached the bottom. Ahead lay a
long stretch of road running straight toward a distant village. Ryan checked his watch. Despite the seemingly endless descent, only seven or eight minutes had passed since
he'd left Son Feliu.

He immediately pulled over to consult his map. What
had the scorpion man said? What was that name? Yes,
there it was, Valldemossa, lower down on the western side
of the island. But if he followed this route, crossed the
plain, turned left, he'd have to pass through Palma, then
take an interior road that led up to Valldemossa. He had no
desire to pass through Palma. By now, it was possible that
every policeman in Majorca had the license number of this
car.

Then Ryan saw another, fainter line on the map. A line
that led almost directly over the mountains, joining the
Valledmossa road higher up the coast. The turnoff to this
road was only a kilometer or two away. He'd try it. He'd
make an end run.

Ryan set off immediately. He reached the junction
within a couple of minutes. At first he almost missed the
narrow opening, it looked more like a paved driveway,
where this smaller route branched off the main road. Hard
to find, unless you knew it was there . . . which might help
keep people from tracking him. He made the turn, and almost immediately found himself climbing back up into
mountains. More switchbacks, more hard driving. A few
kilometers farther along he turned off onto an even more

narrow road, with a rough, potholed surface. So far he had
not seen another car, nor had he passed through any town.
There was nothing around him but bare eroded uplands,
with an occasional isolated farmhouse. Now the landscape
grew even more bare, forbidding, wonderfully deserted. It
was not until the road dipped downward again that Ryan
began to encounter more signs of civilization: bigger farmhouses, tiny villages. Down, down, down, more switchbacks, and then he was in the small town of Fornalutx,
driving through its narrow streets. With relief, Ryan saw
many non-Spanish faces. He was obviously in an area full
of foreigners. He would not stand out.

Then through a larger town, Sóller, a busy place. Past
the town, the roadway rose high, with Sóller lying below,
a smear of houses, fields, a big church, all flanked by massive cliffs. He had now rejoined the main coast road. The
road climbed higher. Ryan encountered scenery right out
of a Roman wall painting ... stone walls holding thin
rocky soil in place above a sheer drop that fell away to the
blue vastness of the Mediterranean. Rocky fields studded
with ancient olive trees. An occasional flock of sheep. Little stone aqueducts, bringing water to isolated trees or to
a tiny field of fava beans. Remnants, in this tourist-cursed
land, of a way of living that had remained more or less the
same since the Carthaginians had first colonized the island
twenty-five hundred years ago.

Another village to pass through, an awesomely beautiful
place, tucked into a steep mountain valley, almost a gorge.
The old part of the town—what had probably once been
the citadel, now just a church and some very old houses—
sat perched on top of a steep hill, with terraced olive
groves falling away into the gorge below. The lower part
of the town was newer, with many buildings less than a
century old. There were many foreigners in the streets:
pale, scrawny Swedes and Germans; more robust Dutch;
smaller, ill-fed English; even smaller French, swaggering
through the streets with cigarettes dangling from the corners of their mouths in bad imitations of Humphrey

Bogart. Ryan noticed a smattering of Americans, most looking as if they had not bathed in a month. The faces of most of the foreigners showed signs of a long debauch of alcohol, drugs, and sex. Which would probably not end until the winter rains arrived and drove them back to their northern holes. The setting of the town was stunning, but the people on its streets indicated a tourist garbage pit.

More winding road, past scattered olive trees. Some of the more ancient trees were actually growing out of sheets of bare rock from which the soil had long ago disappeared, their roots reaching deep for what little sustenance remained in this barren area. The agony of this borderline existence, centuries of it, more than a thousand years for the oldest trees, was reflected in their incredibly gnarled trunks. Ryan saw one thick, squat tree, in which he was certain he could make out the forms of two naked people, a man and a woman, entwined around one another, as if making love. Buried in the trunks of other trees lay a phantasmagoria of shapes, a treasure house for vivid imaginations.

Finally, down out of the hills into a high, flat area. A crossroads ahead, the signposts indicating that Valldemossa lay to the left. A smaller road branched to the right. The signpost told Ryan nothing useful about that road's destination. He stopped and checked the map again. Yes, the left-hand turning led right into Valldemossa, then out the other side, south, toward Palma. In Majorca, all major roads seemed to lead, eventually, toward Palma. But the man who'd died in the pit had definitely said two kilometers *north* of Valldemossa. So Ryan took the right hand turning, which at first seemed to lead nowhere . . . until he caught a glimpse of the sea below. A little farther along, then, there it was, as the Japanese had said, a big stone gate, and above that gate, a worn sign saying "Son Jordi."

Ryan drove on past, barely slowing. To drive through that gate and down the dirt road beyond it might be to drive straight into trouble. He continued on for another two hundred yards. The ground was higher now; he could see glimpses of an inlet below. But no boat.

Just ahead, another narrow track branched off the road. The car's suspension protested as Ryan forced the vehicle up off the pavement, onto what was little better than a mule track. Within fifty yards he had rounded an outcropping of rock that would adequately hide the car from the main road. He stopped, killed the engine, listening, in the deep silence, to small chirping sounds as the engine block cooled.

Aware of the silence, and of how far sound carried in this rocky land, Ryan opened the door and got out of the car as quietly as he could. Even so, the sound of his shoes crunching on the hard soil sounded way too loud. He could hear nothing else, just the sounds that he himself was making. Nobody calling out, no voice raised in alarm, warning about the car. No advancing footsteps. Perhaps he had not been heard after all. Perhaps he had not been heard because he was in the wrong place. Perhaps, even in his terror, his Japanese captive had kept faith with his comrades.

Ryan walked away from the car, heading toward where he'd seen that glimpse of sea. He'd gone about a hundred yards when he decided to start protecting his identity. Out came the phony passport, with its supporting documents. He did not dare burn them; the smell of smoke might carry the wrong way. So he pried loose a large stone, then shoved the documentation beneath it. He carefully set the stone back into place, smoothing the earth around it so that it looked undisturbed. With luck, the phony passport would remain undiscovered for a hundred years. Or until some hungry developer decided to built a tourist hotel on this particular spot.

Ryan walked on, keeping, as much as possible in this barren area, under cover of olive and algorraba trees. Below him, the shape of a deep inlet was coming into view. A narrow opening screened the inlet from the sea. High limestone cliffs rose above the water, far too sheer to easily climb, either up or down.

Finally, Ryan saw it, at first just the tip of one mast, then, as he neared the edge of a cliff, two more masts. He got down onto his belly, inched forward until he reached the edge. Screening his face behind a scrawny bush, he peered downward.

Jackpot. A large three-masted schooner, almost directly below him, lying at anchor. And on its deck, a number of men, scurrying in every direction, some of the men bringing supplies aboard from the beach, others carrying those supplies down hatchways. Voices, floating upward to where Ryan lay hidden, voices speaking in a mixture of Arabic, Japanese, and English.

Obviously, the scorpions had done their job very well.

17

The inlet—actually, it was a bottle-shaped cove—was about twice as long as it was wide. The schooner, perhaps ninety or a hundred feet long, was moored alongside the cliff opposite Ryan. The water was very clear. He could see the bow and stern anchor lines fading away below the surface, until very near the place where they touched bottom. Patches of light green showed where there was a sandy bottom. Closer to the beach the water was darker, indicating rocks or coral. Near the inlet's entrance, the water took on the deep blue of considerable depth.

Someone had done a good job of bringing such a big boat into the inlet. Probably motored in. Ryan thought he could see a screw underwater, beneath the boat's stern. He could understand why they'd use this cove, despite the difficulty of getting in and out . . . the narrow entranceway would screen the boat from view seawards, while the high cliffs made it difficult to see it from the land.

Watching, sometimes with only one eye, to minimize the chance of being seen, Ryan studied the boat for about an hour. He noticed that some of the cargo being brought aboard consisted of large crates. From the way the men strained with the crates, they must weigh a lot. Perhaps they contained machinery. To build the bomb?

His attention was diverted from the crates when suddenly the door of one of the deckhouses opened and two men shoved a woman outside. Ryan stiffened. It was Petra. He could see, by the way she was moving, that she must be very much afraid. He watched as she was herded into the doorway of the hatch nearest the stern. The last he saw of her, she was being prodded below again, with two men right on her heels.

Ryan slid backward from the edge of the cliff. When he figured he'd gone far enough, he stood, then ran back to the car. He reached in through the open window for his binoculars, then trotted back to the cliff edge. Sliding forward on his stomach, he quickly studied the boat below, not yet using the binoculars. Nothing much had changed; some of the men were still stowing cargo, while others were beginning to pay attention to the rigging, coiling lines over taffrails and loosening the bindings on the canvas sail covers.

One man seemed to be in charge, a tall, slender, dark figure standing near the forward deckhouse, pointing here and there, apparently issuing orders. Ryan checked the position of the sun. It was to one side and slightly behind him, dipping down toward the western horizon. There should be no reflections off the binoculars' lenses. He put them to his eyes. They were ten-by-fifties. The deck was suddenly quite close. He studied the tall slender man, saw that he had an equally slender face, hawklike, with dark, brooding eyes and a strong nose.

Another man was prowling the deck, not doing much actual work but watching as others worked. Ryan swung the glasses onto him. Japanese. A powerfully built man, perhaps five feet eight or nine, with a long Japanese torso. In the binoculars, the man's face was absolutely expressionless.

The man was pacing. Ryan noticed that every time he passed near the port rail, his hand dropped down to touch something. Ryan adjusted the binoculars for finer focus, saw a *katana,* a Japanese sword, sheathed, leaning against the rail.

Yes ... the man had the manner of a swordsman. Of someone who had studied the martial arts. His feet were solid against the deck, but not heavy. His balance appeared, even at this distance, to be perfect. And, from the expression on his face, Ryan doubted that anything would perturb him.

There was a shadow of movement in the doorway of the forward deckhouse. The Japanese turned in that direction, as if someone had spoken to him. Ryan raised the glasses a little higher. He thought he could make out a woman's form standing just inside the doorway, but, in contrast to the bright sun out on deck, the cabin was dark inside; he could only make out a shadowy outline. Nevertheless, it probably was a woman. Tetsuo Hidaka? He wished that whoever it was would step out on deck so he could make certain, but the figure disappeared back into the deckhouse, and the Japanese on deck turned away, to resume his pacing. Ryan swept the glasses over the deck again, studying the aft hatchway. Petra had not reappeared. They must be keeping her below. At least he now knew she was still alive.

Ryan turned to his right, studied the sun. In another hour it would be dark. Time to start planning. Common sense told him to return to his own boat, put out to sea, and send a coded message describing the boat below. It could then be intercepted at sea. That was the safe way to play it. Unless it didn't work. Perhaps the plutonium was not on board. Perhaps, after the boat sailed—and from the preparations it looked like it would sail before dawn—the plans for the bomb might be transferred to another, faster boat before help could arrive.

The plans. They were the most important consideration. They were probably aboard. If he could get the plans, then the building of the bomb would be delayed, perhaps for long enough so that the terrorists' use for it would wither away. Or, until the terrorists themselves could be destroyed. Then there was Petra to consider. As soon as the boat put to sea, she might be killed, her body dumped overboard. He had to get her out. Now.

So, get the plans and the girl. After that, let the bastards sail. Let Central's promised backup lay in wait for them, then pounce. Once that had been done, Ryan's mission would be accomplished.

One particular thought kept teasing Ryan's mind, a thought he did not want to listen to ... that the real reason he wanted to do something right now was because he was pretty sure Tetsuo Hidaka was aboard. If he played it alone, he might have a chance to even the score. Personally. To look into her face as he killed her, remembering Yoshiro, making her remember Yoshiro.

No ... better not think about that. Just go ahead and act. But act with a plan. Ryan swung the binoculars over the cove, studying the terrain. He'd definitely decided to slip aboard the boat tonight. Time to look for the best approach.

The beach was very small, made up mostly of rocks. A dirt road ran down to where the rocks began. A large truck sat at the end of the road, just short of the rocky beach. The men had to hump their cargo from the truck, over the rocks, to a dory with an outboard motor, which took the cargo out to the boat, where it was winched aboard. The beach was the farthest point from the boat, at least two hundred yards. Swimming straight out from the beach, even on a moonless night, would be very foolish. There might be phosphorescence in the water ... they'd see his track all the way out.

Ryan scanned the cliff across from him. It would be better to swim along the base of that cliff, moving from one rocky outcropping to another. The boat's stern was probably less than twenty yards from the cliff. He'd be partially concealed all the way.

Ryan stiffened. He thought he'd seen something moving partway up the cliff. There it was again, a slight puff of what looked like smoke. He focused the glasses again, studied the face of the cliff intently for several minutes. Then he smiled. He now knew how he was going to get aboard the boat.

He remained on the cliff for another hour, until it began to grow dark. Apparently, the loading was finished. The last boatload left the beach half an hour after the sun had set. They simply left the truck sitting on the beach, abandoned.

Ryan had hoped that darkness would lead to a lessening of vigilance aboard the boat. No such luck. He watched as a guard was set. Powerful lights were turned on, illuminating the water for fifty yards to port and starboard. Only the water under the stern and bows remained in relative darkness. The deck was still a beehive of activity, with much last-minute tying down of equipment and testing of lines. Unless he was reading the signs wrong, Ryan suspected that the boat would sail soon, perhaps even during the night.

He left the cliff, walking carefully through the dark, not wanting to stumble over anything. He passed by the car; there was nothing inside it he'd need. He walked nearly all the way to the road, until he found a path that led to his right, in the direction of the cove. As he'd expected, he'd gone inland far enough so that the path led, by a fairly gentle gradient, down to the beach. When he reached the end of the path, he found that it was quite dark on the beach; the boat's lights did not reach this far. He crouched behind a bush and watched the boat. Still a lot of activity.

He settled down to wait. An hour passed, then another. It was so dark that he could not see his watch. He remembered the old days, when watches with luminous dials had been all the rage. He'd never used one, had never wanted to be caught, lying hidden somewhere, glowing in the dark. He'd long ago graduated to cheap digital watches. They kept damned good time.

He moved around behind the truck, held his watch close

to his face, pushed the button that illuminated the dial. Ten o'clock. Time to move.

Walking back into the brush, Ryan began to undress. He took off his shirt first, putting it down onto the ground, beneath a thick bush. He placed the Rogak on top of the shirt. The rest of his clothing followed. All of it, including his underwear. When he went aboard the boat, he did not want water dripping noisily off soaked clothing.

He hesitated about the knife. Finally he shrugged, and unstrapped the *tanto* from his lower leg. He did not want it banging against the hull when he climbed aboard. Besides, if he got into serious trouble aboard a boat loaded with trigger-happy terrorists, the knife was not going to help him much.

He made certain his possessions were covered with a layer of brush, then walked in a wide circle around the beach, crossing it far to one side. He moved slowly; the damned rocks hurt his feet. Finally, he reached the water, near the cliff edge opposite the other cliff, from which he'd earlier been watching. He slipped into the water. The water temperature was fairly high, not tropical warm, but warm enough so that he would not be fatigued by fighting against its chill. He let himself sink down into the water, getting used to it. Then he began to swim, slowly, a modified breaststroke, trying to make certain that neither his feet nor his hands broke the surface, where they might splash.

He coasted from rock to rock, stopping at times to observe the boat. Activity on deck was slowing down. No doubt many on board were tired and were going below to get some rest. There were, however, enough men still around to make Ryan's slow approach very dangerous.

Finally, he reached the brightly illuminated area. Now he swam even more carefully, underwater at times, still moving from one place of concealment to the next. Once, he came up too quickly, making a splash. Somebody called out on board; he couldn't understand the words, but he had no doubt it had something to do with the splash. He pasted himself against a rock, with his nose barely above water. A searchlight clicked on, began to sweep over the rocks. Ryan held perfectly still, hoping that no ripples were radiating out from his position. Finally, he heard muttering from on board, perhaps someone saying it must have been a leaping fish. The searchlight went out.

Ryan remained motionless for another half hour. He knew he could not stay here forever; eventually he would grow tired, chilled. He would have to make his move now. And hope that what he'd seen from the other cliff really existed.

He coasted into the circle of light around the boat. A slight swell was running, making him bob up and down. The Mediterranean, being a landlocked sea, does not have tides. Nor does it have, unless there's a storm, much wave activity. Still, there was at the moment a slight swell, perhaps the sign of a distant storm. As the water level dropped, then surged up again, Ryan looked straight up, moving his head dangerously far out of the water. Yes, there it was, above him, that little puff that looked like smoke. He was in exactly the right place.

Ryan began to breathe deeply, pumping his lungs and tissues full of oxygen. His last breath was an especially deep one. Then, taking hold of a ledge of rock, he pushed himself downwards, as deep as he could.

Once underwater, he upended, then began swimming slowly, searching the rock face in front of him. The light from the boat helped, but still, it was very dim.

He did not find what he was looking for. He finally had to surface, his lungs bursting, but he forced himself to let his air out slowly, then fought to breathe normally, to minimize noise. More hyperventilating, then he went under again.

He found it this time, just as his air was beginning to run out. A black hole in the cliff face about two yards beneath the surface. For an instant he contemplated resurfacing for another lungful of air, but, aware of the chance of discovery, he swam forward, into the blackness of the opening. Would it be too narrow inside for him to pass through? Would he become trapped, would he drown, soundlessly, just a few feet away from the boat?

Fortunately, the opening remained wide, and there was not far to go, only a yard or so of rock overhead, then the hole opened out into a large space, with a glimmer of light coming from above. Ryan let himself rise. A moment later, he popped to the surface.

The light was quite dim, but he could see that he was in a good-sized cave. He swam to a ledge, pulled himself up, lay, gasping, drawing in big gulps of air. He doubted they'd be able to hear him in here; there was a considerable sucking and sighing of water as the surge rose and fell.

Brighter light was coming from farther up. It was a fairly easy climb. In a few minutes he was looking out a small hole in the cliff, straight at the boat, which was anchored no more than fifteen or twenty yards away.

He'd guessed right. Most of this side of the island was made up of limestone. Limestone dissolves in water, very slowly. Caves form. He was now in such a cave. That puff of smoke he'd seen against the face of the cliff, while he'd been watching from the other cliff, had not been smoke at all. It had been vapor, expelled from this damp cave as the surge rose, increasing air pressure inside the cave's closed space. That had suggested to Ryan that there had to be an underwater opening into the cave. And he'd found it. Now, here he was, safe and dry, only a short swim away from his objective.

There was still some activity aboard the boat. Ryan watched for a while through his small stone aperture. Not much he could do now. They were too alert.

He climbed back down to the stone shelf, near the water's edge. There was a long wait ahead. Best to spend it resting. He stretched out on the stone, closed his eyes, setting his mental alarm four hours ahead. He actually slept from time to time, dozing lightly, but with his senses always alert. What he hoped not to hear was sounds of the boat departing.

He began to grow cold from the wetness of the stone on which he was lying. He finally sat up; he figured it must be about three-thirty or four in the morning. He spent a few minutes stretching, doing warm-up exercises, to work the cramp out of chilled muscles. Then he climbed up to the stone vent.

The boat was still there. Nothing moved on its deck. Most of the lights had been cut off, which should be a big help. Only a couple of dim deck lights were still burning. But what was that ... there ... a brief glow in front of the mainmast, fading away, then burning brightly again? A cigarette? It must be a cigarette. Probably a guard, smoking, trying to keep himself awake. This was the time of night Ryan had been waiting for, a couple of hours before dawn, when the human organism is at its lowest ebb. The time of night when his enemies would be least alert.

Ryan climbed back down to the stone shelf, then slipped into the water. After the chill air of the cave, the water felt warm, comforting. He pushed his body down, began swimming underwater, looking for the opening that led outside. The boat's bright deck lights had helped him before, now they'd been turned off. Underwater, it was completely dark. He had to feel his way through the rocky opening.

A minute later he was free, no more rock above him. He swam upward, working his way along the underwater portion of the rocky cliff wall. His head broke water. Once again he forced himself not to let his air escape in a rush, made himself let it out slowly. Then he drew in a careful lungful.

It was quiet. Very quiet. No sound at all from the boat, only a gentle lapping of water against its hull. The boat's stern lay less than twenty yards away. He took in a big gulp of air, then ducked underwater and began swimming. On and on. The black mass of the hull loomed ahead of him. He stopped swimming, let himself surface slowly, careful to keep clear of the hull itself, fearful of barnacles, whose sharp shells might lacerate his flesh.

His head broke the surface of the water. The hull was less than a yard away. He blinked his eyes free of water, looked up. There . . . as he'd noticed earlier. A line trailing down over the stern into the water. Probably for tying up the dory, which had already been lifted aboard. Ryan took hold of the rope, began to climb up it, hand over hand. A little water dripped from his body, but without clothing or gear very little water had clung to him. He went up as silently as he could, hoping the other end of the rope was fastened to something strong.

Finally, the stern railing. He transferred his hold onto wood, heaved himself up, swung his torso across the rail, rolled inboard, trying to hit the deck with as little impact as possible.

He lay below the rail, in darkness, listening. Nothing. Just the lapping of water, as before. Then a distant sound, a man clearing his throat. The guard. Smoker's throat.

There was no way, of course, that he could successfully search the entire boat for the bomb plans. Not cold, not with no idea of where they might be. Particularly, not with so many people aboard. Petra would have to be his key.

He moved forward slowly, heading for the rounded rise of the after hatch, the one into which he'd seen them shove Petra. The mainmast lay just ahead of him. He could make out one of the guard's shoulders; he was sitting in front of the mast and a little to one side. Fortunately, he was facing forward, away from Ryan. Ryan debated taking the man out, then discounted the idea. All he'd need would be for a replacement to come on deck and find the guard missing.

The hatch rose about five feet above the deck, with a door set into it vertically. Fortunately, the hatch door was not locked. Ryan opened it carefully, dreading shrieking hinges. It opened silently, and a moment later Ryan closed it behind him. A ladder lay below him. He started down the first steps.

This particular hatch was obviously an entranceway to the lower decks. When Ryan reached the bottom of the ladder, a long companionway stretched ahead of him with closed doors spaced along it. A low-wattage light bulb dimly illuminated the companionway.

Ryan moved to the first door, put his ear to the wood. He heard loud snoring from within. The same with the next two doors, one on either side of the companionway. Rooms full of sleeping men.

The door at the far end of the companionway was smaller. And, unlike the other doors, it had a key in the lock. Ryan moved to the door, tried the handle. It did not turn; the door was locked. From the outside? Curious. Ryan slowly turned the key in the lock, heard it grate, flinched at the sound. Then he opened the door, looked inside. Blackness at first, then, helped by the small amount of light seeping in from the companionway, he saw a small room. He also saw that he had made the right choice. The room was a gear locker. And, lying on a pile of canvas and cushions, one hand held apprehensively in front of her throat, was Petra.

She now sat bolt upright, her eyes huge. Her mouth was beginning to open. He knew she was about to call out, perhaps scream. "Shhhh," he hissed. In Spanish he continued, "Don't make a sound. It's me, Ryan."

"B-but," she stammered. "But ... you ..."

Then he realized ... a naked man bursting in on her, after the horror of the battle at the house, the terror of capture.

"Did ... did they capture you, too?" she blurted.

He quickly shut the door, plunging the room into inky blackness. He moved toward the girl, sat on some canvas next to her. "No. I came here on my own. To get you out of this place. I ... had to swim. That's why I'm not wearing any clothes."

"Oh." Then elation. "You're going to take me away from them? Oh, please, let's go now. There are terrible people here. I've been so afraid. . . ."

"Yes. We'll go soon. But first . . . did you see what they did with Dr. Kranek's briefcase?"

"Oh . . ." distractedly. "They picked it up on the trail."

"I mean, did you see where they put it on this boat?"

"I . . . as soon as we got on the boat, they all went into one of the little houses on deck. I . . . I think they had the briefcase with them. Now . . ." Her voice began to grow desperate. "Can't we leave right away?"

"The briefcase, Petra. We have to try and find it. Dr. Kranek would have wanted us to find it. These people mustn't have it."

A moment's silence, then the girl spoke again, this time in a more controlled manner. "You don't have to talk to me as if I were some hysterical child. Yes, I've been very much afraid. And with you appearing so suddenly . . . the way you did . . . But I know you're right. He would have wanted us to at least try and find his briefcase. It was of great importance to him to keep it away from them. He . . . gave his life trying to do just that. Didn't he?"

He nodded, forgetting that she wouldn't be able to see the nod in the dark. He was impressed. Yes, she was terrified, but she seemed to be able to control her terror. That would help. He wouldn't have to worry about hysterics. "Let's go," he said.

He reached out to help her to her feet. Her hand missed his, collided with his naked flank. He sensed her draw her hand back sharply. Considering her history, she had probably not been around too many naked men. Except for that one occasion, with her uncle. Which would make her memories of naked men very bad indeed.

Ryan slowly opened the door, just a crack, peered out. No one in the hallway. He was about to step through the doorway when he felt cloth brush against his back. He turned. Petra was holding a garment out to him, some kind of light coat that she must have picked up from among the room's junk. He quickly slipped into it. The coat was not very long, it left his legs bare from just above the knees on down, but it felt good to be wearing something again. Being naked around clothed people tended to make a man feel at a disadvantage. Plus, if he went on deck naked, what little light there was would reflect off his bare skin. "Thanks," he muttered in English.

They quickly passed along the passageway, then up the steps to the hatch door. Ryan slowly opened the door. He saw nothing moving outside, not even the guard posted amidships. Ryan hoped he was the only guard. He leaned over to whisper in Petra's ear. "Where was it you said they went when they first got here?" he asked. She'd said something about a little house.

She pointed—behind them, fortunately—at what Ryan guessed must be the chartroom. Good. They wouldn't have to make their way forward, past the guard.

Somewhere Petra had lost her shoes, so her feet made little sound against the deck. No more than Ryan's. They stole around behind the deckhouse she'd indicated. Faint light filtered through a porthole. Someone working early? Another guard?

Ryan peered inside. No one there, just a small light burning low over a chart table. He tried the door. It opened. He waved Petra inside, followed her, shutting the door behind him.

Now ... the briefcase. For the next five minutes, he and Petra searched the room thoroughly. No sign of the brief-case or the plans. Ryan finally turned toward Petra. "You say you saw them take it in here?"

She tried to think hard, working around her fear. "They ... a lot of them came in here as soon as we reached the boat. That awful woman, the Oriental one ... I saw her take the briefcase from one of the men. She seemed to be very happy. They locked me up in the little house at the front of the boat for a while, inside a closet. Then I heard a lot of them come in. The woman was one of them. When they opened the closet to take me out, she looked at me in a strange way, smiling, but not really smiling. A terrible look. She said something to them in another language, not

English, then they took me out on deck and put me down in that other place."

"So . . . they could have taken the briefcase to that other deckhouse . . . even if you didn't see them do it."

She nodded. "Yes. It could have happened that way."

Ryan nodded back. Morosely. Well, it had been too good to be true, the hope of finding the briefcase, complete with plans, tossed casually into the chartroom. Tetsuo Hidaka must have it. He had no doubt that the "terrible woman" Petra was talking about was Tetsuo Hidaka. It must have been Tetsuo herself he'd caught a glimpse of, her shadowy form inside that forward deckhouse. She'd have the plans with her, and she'd be well guarded. Under those conditions, to go after her or the plans would be suicide. He turned toward Petra. "Can you swim?" he asked.

She nodded vigorously.

"Time to leave, then."

He was about to turn toward the doorway when he became aware that a chart lay on the chart table, pressed beneath a sheet of heavy plastic. He hesitated. The plastic had been well marked at various places over the chart. He leaned forward, taking a closer look. It was a large chart, showing coastal conditions, depths, reefs, all around an island. Minorca, that was the name on the chart. He remembered that name from his own charts aboard his sloop. Minorca was one of the Balearic Islands, like Majorca and Ibiza. It lay to the north.

There were particularly heavy markings on the chart around a deep cove that opened out between steep cliffs. Another chart, this time of the entire Balearic chain, lay under another sheet of plastic. A bold black course line had been charted from Majorca to the cove on Minorca. That must be where they were heading!

Ryan felt a rush of triumph. With the terrorists' destination now known to him, he would be able to sail after them, stake them out, perhaps call in help if it was needed. Which would probably be the case.

"Come on," he said to Petra. "Let's move!"

She nodded eagerly, relieved. He wondered how he would manage getting her down to the water without making a lot of noise. He hadn't bothered to ask if she could climb a rope. He'd tie it under her arms and lower her. He took her by the elbow, guiding her out the charthouse door, onto the deck. He was just starting to turn toward the stern when suddenly bright lights flared on all around them.

Both Ryan and Petra froze in place. A moment later a voice called out in accented English, "Stop where you are . . . or you'll be shot before you can take two steps."

18

No doubt about it, they probably wouldn't make it even one step. A man with a machine pistol was standing two yards away, the muzzle of his weapon pointed straight at Ryan's belly. There were flankers on either side, and when Ryan turned, very slowly, very carefully, he saw another man standing on top of the chartroom, covering them.

The hawk-faced man whom Ryan had earlier noticed directing activities on deck came walking around the corner of the chartroom. The area was brightly illuminated; all the lights that had been on earlier in the night were on again. The man stared at Ryan for a moment, ignoring Petra. His eyes widened. "You!" he said in his lightly accented English. "You're the man from the house in Son Feliu!"

Ryan said nothing, glanced around him, trying not to look as if he were doing what he was doing . . . searching for a way out of this. He could see none.

"So," the hawk-faced man continued. "You survived the grenades. Tsunogi was right after all . . . we should have searched the wreckage until we found you."

Ryan still said nothing. He glanced at Petra. She was

chalk-white, but seemed to be holding her fear under control. Well . . . she was no worse off than she'd been before.

Hawk-face gestured to the men surrounding Ryan and Petra. "Bring them," he snapped. The men closed in. Ryan knew this might be his chance. If they got close enough . . .

No, the odds were too long. Two of the men held back, their weapons covering Ryan as two others seized him by the upper arms, then propelled him along after Hawk-face. Besides, there was Petra to think of. If shooting started, she was very likely to get hit. He could hear her choked cry from behind him. She was undoubtedly being shoved along, too.

Ryan was pushed into an open area amidships. More people were coming up on deck. The men who'd ambushed him at the chartroom had been Arabs. Now a small group of Japanese approached. Ryan recognized the man he'd seen on deck earlier, the man with the sword. He stopped a yard away from Ryan. "You!" the Japanese burst out, his face probably as close to showing emotion as it ever got. "You kill many good men!"

Wham! The Japanese foot slammed into Ryan's belly; Ryan never saw it coming. Even as he was falling, with the wind knocked out of him, he found himself thinking that the man was very good. Fabulous timing, no telegraphing at all; one moment, standing in place, the next moment, his foot in Ryan's gut.

Ryan lay on the deck, painfully sucking in air. He feigned greater injury than he really felt, lying on one side, but keeping the man's feet in view. If he tried to kick him again . . .

"Tsunogi! Hassim! What is all this disturbance?"

A woman's voice, speaking pleasantly accented English. Ryan looked up. Tetsuo Hidaka was standing just a few feet away, her eyes darting from himself, to the Japanese, to Hawk-face.

It was the Arab who answered. "One of my men thought he heard someone talking to the Spanish woman belowdecks. At first he thought he was dreaming, then he heard somebody going up on deck. He checked the room where we had put the woman. She was not there. He awoke me. I took some of my men, and we caught them coming out of the chartroom."

Hidaka came a little closer, looked down at Ryan. He considered, for a moment, that if he moved fast, he might be able to break her neck before anyone could help her. But . . . there were probably more pleasant ways to commit suicide. He probably wouldn't even be able to get to her. The Japanese was standing just as close as Hidaka, and from his stance, Ryan knew he was ready to move instantly.

"Who is he?" Hidaka asked Hawk-face, her voice only mildly curious. Or so it sounded.

"The man who held us up so long at the house where we found Kranek," Hawk-face replied.

The woman nodded. "Ah," she said. "The one you were so certain was dead, Hassim. So . . . Tsunogi was right after all."

Hassim. Tsunogi. Ryan was beginning to put names to people. Hassim was Hawk-face. Tsunogi must be the swordsman.

"And the two men who did not return, the men you left behind," she continued, looking obliquely at Hassim, her voice light and lilting, but her meaning clear. "Perhaps this . . . dead man . . . helped them disappear."

Ryan saw Hassim stiffen. No Arab was likely to enjoy taking criticism from a mere woman. But Hassim said nothing. Ryan glanced around the deck. For the first time, he noticed that there were more Japanese than Arabs. Perhaps Hidaka had the bulk of the fighting force. So, then, why did Hassim seem to have so much authority? Or was that authority slipping? Ryan thought back to the fight at the house. He and Kranek had killed a lot of men. Most of them had been Arabs. Maybe Hassim was running out of fighters.

One of the Arabs called out something in Arabic,

pointed to Ryan. Hidaka turned questioningly to Hassim. "He says this man is wearing his coat," Hassim translated.

Hidaka looked down at Ryan again, smiled a small, cat-like smile. The coat had come open. There was no doubt in anyone's mind that Ryan was naked beneath the coat. "Well, then," Hidaka said. "Tell your man to take his coat back."

Hassim hesitated, then snapped an order. Two Arabs stepped forward, jerked Ryan to his feet, then stripped the coat from him. He stood, naked, facing Hidaka. She began to walk slowly around him. "My, my," she murmured. "Such a strong-looking man."

Some of the Japanese were suppressing giggles as Ryan stood naked before their leader. The Arabs looked a little ill at ease. Having a woman—two women, counting Petra—faced with a naked man was not right.

Hidaka stopped a couple of feet away from Ryan, looked straight into his eyes. He looked straight back, studying her as much as she was studying him. Up until now he'd only seen photographs of her. Old photographs. She'd been much younger, then, not beautiful, but pretty, with a round face, an adequate, somewhat plump shape, and long, straight black hair.

What he'd noticed in those old photographs was her eyes. The somewhat strained look about them, the almost hesitant way she had been looking into the camera. Years had passed. The once-plump young body had slimmed down, become somewhat gaunt. So had the face. And now, no hesitancy at all showed in the eyes. Thinking back, Ryan began to believe he must have misinterpreted that hesitancy. Perhaps those younger eyes had been trying to mask the cold cruelty, the incipient madness he now saw looking out at him. Was that what made her so attractive to her followers? This air of mad, potential violence? Whatever the reason, this was one hard, dangerous bitch.

"Who are you?" she asked abruptly.

Ryan hesitated only a moment. "Peters," he finally replied, giving his latest cover name. "Martin Peters."

Hidaka nodded. "Oh, yes, of course. Mr. . . . Peters."

She turned. "Tsunogi?" she prompted gently.

Tsunogi's foot again, that short, sharp, front snap-kick, a *mai-geri,* whipping out and back, not a very large movement, but a kick with Tsunogi's entire body behind it. Perfect stance, no loss of balance, no kung-fu-style wasted energy and movement, no flailing arms and leaping body. Just perfectly efficient force. Trust the Japanese to do it right.

This time the kick was a little higher, digging under Ryan's floating ribs. He could have stayed on his feet, but he chose to go down, to once again feign greater injury than he felt. He lay on the deck, grunting and moaning, only half faking that part. Damn, but that man could kick!

Two men hauled Ryan back onto his feet, holding him up facing Tetsuo Hidaka. She looked down at the deck, near his feet, almost deferentially. "You know what kind of answers I want," she said softly. "I want to know who sent you. I want to know what they know about our plans."

She looked up now, straight into Ryan's eyes. "If you do not tell me what I want to know," she said, "you will be hurt very badly." She smiled. A smile that left Ryan in no doubt as to how much Tetsuo Hidaka would enjoy watching him get hurt.

She started to turn toward Tsunogi again. Ryan flinched away. It was important that he show fear. Maybe then they'd believe the lies he was about to tell them. He had to make them think there was a whole army already on the way. What he must not do was let them know how completely alone he was. Once they figured that out, there'd be a bullet in the head, and he'd be feeding the fish.

"The plutonium," he blurted. "We know you took it. We know what you're going to do with it."

Hidaka looked amused. "Our atomic bomb?" she asked. "The People's Bomb? What do you know about that?"

"We knew about Kranek. That he was your bomb builder. It won't work. There are too many people onto you. We know about this boat, they're tracking it now. They'll stop you, and get the plutonium back—"

This time it was Hidaka who hit him, a slap across the face. Nothing compared to one of Tsunogi's kicks, but Ryan cringed backward, trying to make his fear look convincing. Not that he wasn't genuinely afraid. But he was also constantly assessing his chances, constantly alert for advantages, both verbal and physical. "Lies," Hidaka hissed. "You obviously know very little. You don't even know that the plutonium is no longer aboard, that it is now safe ... somewhere else. You ..."

Suddenly, he saw a slight look of confusion come over Hidaka's face. She stared at him intently. "I know you from somewhere," she said. "Your face looks very familiar. But you were younger then. . . ."

Standing this close to the woman who, for so long, he'd wanted to kill, Ryan temporarily forgot caution. "Yes," he said, his voice no longer uncertain. "We had a mutual acquaintance."

"Who?"

"Yoshiro. Nakashima Yoshiro."

She looked genuinely puzzled. Ryan felt overwhelming anger sweep over him. The bitch did not even remember the young man she'd sent to his death!

"He killed a man for you," he said icily. "A politician. Then he killed himself, committed *sepuku.*"

Another moment's confusion, then Hidaka smiled brightly. "Of course! That nice boy! You knew him? Oh yes, I remember now. I saw you with him once."

Ryan let a moment's silence pass. "I've been looking for you ever since his death. The way he died ..."

A moment's bafflement, then Hidaka broke out laughing. Genuine, amused laughter. "So?" she asked. "This is simply for revenge? Oh, how romantic!"

She turned toward Tsunogi, who was looking at them stolidly. She quickly explained in Japanese who Yoshiro had been, and Ryan's quixotic quest, neither of them aware that Ryan could speak Japanese.

"So," Tsunogi finally said. "He is here on his own. Let me kill him, and we can get some sleep."

But Hidaka was frowning now. "No. His explanation comes too easily. And it only raises new questions. For instance, how did he manage to find us? How did he know about the plutonium? How did he know where to look for Kranek? He may have his own personal reasons for being here, but he had to have a great deal of help. Someone sent him, used him."

She turned back to face Ryan. "And we have to find out who that someone is. How much they know. If he was telling us the truth, and they know about the boat . . ."

Tsunogi started to step past her. "Give me an hour with him," he said, still in Japanese. "Then I will know everything that he knows."

Hidaka shook her head. "No. For one thing, it is almost dawn. We were going to sail at dawn. But if the boat is known . . ."

Tsunogi shook his head. "Would he be here alone if others knew about the boat? I don't think so. He came here for his own reasons . . . to take revenge."

Hidaka hesitated. "Perhaps. But I have to make certain. If he really is here alone . . ."

"An hour," Tsunogi insisted. "Just an hour with him, and I'll know."

Hidaka shook her head firmly. "An hour is too much time."

Then she smiled. Ryan was learning that her smiles usually meant bad news. He remained standing, dumb, unresponsive, anxious to keep them from knowing he spoke Japanese. Not that his knowledge of what they were saying was making him feel any better. An hour with Tsunogi would undoubtedly seem like a year in hell.

"The girl," Hidaka said to Tsunogi, still smiling. "The first thing he did when he got on board was look for the girl. She must mean something to him."

This last statement was made almost with wonder, as if Tetsuo Hidaka could not quite understand someone risking his life for the good of another. Her smile hardened. "We will use the girl."

She looked past Ryan's shoulder, spoke in English. "Bring the Spanish girl closer."

Petra was shoved past Ryan. Their eyes met for a moment. She appeared to be very frightened . . . as she should be. Hidaka stood in front of Petra, studied her face. Then she turned toward Ryan. "I will not bother to ask you again; you would only lie . . . for now. But . . . after you have seen the girl suffer, you will be anxious to tell us everything you know."

She turned around to face her Japanese followers. "Strip her," she said.

Initially, the men seemed surprised, then they grinned. Petra had not understood the command; Hidaka had spoken in Japanese. But when two men seized her, and another man tore off her blouse, she began to struggle. "No!" she cried out.

Ryan started forward . . . until he felt a gun muzzle dig into his back, a stupid move, because he could easily turn away from the gun muzzle, hit the man holding the gun, and take it away from him. But there were too many other guns covering him. There was nothing he could do; he could only stand and watch as Petra was brutally stripped. Her clothing was torn from her with such force that her skin was soon marked with welts where the cloth had refused to tear easily.

In less than a minute Petra had been stripped naked. She was left standing in the middle of the well-lighted deck, in the center of a circle of leering men. At first she tried to cover her loins and her breasts with her hands. But it was a futile gesture, and she sensed it. So she finally stood straight, her face tense, her hands at her sides. Dignity, Ryan decided. She would rather show dignity than cover herself. He was impressed.

Hassim stepped forward. "This is not right," he protested to Hidaka. "We do not make war against women."

Hidaka smiled. "We do what we have to do. What about

our mission, Hassim? Don't you want to see it completed? Don't you want to see your people restored to their land?"

"Of course, but . . ."

Hidaka turned away from Hassim. "Then do not interfere," she said curtly.

Now she was facing Ryan again. "She will be raped," she said flatly. "At first only by one or two men. Right here in front of you. If I am not convinced, by then, that you are telling me all you know, then she will be raped . . . more severely. Perhaps instruments will be used to enter her. She will suffer very much."

"Wait!" Ryan shouted. But Hidaka was no longer paying attention to him. Her eyes were on the girl. And her eyes were glittering. Kinky, Ryan thought. Hidaka was going to enjoy this, enjoy the horror of it, the corrupted sexual part.

All eyes were now on Petra. For good reason. God, but she's beautiful, Ryan thought. In Son Feliu, when he had first seen Petra in her uncle's store, he had been impressed by the lushness of her body. Now, with the girl standing naked in the glare of the deck lights, he realized he'd underestimated that lushness. She was full-bodied without being overweight. Her breasts were solid, perfectly shaped. Her belly was taut, but not gaunt. She had full hips and lovely thighs, punctuated by a perfect dark triangle. As she breathed, rather heavily—because, of course, she was afraid—her breasts rose and fell dramatically. The fear itself only accentuated the loveliness of her face.

The Arabs had, at first, showed disapproval when Hidaka had ordered Petra stripped. But by now they were watching her just as avidly as Hidaka's men. All the men had formed into a big circle, with Petra in the middle. Most of them still hung back, but the eyes of every one of them were focused on Petra. Even Tsunogi was watching the girl, although his face still wore that unreadable expression.

Hidaka pointed toward two of her men. "You," she said. "And you, Hidesho. You will take her first."

The men looked first surprised, then pleased, then perhaps a little embarrassed. Attention swung away from Petra for a moment, to the two lucky ones. Almost no one was paying attention to Ryan.

Which was the moment he'd been waiting for, that tiny window of opportunity that he had been trained to recognize. Even as the two Japanese were beginning to tug at the flies of their trousers, Ryan was already moving. Moving without a preliminary giveaway bunching of muscles, moving the same way Tsunogi had moved when he'd kicked Ryan. Moving the way Master Nakashima had taught him to move, instantly, with no warning—one moment immobility, the next moment, blinding speed.

Tsunogi was the first to become aware of Ryan's move. But he, like the rest, had focused too much of his attention on Petra, so his reaction was just slightly slower than it would normally have been. He tried to intercept Ryan as he raced across the deck straight toward Petra. Ryan had already noticed an opening in the side rail, where the gangway had not been closed. He slammed into Petra, knocking her sideways, toward that opening. He heard her gasp, realized he had knocked the wind out of her, which was not good. A moment later they were both through the opening, past the deck, falling toward the water.

They hit hard. He heard Petra grunt just before she went under. That meant she had lost even more air. He seized her arm, dragged her underwater toward the boat's stern. She resisted just a moment, then he sensed that she was cooperating, kicking with her legs, swimming along with him.

They came up under the stern, sheltering beneath the overhang. Petra was gasping, sucking in air. Ryan gave her a moment to breathe deeply. He heard shouting on deck, the pounding of running feet coming their way. Men were calling out in three languages. He heard Tetsuo Hidaka shouting, "The stern! They went toward the stern!"

"Now!" Ryan whispered to Petra. "Follow me underwater. Trust me."

They both upended, digging for depth. Ryan caught a glimpse of a face over the stern rail, the snout of a weapon. Then the water closed over them both.

Ryan swam hard, with Petra alongside him swimming just as hard. She had not been exaggerating earlier; she could really move through the water. But then, she'd been brought up on an island.

The boat's lights helped. Ryan saw the dark maw of the cave entrance directly ahead. He looked back once, saw the lighted surface of the water, saw, also, many splashes as automatic weapon fire churned the surface, saw the bullets strike, then flatten, streak downward for a foot or so, dragging bubbles, then tumble slowly down into the depths, totally harmless.

Fortunately, with the surface being chopped up so badly by the firing, the water had become more opaque. Ryan hoped that the glare of light rebounding off that choppy surface would keep those on the boat from seeing where he and Petra were heading. They were inside the cave opening now. Petra was struggling a little, perhaps running out of air. Ryan pulled her through, past the rocks, then they were rising.

They both made a lot of noise when they broke the surface, but Ryan doubted anyone outside could hear. Not with all that shouting and firing. "Up," Ryan whispered to Petra. They both hoisted themselves onto the underwater shelf. Just in time. The water surged. Ryan heard a dull boom outside. They were using grenades!

More dull underwater explosions. The water below their legs surged again. If they had still been swimming, the force of the explosions might have ruptured their lungs. Which was undoubtedly the plan.

Finally, Ryan heard Hidaka shouting, "Stop throwing those grenades! Do you want every policeman on the island heading this way?"

The noise level from the boat began to diminish. "Put the dory over," he heard someone call out. It sounded like Hassim. Ryan heard the sound of wood striking against wood. He leaned down, whispered into Petra's ear, "Stay here. I'll be right back."

She grabbed his arm. In the faint reflected light Ryan could read the alarm in her eyes. Perhaps she thought he was going to swim back out into the cove. He pointed upwards, then began to climb. In a moment he was at the little hole in the cliff, looking out.

Yes, they were putting the dory over. Too fast, too sloppily. The little boat hit the water bow first and almost went under. After a lot of shouting and swearing, five men jumped into the dory, all of them carrying Kalashnikovs. Two rowed, while the other three crowded toward the bow, weapons ready.

They headed straight toward the cave. Ryan tensed, then relaxed a little. It only made sense for them to come this way; it was the last direction in which he and Petra had been seen heading.

Ryan held his breath as the boat coasted along the cliff face . . . right over the entrance to the cave. But the men were not looking down, they were examining every rocky outcropping that might shelter someone trying to hide. One of the men fired once, probably at a shadow. There was a loud query from the boat, but the man sheepishly answered that it was nothing.

The dory prowled the cliffs for half an hour, while searchlights played over the water, alert for surfacing swimmers. Then the dory went around and around the boat itself, on the off chance that Ryan and Petra were hiding beneath the shadow of the hull.

Finally, a cry from the boat. Hassim's voice. "They must be dead. No one can stay underwater that long. The grenades must have killed them."

Hidaka's acid reply. "Ah, Hassim . . . isn't that what you said when that bastard was trapped in the house?"

A quick explosion of anger from Hassim. "Do you have any other ideas, woman? Would you like to drain the sea, so we can find their bodies?"

Silence. "No, of course not. You are right. And more

importantly, we must get out of here. With all the noise we've been making ..."

Ryan watched while the dory was hoisted aboard. There was great activity on deck, the kind necessary to get such a large boat moving. Ryan heard an auxiliary engine fire up, then, a minute later the *clank, clank, clank* as the anchor was slowly warped up toward the cathead.

No point in staying up here any longer. He could see the white blur of Petra's body below. He realized that it was growing light outside. A good deal of that light was filtering into the cave. There must be another opening, a larger one, higher up.

He climbed down to Petra. Her eyes sought his. He could see that she was shaking. At first he thought that fear was overcoming her, until she said, "I'm cold. So cold."

He nodded. It was indeed cold. And damp. And neither of them had any clothes on ... although Petra no longer seemed aware of her nakedness. Perhaps there had been too many other things to consider. Like surviving.

Ryan moved close to the girl, took her in his arms so that they could share each other's body heat. For just a little while her damp flesh felt cold against his. Then her skin began to warm. To grow very warm indeed. He glanced at her, and in the growing light, saw that she was looking at him intently.

They continued to look into one another's eyes for several seconds. Then Petra suddenly grasped him tightly against her. He could hear her breathing quicken, sense her flesh growing even warmer, searing against his own.

He'd seen it happen before, a peculiar sexual intensity brought out by the nearness of death. Perhaps it was an instinctive reaction of the organism to danger, an urge to reproduce when the organism's existence was most threatened.

The hell with rationalizations. A naked woman, of uncommon beauty, was panting beside his own naked body. His hands began to roam. When he brushed a palm over

Petra's breasts, he felt her nipples stiffen, heard her utter a short, sharp little gasp.

It was all instinct after that, a natural progression of events. There was a certain clumsiness in Petra's reactions, a sense of pleasant shock, of delighted discovery each time Ryan touched her in a new place. Kranek must have been right when he'd suggested that Petra had not been touched by another man since her uncle had raped her.

It was like making love to a virgin—except for the usual difficulty of entering a virgin. With Petra, there was no difficulty at all, the way had already been opened for Ryan, years before, in an ugly act. There was no ugliness now. Petra, perhaps with that old memory still in her mind, seemed astounded that this time it could be so wonderful, feel so good, be so incredibly exciting.

The first time was short and wild, an instant coupling, with quick, hard intakes of breath, a sudden, uncontrollable shuddering from each of them, then they were temporarily spent.

Ryan pushed himself up onto stiffened arms, looked down at Petra. She was looking back up at him. Her face was still flushed from her passion, but her eyes were also wonderfully calm. She studied Ryan's face for half a minute—it was not quite light. It was a proprietary kind of scrutiny. A look Ryan had seen before, from other women. A look that had always made Ryan nervous.

The hell with it; by God, they were both alive. Very much alive. He was aware of Petra's naked warmth all along the length of his body. It was not easy to pry himself away, but he had to see what was happening outside. He could hear the sound of distant engines.

He rose away from Petra. He heard her gasp as he pulled out of her body. Then he was climbing toward the spy hole.

The boat was already halfway through the inlet's narrow entrance. He watched as its stern disappeared around the headland. Gone. He and Petra were safe . . . at least for a while. Unless this was one of Tetsuo Hidaka's little tricks.

Perhaps she intended to take the boat just out of sight, then send the dory back in for an ambush when he and Petra left their hiding place.

Better to stay here in the cave for a while, remain hidden. It was frustrating not to be on the move, but . . .

Ryan looked down at Petra. She was propped on one elbow, looking up at him. Gravely. He noticed that even though she was lying mostly on her back, her breasts had not lost their shape. She was incredibly beautiful.

Yes, perhaps hiding here for a while longer might be a damned good idea. He began to climb down. Petra continued to look back up at him. Gravely. Expectantly.

19

Ryan and Petra remained in the cave all day, wondering when the police would arrive. He and the girl drank from little rock pools higher up in the cave, where fresh water had seeped down through the limestone. However, there was nothing to eat. Nothing for them except each other.

For a while Petra was conscious of her nakedness, but after they had made love a few times—and each time seemed to bring new revelations to the girl—she seemed, to Ryan, to actually begin reveling in that same nakedness.

Hunger drove them out just before dark. There had been no police; either the shooting had not been heard or no one had reported it. They left the cave through the underwater entrance, then swam toward shore, coasting along the rocks. When they walked out of the water up onto the rocky beach, they found they were not alone. Two boys in their early teens were standing fifty yards away, gawking at Petra. But they did no more than stare, accustomed to skinny-dipping tourists.

Ryan led the way to where he'd hidden his clothes. To his relief everything was still there, including the pistol and the knife. Unfortunately, Petra had no clothes; hers were still aboard the schooner. Ryan draped his shirt over her; it barely covered her groin. He wore only his trousers, carrying the pistol in one hand, rolled up in his underwear.

They climbed the path that led to the car. Before he'd left Palma in the morning—my God, had it been only that long ago?—Ryan had thrown a small bag with extra clothes onto the backseat. It was still there. He found a longer shirt, and a pair of shorts for Petra. The shorts bagged around her waist, but her hips held them up well enough. Now she lacked only shoes.

Half expecting hidden police to jump out at any moment, Ryan drove the car onto the road. He was going to have to be constantly alert about police. Although there were none in sight now, there would be others to face later. Fortunately, there was nothing to link all this trouble to John Stevens, boat owner. The car he could ditch, as he'd already done with the false identity papers he'd used to rent it.

But what about Petra? Undoubtedly the police were looking for her. Strenuously. By the time the police had arrived at Kranek's house, there had been no bodies, the terrorists had seen to that, but there had been plenty of blood. And, of course, the wrecked house itself. Petra was tied to that house. And to Kranek. In a village that small, everyone would have known about it. And now Petra was missing. Yes, the police would definitely be looking for Petra, either as a victim or as a witness. If she simply returned to Son Feliu, she would immediately be brought in for questioning. Lots of questioning. She would, in time, tell the police everything she knew. Which was too damned much. Word would get out that terrorists were building an atomic bomb. Then, of course, terror would follow. General terror. Public terror. Which was exactly the kind of thing Ryan was supposed to prevent.

So Petra would have to stay out of sight until this entire mess was over. The best way to keep her hidden would be to keep her with him. He doubted she would mind. At the moment, as she sat next to him in the front seat of the car, she was looking very, very satisfied. No, she definitely would not mind.

Nor would he mind. But that was a stupid way to think. To become emotionally involved now . . .

He must not be trapped by what he and Petra had shared in the cave. He must find a way to get rid of her. But how? This was a rather small island. He did not consider, even for a moment, the idea of harming Petra. There were no easy answers. And tugging at him were . . . incentives. Feelings that made him want to keep her close by . . . the sweet smell of her body, memories of the wild way she had responded by his lovemaking, his general level of stupidity where women were concerned.

He could keep her on the boat. Yes, that might be the best answer. He'd leave her aboard when he went after the bomb plans. He was certain that he was going after the plans. For the past few hours he'd been thinking about those charts he'd seen, the ones on the chartroom table aboard the schooner. Thinking about the course plotted for Minorca. And that cove, with all the markings around it. Could he remember where that cove was? He hoped so, because he was going after the schooner. The bomb plans. The plutonium. And Tetsuo Hidaka. Petra would go with him.

When they reached the main road, Ryan turned toward Valldemossa. Most businesses were closed at this time of day; it was nearly eight P.M., beginning to grow dark. But Valldemossa was a tourist town. Nearly all of the dozens of huge buses, packed with fat sunburned English, German, Scandinavian, and American tourists, had already left the huge tour bus parking lots. But there were still a few tourist shops open. Ryan went into one, where he bought clothing for Petra: a summer-weight dress, some jeans, shirts, and two pairs of shoes. Returning to the car he tossed everything into the backseat, then they drove out of town. A few miles past Valldemossa he turned off the main road, into a little grove of trees, where Petra dressed.

Then on to Palma. It was quite dark now. While Petra

had been dressing, Ryan had knocked out the little light that illuminated the license plate. He'd already noticed various bits and pieces of running gear missing from other cars, so he doubted this particular equipment omission would stand out.

He took a chance, driving most of the way into town. Then, near the Plaza España, he parked the car on a dark side street. Taking his bag, stuffed with his own belongings plus Petra's new clothing, he let Petra guide him across the Plaza España into a warren of narrow streets near the Mercado Central. "I'm hungry, aren't you?" she said hopefully.

Ryan was starving. "We can't go to a big place," he replied.

She nodded, then led the way down a very narrow street that ran off Calle Olmos to an *economico,* one of the tiny restaurants that sold food the average working man could afford. There they wolfed down soup, salad, bread, fish, meat, and wine, all at one fixed price. Ryan ate two meals, sharing part of the second one with Petra.

Now, the boat. Would it be staked out? It was only about half a mile to the docks. They walked through the older areas, through narrow, twisting, poorly lighted streets, staying away from the big avenues. Finally, they reached the Paseo Maritimo, a broad thoroughfare that overlooked the harbor. Ryan stopped in the shadow of some trees, studying the entire dock area. He could see the boat; there seemed to be no one near it. As far as he could tell, there was nothing out of the ordinary anywhere within his line of sight.

Which meant nothing. He pointed the boat out to Petra. "Walk by," he murmured. "If you don't see anyone watching, go on board and sit in the cockpit."

She nodded, then walked away. He watched her go, feeling tension. Not for Petra, she would be safe enough, physically. The only people who might have a reason to watch the boat would be the police. If they took her into custody, they would have no reason to harm her. Of course, the questions would begin, but she would probably play dumb long enough for Ryan to take some evasive action. He'd be free for at least a little while. He'd be cut off from his base, of course, from his radio, his identity as John Stevens, but that was a lot better than being arrested.

Petra stepped aboard the boat with no apparent trouble. Ryan watched her descend into the cockpit. He could barely make her out. As far as he could tell, no one was paying her the slightest bit of attention.

Five minutes later, Ryan followed. When he stepped aboard, Petra ran her hand affectionately over his shoulder. To Ryan, she appeared totally calm, as if she did this kind of thing every day. He was very pleased; she had done as he asked without any hesitation. He remembered her courage at the house during the fight. And later, aboard the schooner. Perhaps she would turn out to be an asset, rather than someone to worry about. Or so he kept telling himself . . . when he wasn't remembering her naked body, and the way she'd responded to him, as if she'd been starving for sex all her life. Which was probably the case.

To his relief, once they had gone below Petra seemed more interested in sleep than in sex . . . until the morning light began to seep into the boat. Then she rolled against him in the bunk, her thighs parting as she lifted one leg over his hips, opening herself to him. Groggy, but not that groggy, Ryan realized that even though Petra was still half asleep, she was already very wet. Perhaps she'd begun to wake up in the middle of a particularly sensuous dream. When she'd become conscious of the reality of warm flesh lying next to her, she had proceeded instinctively.

Her eyes were half open, smoky, dreamy. She was making a self-satisfied little humming sound deep in her throat. Ryan could not resist.

Later, they walked to the yacht club's showers separately, where they washed away yesterday's dried salt water. With Petra back below deck, Ryan took aboard fresh water and a supply of food. Then, with the sun barely above the horizon, he motored out of the harbor. When they were past the breakwater, Petra helped him set the sails. She did not seem familiar with boats, but she was quick to learn. Within an hour Ryan had her at the tiller, while he went below to check the radio.

It seemed functional. And now . . . decisions. Common sense told him to send a message detailing what he had found. Let others close in. But, who would those others be? Would they swoop down in overwhelming force, panicking Hidaka, Hassim, and Tsunogi? Would a fight follow, with all the terrorists killed, without anyone left to tell where the plutonium was hidden? Ryan remembered Hidaka saying, on the schooner, that the plutonium was no longer aboard. So, where was it? On Minorca? And if so, where on Minorca? With other terrorists?

No, the best thing would be to follow that charted course to Minorca, locate the schooner, find the plutonium, and then use the radio. That was undoubtedly what Central had had in mind when he'd given Ryan the assignment. Keep a low profile. Strike only when he had all the information he needed.

A few hours out of Palma, the wind died. They were becalmed for a day and a half, drifting slowly with the current, sails barely flapping, Ryan stewing in the cockpit beneath a canvas awning he had rigged to keep the sun from frying them.

Petra was not at all dismayed. Now that they were out at sea, far from human company, her clothes disappeared again. She seemed to want to make love all day long; she'd discovered a wonderful new toy.

Ryan complied. Not much else to do. Not that he particularly minded. What did bother him was that proprietary light, now growing stronger, glowing warmly from Petra's eyes. She'd found love, she'd found her man. The tight, bitter lines around her mouth were totally gone now, and where before she'd been merely beautiful, she was now awesome. All of which made Ryan very nervous. Petra was obviously not a woman who would be satisfied with the kind of relationship he had with Inge.

And what about Inge? Petra would never permit him to . . .

As the doldrums continued, a subtle change invaded Ryan's thinking. He began to be just the slightest bit pleased with the idea of being with someone who was totally his, and to whom he owed . . . something approaching permanence. With a sinking feeling he realized that his usual priorities were becoming hopelessly scrambled. First, he'd developed a love affair with the boat. And now, this thing with Petra. But was it really necessary to fight either feeling?

On the third day, a breeze suddenly arose, tugging at the sails, heeling the boat over. Ryan quickly adjusted the sheets until the sails were drawing well, then set the course once again for Minorca. He'd expected Petra to be upset once they were on their way again, to pout as if a honeymoon had been prematurely interrupted, but she immediately set to work helping him sail the boat, just as cheerful as when they'd been making love all day. Once again, she had impressed him. This damned mission, he thought. Get it over with quickly. After that, well, a year or two sailing the Med with Petra might be . . . a consideration. Might be . . . damned wonderful.

They sighted Minorca on the morning of the fourth day. Majorca had its share of cliffs, but the cliffs around Minorca were awesome . . . sheer walls of limestone rising straight out of the sea. Ryan debated putting into the capital, Mahón, but decided against it. He kept looking at his charts, trying to remember which cove had been marked on the schooner's map. Finally, he decided to simply sail around the island, looking.

They found it late in the afternoon, the schooner, partly visible, tucked away in a tight little cove. Staying well out to sea, Ryan studied the schooner through his binoculars for several minutes.

Yes, it was definitely Tetsuo Hidaka's boat. Ryan's hunch had been right. Hidaka and the others had headed straight for Minorca. Where they probably were even now constructing their bomb.

He and Petra exchanged troubled looks. The honeymoon was definitely over.

20

They continued sailing, well offshore, with Ryan studying the schooner through his binoculars, keeping low, with most of his body hidden inside the cockpit, just in case someone from the schooner might be studying him.

No sign of life on the schooner's decks. Uh-uh, wait . . . one man, moving slowly near a deckhouse. Moving like a bored guard. And like a guard whose superior was nowhere near. He must be the only man aboard. Where, then, were the rest? Probably ashore.

But where? Ryan scanned the area. Rocks. Sheer cliffs rising straight out of the water. He did see a path leading up from the cove where the schooner was anchored. A narrow, twisting path. How the hell would they have been able to get all that equipment up that completely inadequate path?

He and Petra sailed on by. Now Ryan noticed two or three cave mouths up on the sheer sides of the cliffs, near the cove. Dark, empty holes gaping in sheets of weathered, pale limestone. Did those caves cut through to anywhere? If so, Hidaka and her people might have been able to drop lines down from the cave mouths, temporarily moor the boat beneath them, then haul the cargo straight up off the boat's decks. If those caves were anything more than shallow holes in the cliff face.

The cove that sheltered the schooner fell behind until it was out of sight. Ryan continued sailing along beneath the cliffs. A mile farther along he saw a gap in the cliffs leading into a small cove. He put over the tiller, heading to port. He called out to Petra, asked her to go forward and watch for rocks and reefs. When he was just offshore, he lowered the sails and started the little auxiliary. They inched in, with Petra leaning over the bow, trying to see beneath the water, which was not too difficult, because the water was quite calm; she could look far down into its depths.

There were reefs, but with big gaps that allowed Ryan to motor the boat right into the cove. They made anchor behind a big outcropping of rock that completely sheltered the boat from the sight of anyone who might pass by out at sea.

While Ryan was making the mainsail fast to the boom, he was aware of Petra watching him. Looking at him intently. When he had finished his task and turned toward her, she asked, her voice low, "What are you going to do?"

He pointed back in the schooner's direction. "Find out where they are. Those people. Go after them."

She looked puzzled. "Why? You've seen the boat. You already know they're here. Isn't that enough? Can't you . . . get some kind of help? Let someone else do it?"

Ryan turned away, sat next to the tiller while he looped lines over it, fastening it in place. What could he tell her? That this was as much a personal as a professional matter? Why bother? She wouldn't understand. Hell, he wasn't sure that *he* understood. "It's what I have to do," he said flatly.

She continued to look steadily at him for several more seconds. Then she nodded. "I understand. Sometimes men have to do things."

Her face was not happy, but it was calm. Quite a woman, Ryan reflected. What was it? Her Spanish heritage, that long history of suffering and trouble that went all the way back to her people's seven-hundred-year fight against the Moors? Or just Petra herself? He laid his hand on her shoulder. She smiled, moved closer to him. He caressed her cheek. She pressed it against his hand.

Time was short; it would be dark soon, and he had to get moving while he could still see where he was going. He went below, into the cabin. Petra followed. He was aware of her somber gaze as he thrust the Rogak into its holster at the back of his belt, then strapped the *tanto* onto his lower right leg. As he turned to go on deck, she clung to him tightly, one long, yearning embrace. Nothing of panic in it, just . . . longing.

Going on deck, he hauled on one of the anchor lines, drawing the boat close to a low outthrust of rock. He jumped, landing on the rock. He turned back for a moment, to look at Petra. She was leaning against the little cabin, watching him. A wave from him, an answering wave from her, then he began to work his way along the cliff. It was not difficult; low ledges and rocky outcroppings stretched all the way to the usual rocky beach. He'd already noticed a small trail leading up to the top of the bluff. Once on the beach, he studied the trail carefully. It looked rough but passable. He started climbing. The trail switchbacked over a series of increasingly high outcroppings, where weather had worn away the face of the cliff. It was a steep climb, but not particularly dangerous. In less than ten minutes he was at the top. He halted for a moment, looking down at the cove, far below. The water was so clear that his boat seemed to be floating in the air, thirty feet above the greenish rocky bottom. He saw that Petra was still watching him. He waved one last time, she waved back. Then he turned and passed out of her sight over the top of the cliff.

It would be dark soon; he had to move quickly. He trotted along rocky paths, seeing no one. He had already been told by Petra that Minorca was not nearly as heavily populated as Majorca or Ibiza. This particular area seemed to be completely uninhabited. He could see why ... the rocky, barren soil barely supported weeds.

But within twenty minutes he spotted the roof of a house, perhaps two hundred yards ahead. He instantly dropped to the ground. As far as he could figure, from the distance he'd already covered, that house must be right above the cove where he'd seen the schooner.

Using every available bit of cover, Ryan worked his way toward the house. Within fifteen minutes he was lying on his stomach in a patch of boulders only a hundred yards from the house's front door.

He studied the area through his binoculars. It was barren, just like the land he'd already passed through. A steep hill rose just behind the house. There were no buildings on it at all, just steep, rocky hillside.

Nothing. Nobody in sight. The house itself was quite small, the usual stone and rubble construction, with probably no more than four or five rooms inside. Too damned small a place to house the large crew he'd seen aboard the schooner. Way too small a space for the building of an atomic bomb.

So where the hell was everybody? Had they abandoned the schooner? Had they gone somewhere else on the island? Or perhaps they had transshipped their equipment to another boat and sailed away. If so, he'd probably lost them. If that was true, then his gamble of following the schooner on his own had not paid off.

Ryan had nearly convinced himself that the house was merely some goatherder's headquarters when he saw movement inside the doorway. He raised the binoculars again. He saw a man standing in deep shadow. Definitely a man. Or a woman in trousers. The light was fading fast. Ryan continued to stare through the glasses. He saw whoever it was lean something against the door frame, then step outside, into the fading light.

A Japanese. Here in this isolated place on Minorca. And

what he'd leaned against the door frame appeared to be a Kalashnikov. By God, he'd found them after all!

Ryan watched the man, obviously a guard, scratch his crotch for a while, then go back inside the house. Yet, no lights shone from the windows, and it was now almost dark. What was going on?

Ryan continued watching for another half hour. An inky blackness settled over the area. No moon tonight, and no city near enough to light up the sky. It was this intense blackness that eventually showed him what he had hoped to see. The sky blazed with stars, vivid against the velvety black of the sky itself. The Milky Way stretched overhead, a broad shimmering band. The starlight was almost enough to block it out, but then Ryan saw it, faintly, a glimmer of light set against the dark mass of the hill that rose behind the house. Light where there should have been only barren hillside.

Ryan, moving with great care in the intense dark, guided only by starlight, worked his way down off his perch, across flat land near the house, and up the side of the hill. It was probably no more than two hundred and fifty yards, but it took him an hour.

Here, the light was brighter, a glimmering from inside the hill itself, outlining an irregular opening. A cave mouth. Not very large, but large enough to allow light to escape. And large enough for Ryan to enter.

He crawled inside, between crumbling limestone boulders, inching his way along, intent on not disturbing stones or soil, or making any noise that would give him away. The light got brighter, his progress even more careful. The cave was growing a little wider; before, he'd felt rock pressing down only a couple of feet above his back. Now he could see that the cave roof was at least eight feet high. He could easily have risen to his feet, but he preferred crawling, so that he could check out the way ahead of him with his hands.

He had a sudden, vivid memory of the old *deposito* near Son Feliu, and of the mass of scorpions who inhabited it.

He remembered the dying screams of the man who'd fallen into the *deposito*. Would his fingers come up against anything like that? Something scaly, with lots of legs? He shuddered, but kept on.

More light now. The cave he was in ended a few yards farther along. But not in a blank wall. It ended in space, in a ragged, well-lighted opening. He crawled to the edge of that opening and looked down. Into bright light. He was above a long tunnel that ran at right angles to the one he was in. A big tunnel, a long corridor, probably originally a natural cave, was about four yards high. Concrete smoothed the cave's floor. Electric lighting was strung along the ceiling. Farther along, he could make out dark gaps in the cave's wall, openings like the one he was currently looking out of. And damned if a couple of those openings didn't have doors set into them.

Suddenly he heard the sound of heels slapping against concrete. The sound echoed loudly off the walls. Two men came into sight, walking together, Arabs by their appearance. Walking somewhere with an air of purpose. Ryan slipped back into his cave, lay for a moment, thinking. Yes, he'd found it. He had no doubt about that. Found the place where they were making their bomb. What had Tetsuo Hidaka called it? The People's Bomb.

21

It was beginning to grow light by the time Ryan once again reached the clifftop above his boat. How peaceful the little craft looked, swinging gently against its anchor line. How inviting, considering that Petra was aboard. How tempting to simply sail away, forget Tetsuo Hidaka, the bomb, everything.

Perhaps he would do just that. He started down the path. It was steep and rocky; he could not help dislodging small stones, some of which bounced all the way down to the water. It was these small splashes that brought Petra out on deck. Ryan felt something leap inside himself when he saw her wave happily up at him. Something very good had happened to him on this mission, something totally unexpected. Petra herself. An incredible gift.

When he boarded the boat, she pressed hard against him, her arms tight around his body. He hugged her back. When she looked up, her eyes were misty. "I was afraid for you," she said simply.

"So was I," he replied, grinning.

She lit up at his grin. "We can leave, then?"

He stopped grinning. "Maybe. I . . . don't know."

He went below, lay on the bunk, staring up at the ceiling, while Petra fired up the butane stove, then cooked some eggs and sausages. He began to eat, mechanically at first, until he realized how hungry he was, and how good the food tasted. He looked at Petra once, then looked away. She obviously wanted to leave here very much. When he'd eaten, Petra turned away to wash the dishes. He stopped that by pulling her down onto the bunk with him. Within less than a minute they were making love. Wild, grasping love, as if their closeness was something out of their control, some caged animal that was about to make its escape, was something that had to be used up now, before it was gone forever.

Afterwards, Ryan slept. He awoke in the late afternoon, feeling well rested. Petra still lay beside him, naked, asleep, her face peaceful. Ryan watched her for a long time, watched her breathe, listened to the small sounds of her sleeping. Amazing, he thought. The longer he knew her, the more beautiful she became.

He got up. His movements awakened Petra. He smiled, then prodded her off the bunk. To get to his radio, the bunk would have to be folded out of the way. She watched, curious when he opened the countertop, even more curious when she saw all the equipment inside the hidden compartment. "I have to send a message," he told her.

He'd decided to do it. Call in the big guns. Not take any more chances of losing Tetsuo Hidaka and the plutonium. It took him an hour to draft a message that he considered both sufficiently succinct and sufficiently informative. The final message was longer than he might have wished it to be, but it did describe the whereabouts of the terrorists and their bomb factory.

When he had finished writing out the message, he encoded it, using the cipher book Central had provided with the radio. Then he recorded the message in voice, a meaningless collection of words. Now, all he had to do was put the tape in the machine, tune the set to the right channel, push a button, and the message would be sent in a quick, high-speed burst that would last only a few seconds.

But he did not press the button. The tape remained inside the machine, its message unsent.

Ryan sat on the edge of the half-folded bunk. It was tempting to simply send the message, then sail away. With Petra. With this beautiful woman. This sensual, courageous woman. Easy. Yes, the easy thing to do. But the reasons that had sent him into the cave in the first place were pushing him to go in again. It was simple enough . . . he had not yet located the raw material for the bomb. The plutonium itself. He knew how heavy-fisted the response would be once he sent the message. A sledgehammer approach. Lots of killing and shooting. But where, in those labryinthine caves, was the plutonium? Was it even there at all? He had to be certain.

Then, there was the woman. Tetsuo Hidaka. He had not seen her at the cave. Was she there? Perhaps those caves were only some kind of supply point. Perhaps Hidaka and the other terrorist leaders were already on their way to someplace else. Having the caves hit now might only make them lie low . . . perhaps still in possession of enough plutonium to build their bomb.

What disturbed Ryan the most was the possibility that Tetsuo Hidaka might eventually be captured. Alive. Put in prison. Ryan had a mental image of Tetsuo Hidaka, smirking into cameras, justifying her butcher's philosophy to all the little champagne Marxists, those bored yuppy assholes who seize onto grubby movements, or grubby personalities like Hidaka, to try to prove to themselves that their lives are not quite so empty after all. Trendy people, who chant, and wave banners, who never see past the surface of whatever cause they support, who never see the complexities underneath. Who never have the time. Later, feeling virtuous, they return to their greedy, grasping little life-styles. Yes, people like that would hang on that bitch's every word. She'd be a celebrity, and she'd love it.

Then, the worst . . . she might even be rescued from jail by other terrorists.

No. This had to be finished the right way. He would have to go back to the caves. Pinpoint targets, so that when the cavalry arrived, they would not go in blind.

Petra sensed his unease. It was growing dark now, but he could see the look of strain on her face. He turned to face her. "I'll be going back tonight. There's more that I have to do there."

"No," she replied. "You've done enough."

He shook his head. "That's something only I can decide."

She started to speak, then fell silent, sensing that she would be unable to dissuade him. He closed the countertop, and they put the bunk down again. They lay on it together for another hour, while it grew completely dark outside. He told her all about what he had found, the caves, the house. He told her that he thought the people who had killed Kranek were using Kranek's plans to build an atomic bomb.

Mentioning Kranek seemed to settle Petra down. But she still seemed dubious about the role he was choosing for himself. She was looking at him questioningly. He realized that she knew he was holding something back. So he told her. About Tetsuo Hidaka. What she had done to his friend. To his surprise, this new information made a considerable difference to Petra. Made a difference to her Latin soul. Brought up in a remote village, where life's values had changed little over the centuries, mere duty to a distant government must seem unreal to Petra. But revenge . . . that she could understand. "You have to do it, then," she said decisively.

Ryan got up, folded the bunk away, opened the countertop again. He drafted a new message, detailing the location of the caves but asking that he be met at sea in forty-eight hours, fifty miles off the coast of Minorca. He snapped the tape back into place, pushed the button. The tape spun. The radio emitted a high-pitched electronic squeal, then fell silent again.

Time to go. Which was not easy to do. Not easy to leave Petra. "I showed you how to start the engine the other day," he said, his voice a little gruff. "If I don't get back by full light, fire it up, then get the hell out of here."

Petra nodded, her expression very serious. "Do you understand what I'm saying?" he prompted.

"Yes."

He nodded, started to leave. But her arms were around him, holding him fast. One last desperate clutching together, and then he was gone, out on deck, leaping for the rock, disappearing into the night.

Ryan reached the caves quickly. This time, knowing the layout, he did not have to go as far as the house, but climbed right up the hillside. He had some difficulty finding the cave opening. He'd been counting on seeing that faint glimmer of light, but a half-moon had just risen, and it was enough to blot out that feeble flicker. Finally, he nearly fell into the opening. Catching his balance, he wormed his way inside.

Tonight he had brought, instead of the binoculars, a small hand torch with a focused beam. Using it, he soon found what he had suspected existed—another passageway running off this particular cave, in a direction that paralleled the main cave.

He was aware of the risk of taking this new, unexplored route; it was a smaller passageway that might peter out, perhaps in a manner that would make it difficult to find his way back. He might even become trapped. But last night, looking out into the big main cave, he'd seen several gaping holes higher up on the cave walls, like the one he was in, indicating the possibility of many other passageways radiating through this porous hillside.

Within ten minutes he was beginning to think he'd made a mistake; the passage stretched on and on, black as ink, with no sign of a way out. Then, finally, he saw a glimmer of light ahead. In another couple of minutes he was looking down at the main tunnel, about fifty yards from his original spy hole.

He had to be careful; the opening was several feet across. He could be easily seen. He stuck his head out into the main cave for an instant, trying to get his bearings. There were several doors spaced along the cement-reinforced walls. Suddenly a door opened, spilling brighter light into the dimly lit corridor. Ryan ducked back, caught a glimpse of a man in what looked like a white lab coat, and behind the man, inside the room, a gleam of equipment. It must be a laboratory, or a workroom of some kind. Now Ryan felt certain that the terrorists were actually constructing the bomb here, in this system of caves. He felt so certain that he decided that he might as well go back to the boat, send an updated message, then head for the rendezvous point.

Just a little more reconnoitering. He decided that he did not like his current position. Another passageway ran off to his left, deeper into the complex, several feet above the main passageway. He crawled along it, moving as quietly as possible, using his small light only when absolutely necessary.

For a while he was lost in darkness. Then he saw another glimmer of light, a very small one, twenty yards ahead. He could hear a murmur of voices. He crawled closer. The light did not gain in strength, but the sound of voices did. Someone was very near.

He finally reached the source of the light, a very small, ragged opening in the limestone, only a few inches across. Ryan raised up a little, looked through the opening. It took his eyes a moment to adjust to the bright lighting on the other side, but finally he was looking down into a chamber, either naturally or artificially carved out of the rock. And inside that chamber, two people were talking vehemently. Tetsuo Hidaka—and Hassim. "No, no!" Hassim was saying loudly. "I reject your idea. Reject it completely. We cannot do it your way!"

"You reject?" Tetsuo replied, her voice full of scorn. "You talk like a professor. Reject?"

"Absolutely. Appearances are all-important. We must be seen to be doing this for the correct reasons. We must be seen to be acting out of principle. Deep principle. We must demonstrate a point that the world cannot misinterpret, cannot ignore. If they think we are simply a group of—"

"And what is this 'principle' you want to demonstrate?" Tetsuo asked acidly.

"A very simple one," Hassim replied heatedly. "A signal to the United States . . . that it must pay for its actions. That it must pay for what it did in the Persian Gulf. The United States must be forced to realize that no matter how powerful and effective its army, military might alone cannot be a complete shield against a just response from those who have been wronged. A response from my people, from the Arab world. After we do this, after we set off the first bomb, we Arabs will be able to hold our heads up again."

Hassim seemed too wrought up to continue. Ryan tried to work into a different position, so that he could see better, but he was packed into a cramped space, and the little crack in the wall was at a height that forced him to crane his neck uncomfortably. Finally, after some silent squirming, he was able to see most of the room. Tetsuo was pacing slowly back and forth, looking up at Hassim from time to time, her face unreadable. "There is this word I've heard, a word that's used often in the United States," she finally said. "I don't believe it's actually an English word, but they still use it. *Machismo*. Are you familiar with *machismo*? What it means?"

Still caught up in his own fervor, Hassim gave a little start. "What did you say? Machismo . . . yes, I think so."

Now Tetsuo was smirking. "Machismo. That's what's running your Arab world. Oh, you poor little things. You've had your pride hurt. They beat you Arabs so easily in the Gulf."

Hassim's face suffused with blood. "Machismo? You

dare admit that you do not know the difference between machismo on the one hand and honor, respect, on the other? Because that is what it is, that's what I'm talking about. Respect. Being able to hold your head up. And, after we destroy New York, after it is known who did it, Arab prestige will once again be restored."

Tetsuo shook her head. "I say that we bomb Washington first. New York is a cesspool. The world would thank us for destroying it. But, to wipe out the central nest itself, Washington . . ."

"And what have we gained if we do that?" Hassim snapped angrily. "We will have wiped out the center, the nerves, the brain. Then who will we negotiate with when we threaten to set off a second bomb?"

"Negotiate?" Tetsuo asked scornfully. "Now you sound like a politician. Don't you understand anything at all? Setting off the bomb is its own end. Terrorism is an end in itself!"

Hassim shook his head slowly. "Terrorism without a goal is barbarism. I want justice for my people. For the Palestinian people. Pressure must be put on the Zionist entity to give us back our lands. That horde of European Jews must leave the Middle East. My religion forbids barbarism. But it does permit holy war. If the world does not care about justice, if no one will listen to reason, then they must discover that they will have to listen to terror. If not to the terror of the Kalashnikov, then to our bomb . . . the ultimate terror."

Tetsuo was leaning against the side of the chamber, her expression still cynical. "And there's the money, of course. They'll furnish you with money when you threaten to set off a second bomb. That's what you're counting on, isn't it?"

Hassim flushed. "Revolutions cannot be fought without money, without weapons and supplies. The old sources of money have dried up. Russia is a pauper state. The oil sheiks have gone over to the Americans, to their 'New World Order.' So, we must take money from our enemies.

Force them to finance the movement that will eventually destroy them. Out of fear of our bomb."

Tetsuo laughed. "Another saying I learned about in the West . . . backing the wrong horse. You Arabs backed the Communists . . . and now communism is collapsing. Don't you ever learn? Why don't you just . . . terrorize?"

"You?" Hassim said unbelievingly. "You, the leader of the Red Dragon Brigade, can sneer about connections to communism. Why, you—"

Tetsuo waved her hand in a gesture of dismissal. "Communism? I never cared anything about communism, Marxism, Leninism, Maoism. They were simply sources of funds to promote our . . . activities. To promote what the world needs . . . terrorism . . . anarchy. A terror that will lead straight to our own New World Order."

Hassim shook his head slowly. "You're not interested in promoting anything but yourself. Your whole group . . . they're middle-class idiots. You have no goal at all, except to feed your own diseased egos. You're rejects, you're the sick by-products of a society that drowns itself in aimless work producing a deadening glut, an ocean of material objects. You have no goal but your own gratification. You keep bringing up American slang words. I can think of one that describes you and those psychopaths who follow you. *Kinky*. You act out of mindless kinkiness."

Tetsuo stared steadily at Hassim. Uncomfortable with her gaze, he turned away. "I've never liked working with you, Tetsuo. And my dislike has led me to some private thinking. About this thing that we plan to do. Perhaps what we should really do is simply set off our first bomb where it will harm no one. Or very few people. Then, having demonstrated what we can do, we can force the West into real negotiations."

Ryan, looking down from his vantage point, could see what Hassim could not see . . . a twisted spasm of shock and anger pass over Tetsuo Hidaka's face. "You . . ." she said in a strained voice. "You'd go ahead and destroy our plan now? You . . ."

Hassim turned, saw how upset Tetsuo was. He smiled coldly. "You would hate that, wouldn't you? To see us act like rational people."

He paced around the room. "Yes," he half murmured. "I like that idea ... demonstrate our power, and at the same time demonstrate our sense of compassion."

Tetsuo started to say something. Hassim cut her off. "After all, I was the one, me and my men, who took the plutonium in the first place. We were the ones who cultivated Kranek. We made this all possible. And, as you may have noticed, it is my men, my brother Arabs, who have been doing most of the bleeding and dying. There are so few of us left."

He turned away again. "No more discussion. We will do this thing my way."

Ryan could read in Hassim's manner, in his words, a culmination of frustration. It must have galled him from the beginning to find himself, an Arab male, a Moslem, having to treat a woman as his equal. Ryan wondered how the relationship had lasted this long without a fatal rupture.

Perhaps Tetsuo came to the same conclusion, saw the venue shifting, in some way known only to herself, toward male-female relations. For years she had controlled her followers with her strange brand of sexuality. Hassim had used the right word. *Kinky.* The societal rejects Tetsuo had chosen as her sex victims probably could not have responded to any other kind of sexuality.

And now she made the mistake of trying to use the same kind of control with Hassim. Is she crazy? Ryan wondered, immediately realizing he already knew the answer to that one. Was she out of her mind as she forced the ugly, vicious look from her face, twisting it into a parody of sexual allure? She moved forward, her hands stroking slowly over Hassim's shoulders from behind. "Why do we fight?" she asked, trying to make her words sound seductive, to turn what she was saying into a soft purr, but her voice still betrayed the strain of her anger. "Why don't we ... become closer to each other?"

Hassim turned, disbelief on his face as he looked down into Tetsuo's eyes. She had lowered her head, and was looking up at him from under her lashes with the most awful parody of coquettishness that Ryan had ever seen. Her hands were on Hassim's shoulders, from the front now, still gently stroking. She started to move closer, to press her body against his.

Hassim shoved her away. Hard. Brutally. "Stop!" he hissed. "You . . . disgust me. You are . . . the mother of all whores. I've seen you with your men, I know the way you control them. We are warned about that in my culture. Women, if given too much rein, become the source of all mankind's misfortunes. Get away from me, bitch. You make me feel dirty."

He turned away from Tetsuo once again. A terrible miscalculation. His remarks, filled with an obvious cold loathing, had struck home. Ryan could never completely know, of course, what really drove Tetsuo Hidaka. What secret horrors she kept locked up inside herself. What her image of herself might be. But he did recognize the look that came over her face. A look of uncontrollable rage. The weapon that had always served her so well had been rejected, ridiculed. She obviously could not let that ridicule go unanswered.

She moved very quickly. Before Ryan could determine what her intention was, she produced a long, thin-bladed knife from her clothing, leaped forward, and buried the blade deep in Hassim's back. "You . . . you male swine!" Ryan heard her hiss.

Hassim's back arched, a strangled cry escaped his throat. He stood for a moment, his hands twisted behind him, clawing ineffectually at the knife hilt jutting from his back. He managed to turn around, to look into Tetsuo Hidaka's distorted features. Then he fell, hard, onto one side. He lay on the floor, struggling feebly.

Ryan, shocked by the speed with which it had all happened, was still reacting. God, that expression on the woman's face! Then he was reaching around behind him for the Rogak. One of the terrorist leaders was down; if he could kill the other . . .

But it was difficult to work the big pistol into firing position. He shifted his body as much as he could, finally managed to get the barrel through the narrow opening. But in so doing, he could not avoid making a great deal of noise. Tetsuo looked up, saw the snout of the pistol starting to point in her direction. "Tsunogi!" she screamed, then threw herself to one side, running hard.

Ryan fired. And missed. Trapped inside the system of caves, the sound of the shot was incredibly loud, echoing and re-echoing. Ryan heard the bullet spang harmlessly off rock. By now he was looking down at a room that was empty . . . except for Hassim's body. Farther away, he could hear the sound of shouting, of Tetsuo Hidaka's cries for help. Hear also the sound of running feet, converging on his position.

He was in very bad trouble.

22

Ryan scooted backward, working toward another passageway. As he moved away from the opening, he heard shouting from inside the chamber, Tetsuo screaming, "Get him! He killed Hassim!"

The bitch. Ryan knew that he would stand little chance with Hassim's followers if he were caught. Arabs were big on vengeance.

He made it back to the tunnel that led to the opening on the side of the hill. But that was as far as he got. As he was crawling toward the faint glimmer of moonlight shining in from outside, the entranceway was suddenly blocked by a dark figure. A powerful light lanced into the cave. A man shouted something excitedly in Arabic. A moment later there was a spray of automatic weapons fire. Bullets pinged off rock all around Ryan. He had already pulled out his pistol, but a richochet slammed against the receiver, knocking the Rogak from his hand. He groped for it, his hand half numb from the shock, but could not find the pistol in the dark. The man was well inside the entrance now, coming closer. He fired another burst.

Ryan scooted backward again . . . only to be illuminated

by a powerful light from behind. Somebody had come up into the tunnel from the main cave. He was trapped.

Another burst of automatic fire, then an angry shout from the pursuers coming from the direction of the cave. That was all that saved Ryan from immediate death; he was between two groups of pursuers. Neither group could fire without endangering the other.

A moment later men were crowding in close. Ryan felt the muzzles of guns pressing hard against his body. He tensed, waiting for the shock of the bullets. He was vaguely aware of a woman's voice, some distance away, shouting loudly. To his surprise, his captors began to drag him along the passageway until the ceiling was high enough so that he could stand. They jerked him to his feet. When they reached the broad opening that overlooked the main passageway, he was unceremoniously shoved through. It was a fall of almost two yards, but he managed to land on his feet, then roll, as in a parachute jump.

Half stunned, he was aware of a number of people crowding around him. He was jerked upright again by a very powerful hand. Tsunogi. The Japanese glared into Ryan's eyes for a moment, then spun him around . . . to face Tetsuo Hidaka. She was standing a few feet away, looking intently at Ryan. Finally, she walked to within a yard of him. To his amazement, she smiled. "You have more lives than a cat," she said amusedly. "In a little while we'll find out just how many you have left."

Her gaze grew intense again. "Hassim's men will want to take most of those lives. After what you did to their leader."

Ryan stared straight back at her. No point in trying to tell the others that it was Tetsuo who'd killed Hassim. They would never believe him. In the meantime, Tetsuo was very close. The men who had caught him in the cave had made a perfunctory search for weapons, but his empty holster had predisposed them to believe that he was already disarmed. They had not searched far enough down his right leg to find the Japanese knife. He wondered if he would be able to get to it quickly enough to kill Tetsuo. He decided that he could not. He was very aware of Tsunogi's presence right behind his shoulder. Maybe later, if there was going to be a later, he'd have his chance.

Tetsuo was still looking straight at him. "How did you know where . . .?" she started to say. Then she answered her own question. "The chartroom! Of course. When we caught you on the boat, you were coming out of the chartroom. You saw our course, all plotted out for you to follow. Clumsy of us. Particularly clumsy of Hassim; he was always leaving things lying around."

"Or turning his back," Ryan replied evenly.

He saw a quick spasm of anger pass over Tetsuo's face. Just the slightest loss of control. "If you wish to talk about that," she hissed, "you will not live another ten seconds."

Ryan said nothing, but kept staring intently into her eyes. He knew he was a dead man, but he'd be damned if he'd cringe in front of this bitch. He'd faced death too many times to be terrified of it. Afraid, yes, but terrified, no.

The smile came back onto Tetsuo's face. That strange, half-shy, half-vicious smile. If spiders smiled . . .

Tetsuo changed her position, standing hipshot, her chin cupped in the palm of her left hand. "Once again, we have the same problem . . . how much do other people know of what you know? Are others on their way already? And where is the girl?"

Ryan did not reply; there was really nothing he could say. He thought of the message he had sent, off into the ether, not having any way of knowing if it really got through. Or even if all that backup Central had promised actually existed.

Tetsuo, thinking aloud, said, "The very fact that you're here alone makes me think that you have once again been too stupid to let others know. This childish vendetta you've been following over that boy who died . . . What was his name?"

"Yoshiro. Nakashima Yoshiro," Ryan replied calmly. He

wanted her to have that name fresh in her mind if he ever got close enough to kill her.

"Ah, yes. A nice boy," she said, almost absently, then returned to her original train of thought. "Yes, there is reason to believe that you are here on your own. If not, we are in trouble. But we may have enough time to finish what we started, then leave here. Within hours."

She smiled up at him. "We have, you see, almost completed building our first bomb." The smile grew almost warm. "Would you like to see it?"

She started to turn away, then stopped, and said to Tsunogi in Japanese, "Guard him every step of the way. If he makes one wrong move, kill him."

Tsunogi gave a short little bow, then turned and walked over to where his sheathed sword was leaning against the cave wall. He picked up the sword and thrust its sheath into his belt. When he walked back, his right hand was resting lightly on the sword's handle. Tsunogi was smiling, a very slight, pleased smile. Ryan knew that if he did indeed make any quick moves towards Tetsuo, he would feel the bite of that blade. Feel it cutting deep into him. He quickly glanced to each side. Two of the other Japanese also wore swords thrust through their belts. Still living out their samurai fantasy.

Tetsuo turned and walked off, leading the way down the hall. Ryan hesitated. She turned back to face him. "Aren't you coming?" she asked lightly, as if she were giving an invitation to a picnic.

Ryan shrugged, then walked after her. She stayed a few paces ahead, but glanced back over her shoulder from time to time to talk to him. "What we took from that Egyptian nuclear plant," she said, then corrected herself, smiling brightly, "or what Hassim stole . . . if you heard our whole conversation, then you heard him boast about that . . . what we took was plutonium nitrate. In a liquid form. But, according to the late Dr. Kranek, we needed pure plutonium to make our bomb. Well, I don't know all the technical details, but it was a lot of work. Here," she said, knocking on one of the closed doors. "Fuad will tell you all about it."

The door opened. A brightly lit laboratory lay beyond, the same one Ryan had been looking into before, from his first vantage point. A white-coated man, an Arab by his features, held the door open, glanced from Ryan, to Tetsuo, to the others. "What was all the noise?" he asked. Ryan noticed that his voice was not very strong and his manner was vague.

"We have a visitor who just ... dropped in," Tetsuo replied pleasantly. "It seems he's developed a considerable interest in what we're doing here. Perhaps you could tell him all about it."

Fuad seemed confused for a minute.

"About how you converted the plutonium," Tetsuo prompted.

Fuad's face lit up. "Ah, yes ... how we made the plutonium. Well, in reality, only Allah can make plutonium." He gave a little laugh, as if to show he was joking, although Ryan suspected that he was not. Not completely. "What we did," Fuad said, "was take our original material, plutonium nitrate, and, through a chemical process involving heat, convert it into plutonium oxide. Here," he said, stepping back into the lab and waving his hand at various pieces of shining scientific apparatus. "We did it right there. By a shoestring, as I think they say in English. It was very difficult getting all this equipment into the cave, difficult bringing in a generator that could furnish the voltages necessary. But we did it. We completed the conversion. Only yesterday, as a matter of fact."

Ryan stepped into the doorway. He was aware that no one else had done so. Then he noticed a figure lying motionless on a mattress on the floor near the rear of the laboratory. Fuad saw where he was looking. "Ah, yes," he said sadly. "Ibrahim. We have had accidents. You see, at various points during the conversion, large amounts of radiation are released. Fatal amounts."

He turned toward Ryan. "Some die more quickly than others."

And then Ryan knew . . . Fuad himself was dying from radiation poisoning. This entire lab was probably reeking with radiation. No wonder everyone else was staying well back of the door. He made no move to go farther into the room.

Fuad was speaking again. "We had to take our plutonium nitrate—we had so much of it—and convert it to a fluoride. That meant we had to first add oxalic acid, then use heat. When you've cooked out all the water, you're left with a salt. Fluffy green salt. Plutonium oxalate. Then you expose this salt to fluoride gases. Chemically, that's dangerous; you have to heat hydrofluoric acid to five hundred degrees Celsius. Hydrofluoric acid is very caustic. But when you're finished, you have plutonium fluoride. Quite a tedious process."

Fuad had turned and was smiling vacantly at Ryan. "Of course, after we got the fluoride, there was still a ways to go. Dr. Kranek, a very fine man, decided that we should use metallic plutonium for . . . for what we wanted to do. So we took our plutonium fluoride, combined it with metallic calcium and crystalline iodide, exposed that combination to argon gas, and heated it up again. This time all the way to seven hundred and fifty degrees. When you do that, an internal reaction occurs within the mixture, a chemical reaction, pushing the temperature much higher. To sixteen hundred degrees. That's Celsius, sir. In the old system, Fahrenheit, that is the equivalent of almost three thousand degrees. Hot. Very hot. Metals melt at that temperature. And in this case, they also form. Because when you let the mixture cool, you finally have it, a chunk of metal, lying there, within a remainder of the salt. Yellow, flaky salt. A chunk of pure plutonium. All you have to do is wash it with nitric acid. Wash away all that is impure."

Fuad seemed lost in thought for a moment. "Wash away that which kills."

He looked up, past Ryan, toward Tetsuo Hidaka.

"Ibrahim is dead," he said quietly. "He died half an hour ago. Perhaps you could . . ."

"Move him to the doorway," Tetsuo said curtly. Fuad nodded. He dragged the entire mattress into the doorway. Two of the Japanese, using long poles, rolled Ibrahim onto a blanket. Then they dragged the blanket along the smooth concrete floor of the cave. Fuad stayed behind, looking sadly out of his lab. The rest of the group followed along after the corpse. Ryan took a closer look at what was left of Ibrahim, saw huge sores on the exposed skin. "He is radioactive," Tetsuo said, with obvious distaste. "Fuad and his people are . . . a little clumsy. That was one of the reasons we wanted Dr. Kranek. He would not have made so many mistakes."

Then the smile was back on her face. "But Ibrahim, Fuad, and the others who converted the plutonium were not unhappy. They were contributing their lives to the Cause. Offering themselves to Allah. And I'm certain that they are now, as good warriors, as men who fought the good fight, the Jihad, they're now snug in paradise, with all those nice young girls Allah provides for them."

Tetsuo actually sniggered . . . under her breath, very quietly, but Ryan heard her. By now they had reached a large opening in the cave wall. A black, gaping hole. Ibrahim's body was unceremoniously tipped into the opening. It disappeared from view, although Ryan could hear it striking obstructions as it fell. Finally, a distant splash. "That's where we put those who die of radiation poisoning," Tetsuo said. "Four, up until now. Far away from the living. Of course, the others who die, particularly in battle, the heroes, like Hassim, are more properly buried. It gives their followers something to get excited about, and they do like to get excited. I had so much trouble keeping them from firing off those Russian rifles, Klashins, they call them, when we were burying our people near populated areas. Savages. All of them."

She noticed the surprised look on Ryan's face because she was speaking so openly in front of the others. She read the question in his eyes. "Oh, with Hassim dead, none of the Arabs who are left, with the exception of Fuad, speak English. And he should not last much longer."

She started to turn away, but halted, looked back at the ugly black opening in the cave wall. She smiled. "That is where your body will go."

Then she turned away and continued on down the passageway. "But come. You must see our final product. The one we've worked so hard to complete."

She glanced back at Ryan. "And the one you have worked so hard to keep us from completing. But you are too late. We are finishing our bomb."

She stopped at another door, made of heavy planks knocked together. There was a big padlock hanging from a hasp, unlocked. She opened the door herself. Ryan looked into a room much cruder than Fuad's laboratory. The walls were rough, unfinished. Indeed, a ragged opening gaped in the cave wall at the rear of the room.

A man sat at a bench, working with something shiny. He stood up, looking questioningly at the others. Tetsuo pushed past him, passing very close to Ryan as he did so. Ryan tensed. Perhaps now was the time . . .

A slight sibilance. Turning, he saw that Tsunogi's sword was half out of its sheath. Tsunogi's eyes were fastened on Ryan's . . . who realized he was a split second away from an agonizing death.

He relaxed, then moved to the side, well away from Tetsuo. She was now standing right next to the bench. On it were some rather mundane-looking objects, most notably two large shiny metal hemispheres. Almost like stainless steel salad bowls. They lay face up. Ryan could see that a thick layer of something waxy-looking had been plastered over their interior surfaces.

Tetsuo pointed. "Paraffin. Simple paraffin. Enough is put in to line the interior, thick enough so that it will support the plutonium when it goes inside. According to the technical part, both the paraffin and those stainless steel things are good neutron reflectors. So when the plutonium starts to go . . . how do they say? Critical? All those particles moving around feed back on themselves."

But Ryan had already looked away from the stainless steel hemispheres. Farther away on the bench, he'd noticed a big ball of what looked like aluminum foil. Except that it was duller than aluminum. "Ah," Tetsuo said. "You've seen it. The results of our labors."

She walked over to the bench, began peeling off layers of foil. From the way it held its shape, Ryan suspected that it was lead foil. Finally, he caught a glimpse of a round mass of a dull-colored metal. It had to be the plutonium.

He automatically shrank away, remembering Ibrahim's wasted corpse. Tetsuo laughed. "Don't worry. Do you think I'd risk my life? They tell me that when it's a metal, the plutonium is quite safe to handle. Unless, of course, you breathe in a tiny shaving, or let it get beneath your skin. This is it, then. The heart of our bomb. Just short of critical mass. It goes into the hemispheres, then they are covered with a layer of plastic explosive, and when all that explosive is touched off, it presses inwards. Compresses the plutonium. Which then creates an atomic explosion. Oh, not a very big one, of course. But big enough. Everyone within a mile of its center will die. Within a quarter of a mile, nothing will be left standing, everything will have been vaporized. Heat. Incredible heat. Terror. Ultimate terror. Can you imagine? Our boat moored in the Potomac, off Washington, all of us ashore, miles away? The timer we have set goes off. And then . . ."

Tetsuo's voice was becoming a little shrill. Her stare had become vacant. This is turning her on, Ryan realized. Sexually. "Careful," he said dryly. "You'll wet your pants."

Tetsuo's eyes snapped back into focus. She glared at Ryan. "You'll pay for that," she said, her voice gritty.

Suddenly, from far away, all of them heard the sound of a single shot followed by a great deal of yelling. For just an instant Ryan believed that the reinforcements had arrived . . . until he remembered that he'd only asked them to meet him at sea.

Tetsuo glanced around quickly. Ryan thought he could detect just the faintest traces of fear on her face . . . as if she too thought reinforcements had invaded her bomb factory. But, when no more shooting followed, she quickly brought herself under control. She motioned to Tsunogi, who motioned to two other men, who began to hustle Ryan out of the room. He's careful, Ryan thought. Tsunogi was standing back, out of Ryan's immediate reach, while Ryan was well within the reach of Tsunogi's sword.

They moved rapidly along the cave's main corridor. A group of men came bursting around a corner. Tetsuo's men. "We found her inside the house!" one man said excitedly in Japanese to Tetsuo. He held up a pistol, what looked to Ryan like a Colt lightweight Commander. Like his pistol. "She tried to shoot us," the man continued. "We took the gun away from her."

And then Ryan saw, farther back in the group, someone being dragged along. His heart sank when he realized who it was.

Petra.

23

When Petra saw Ryan, her face lit up with hope . . . only to crumple into despair when she realized that he too was a captive. Ryan started toward her, until he was jerked back by the arms. The cordon of armed men surrounding him seemed to have grown. "Petra . . . why?" he burst out.

She looked straight at him. "I had to come after you," she said in an anguished voice. "I couldn't let you do this all alone."

That pistol the man was holding. It *was* Ryan's Colt Commander. Petra must have seen it when he opened the countertop to use the radio. Must have taken it, to come and help him. Courageous, but very foolish. And crushing to Ryan. So far he'd been able to accept his own capture because of the knowledge that Petra was safe on the boat, that she would sail away in the morning if he did not come back. Now Tetsuo Hidaka once again had a pawn to play off against Ryan himself.

But it seemed to be working the other way around. Tetsuo immediately asked for a translation of what Petra had said to Ryan. One of her Japanese, who apparently spoke Spanish, told her.

"So," Tetsuo murmured, walking close to Petra. "They are both alone, then."

She turned to face Ryan. "Could anyone actually be such a fool?"

Ryan said nothing. What could he say? That he had radioed for a rendezvous? That he had also given the position of these caves and a description of the schooner? Such an admission would probably bring instant death. On the other hand, if Tetsuo thought he and Petra had come here alone, they might be killed out of hand as unnecessary nuisances. He would have to play it by ear. Was there any way he could trade off his knowledge for their lives? Not his own life, perhaps, but Petra's. Or merely prolong survival. If they could stay alive until after the rendezvous time, someone might come for them, someone might decide to check out the information Ryan had sent.

Petra. He felt a moment's anger that she had disobeyed his orders, mixed with admiration for her courage and loyalty. A genuine warrior's woman. Too damned bad they weren't going to have any more time to enjoy one another.

Tetsuo was clearly growing frustrated. "I wish I knew!" she half shouted, to no one in particular. "I wish I knew what to believe!"

She turned toward Ryan again, repeated herself, murmuring, "Could anyone *really* be that stupid?" She walked close to Ryan, stared straight into his eyes. "We could make you tell us ... if we had the time," she hissed. "Make you feel so much pain that you would beg to have the chance to tell us nothing but the truth. If we had time."

She noticed, then, that the man who had been working on the bomb was standing at the back of the group, watching. "Get back in there!" she shouted, pointing down the corridor, towards the room where Ryan had seen the partially completed bomb. "Finish your work!"

The man reluctantly turned, then walked away down the corridor, unwilling to miss the show, but also unwilling to incur Tetsuo's anger.

Tetsuo turned back toward Petra. She motioned to

Tsunogi, then pointed toward the girl. "Hurt her," she said in Japanese. "Not enough to kill her, but enough to make her scream. Then we'll see what *he* can tell us."

Tsunogi nodded. He left Ryan's side, walked toward Petra. As he passed by, Ryan could see a slight smile on Tsunogi's usually inscrutable face. Ryan started after Tsunogi. Three men took hold of him tightly, one wrapping his arm around Ryan's throat. Ryan struggled, but with his arms pinioned by two of the men, both of them Japanese, he could do nothing as the choke hold tightened. In a moment or two he would start to pass out, so he stopped struggling, and immediately the choke hold loosened. He turned his eyes to one side, then the other, without moving his head. The man on Ryan's left had a sword like Tsunogi's thrust through his belt. The man's eyes met Ryan's. The hot, eager look in those eyes told Ryan that the swordsman was looking for any excuse to use his weapon.

By now, Tsunogi had reached Petra. He stood in front of her, studying her face. Petra met his eyes well enough, although Ryan had no doubt she was very much afraid. Then Tsunogi's eyes slid down her body, fastened on the swell of her breasts. Almost leisurely, Tsunogi reached out, took hold of Petra's blouse, and tore it away from her. The resistance of the material, as it tore, spun Petra halfway around, with the remains of the blouse hanging from her waist. She had been wearing nothing beneath the blouse; Ryan had not thought to buy her a brassiere after the escape from the boat. Indeed, he'd realized very quickly that she did not need a brassiere.

Now she stood naked to the waist, a little stunned by the deceptive slowness of Tsunogi's perfectly timed attack. Her eyes sought out Ryan. He could read pleading in her expression, mixed with the awful knowledge that Ryan himself was in no position to help her.

Ryan was beginning to wonder if it might not be better, after all, to tell Tetsuo about the message he'd sent . . . if it would save Petra, at least for a little while. Then

Tsunogi was moving again. This time he hit Petra across the face with the palm of his hand, a blow that looked casual, relaxed, but which had the weight of Tsunogi's perfectly trained body behind it. Petra spun around, staggered, fell against some of the men. They had been standing alongside the cave wall, staring at Petra's half-nude body, and now they caught her, which was the only reason she did not fall; she was obviously badly dazed from Tsunogi's blow.

Two of the men, both Japanese, laughed as they fondled the girl's breasts. Petra's head was beginning to clear. She felt their hands on her, tried to pull away, but they held her more tightly. Her mind began to fill with memories of the near-rape aboard the schooner, before Ryan had pulled her over the side into the water. Rape. A reliving of the horror she'd experienced, all those years ago, at her uncle's hands. An experience she'd survived, but with an ugly vacancy in her soul, an invisible scar that had twisted her thoughts for far too long. Until Ryan. Until he had shown her what it was like to really love a man, to share her body with his, to feel fully alive for the first time in her life. To feel clean. Whole.

She saw that Tsunogi was slowly coming toward her. This hideous ape was going to make her feel filthy again. To destroy the beauty of what she had with Ryan. She would rather die first.

She saw the handle of a knife, inches away from her right hand, worn in an unfastened sheath at the belt of one of the men holding her. She moved with the perfect timing of a person who no longer is thinking, but only acting. In an instant the knife was in her hand. She cut at the man holding her. He yelped, leaped backward, away from the blade. As a continuation of the same movement, Petra was already turning, the knife arcing through the air, cutting at Tsunogi, who, his mind full of the sight of the girl's naked breasts—big, full breasts—was caught off guard for one of the few times in his life. Not completely off guard; he pivoted away. But not before the knife had sliced a shallow cut into his left forearm.

The rest was sheer instinct, mixed with rage. Anger at being cut by a mere woman. Shame at being taken unaware. A loss of face that demanded immediate response.

Ryan saw it coming, opened his mouth to shout a warning to Petra, but it was too late. It all happened in a split second, Tsunogi's sword sliding from its sheath in a graceful arc, the arc flattening at the last moment as half the length of the blade sank into Petra's chest, right between her breasts.

Ryan's shout finally surfaced, no longer a cry of warning but a long howl of horror and grief. Petra remained standing for a moment, staring down at the shining steel blade embedded in her body. Then she looked up, straight at Ryan. Longingly. Hopelessly. Knowing she would never again feel his body against hers. Knowing that her life was over.

Tsunogi pulled the sword from Petra's body. A great gout of blood jetted from the wound onto the floor. Petra fell, her eyes already glazing over, moments from death; the sword had pierced her heart, as Tsunogi had intended.

And now Ryan moved. Rage, horror, drove his body. He sank his right elbow into the belly of the man with the choke hold, pounded away the man on his right with the back of his right fist, then smashed the edge of his other hand against the throat of the man on his left. The one with the sword. The swordsman was clutching his throat as Ryan tore the sword from its sheath, then spun, half crouched, sword in hand, facing Tsunogi. His cry, when it came again, was an inarticulate shout of rage, of desire for revenge.

Immediately, weapons began to train on Ryan. He knew that in a moment the men around him would open fire, blast him where he stood. Maybe, just maybe, he could make it to Tsunogi before he died, at least make the effort of killing him.

Then he heard Tetsuo cry out harshly, "Leave him

alone!" She ran forward, pushing aside gun barrels. Ryan saw her do this out of the corners of his eyes; all the rest of his attention was focused on Tsunogi, who was staring back at him coldly.

Ryan took a moment to glance at Tetsuo. She was smiling, she looked pleased. She pointed to the sword in Ryan's hand, then to the sword Tsunogi was holding, its blade red with Petra's blood. Her smile was mocking. Ryan knew the smile was meant for him. "He wants to fight," she called out. "Let him fight Tsunogi. This time, we'll be sure he's dead. As dead as the girl."

She turned toward Tsunogi. "Shame on you for killing her . . . so quickly," she chided. She gestured toward Ryan. "Take a little more time with this one."

More mockery, in her voice, her gestures. She, of course, expected Tsunogi to kill Ryan. No contest. Just a cat playing with a mouse. Looking at Tsunogi, Ryan wondered if she might not be right. Tsunogi was standing like a rock, casually flicking blood from the blade of his sword. Petra's blood. Ryan felt a hot flare of anger. No, he must contain that anger, channel it into resolve. Channel it into killing Tsunogi. Even if he himself was killed in the process. Kill Tsunogi for Petra. For the brutal ending of a life that had just, at last, begun flowering.

He forced himself to look away from Petra's body; it was lying in a huge pool of blood near the cave wall. Tsunogi was moving toward Ryan now, leisurely, each footfall sure, steady, planting itself firmly against the cement floor, sword held out in front of him, still casually, as if he did not consider Ryan much of a threat.

Perhaps Ryan could use Tsunogi's arrogance to his advantage, keep him overconfident, let him grow careless. Neither Tsunogi nor Tetsuo knew of Ryan's years with Master Nakashima, the endless hours spent practicing, not only karate and the bare-hand arts, but also hours and hours of practice with the sword. Nakashima was a master swordsman, he'd been a champion in his youth. He had taught Ryan that all the Japanese martial arts were, at their

heart, similar. In contrast to the flashy showmanship of
Kung Fu and the other Chinese arts, the Japanese arts were
based on a relaxed use of the body, coming from the
body's center, every move supported by perfect balance,
by a kind of relaxed speed, nothing appearing very fast,
but with no wasted movement whatsoever.

And, of course, perfect concentration. Mind like still
water, reflecting, on a mirrorlike surface, all that was happening, every sound, sight, movement . . . including one's
own movements, one's own body, mirrored together with
the movements and body of the opponent. A joining of the
two. His movement is my movement. Sword or empty
hand, it should all feel the same.

Ryan would have to hide his training. He could already
see a slight look of confusion in Tsunogi's eyes, as if he
were beginning to suspect that, with Ryan, he might not be
facing an amateur.

Ryan immediately let his technique fall completely
apart. Holding the sword clumsily in one hand, he advanced on Tsunogi in a series of heavy, stomping steps,
waving the sword, slashing at the air wildly. Tsunogi
smiled, slid his right foot forward, his sword held in two
hands, the tip pointing at Ryan's throat. Ryan tensed.
Where would Tsunogi attack? Then, the merest flicker of
Tsunogi's eyes toward Ryan's left arm let him know
Tsunogi meant to cut him there. Not a serious wound,
merely something that would hurt. The first installment of
a lasting agony.

A serious flaw on Tsunogi's part, that flicker of eye
movement, that looking directly at his target, instead of
looking, not even at the whole man opposite him, but past
the man, seeing everything, missing nothing. Perhaps it
had been a long time since Tsunogi had fought a worthy
opponent.

The cut. Simple, direct, toward Ryan's left arm. And
from the inside. A difficult angle. Perhaps Tsunogi wanted
to show off. Ryan shifted slightly to his right, so that
Tsunogi's blade completely missed his arm, just the slight-

est touch from Ryan's blade deflecting Tsunogi's. Ryan was holding his sword in two hands now, and his hands were rising, the sword following, the blade a little behind the hilt. Immediately, a quick downward cut toward Tsunogi's unprotected head.

And now Tsunogi showed his mastery. He crouched. His hands shot upward, the blade pointing downward, covering his left side, from the head down, a movement made with such perfect grace and timing that Tsunogi seemed hardly to have moved at all. Ryan's sword, deflected by Tsunogi's, glided harmlessly downward, the pressure against it perfect, just enough, so light a touch that there was the barest ringing of steel against steel.

And now, the counterattack, fortunately one Ryan knew well, Tsunogi suddenly standing fully erect, his sword whipping downward, toward Ryan's head, Ryan barely able to block, his sword rising jerkily, nearly knocked from his hand by the force of Tsunogi's blow. Ryan staggered backward, badly off balance. Tsunogi might have finished him then, but he wasted a second looking at his sword. His face darkened as he studied a nick in the perfectly polished blade.

"Haahh!" Tsunogi breathed out, coming back into the on guard position. No toying with his prey this time. Ryan knew that Tsunogi was out to kill him.

Ryan glanced over at Tetsuo. She was no longer smiling. Ryan looked away from her. Time to stop his playacting. He settled himself, sliding his feet along the floor, perfectly balanced. He held the sword in front of him, two-handed, lightly, with his little fingers and third fingers wrapped tightly around the sharkskin hilt, his index fingers half loose, guiding. The sword an extension of his own body. That was what Nakashima used to tell him. The sword an extension of his will.

The two men stalked one another, moving slowly closer, using little sliding shuffle-steps. Nothing more stupid than to put all one's weight on one foot. Or on the toes alone. Toe and heel, solidly against the floor.

The clash, when it finally came, was instantaneous, a sudden attack by Tsunogi, met with such speed by Ryan that it looked as if both men had attacked simultaneously. Their swords crashed together in front of their bodies, between them, each blade pressing against the other from the left, with the tip pointed up above the opponent's head.

Their bodies were close now, less than two feet apart. Neither man dared move; if he did so he would provide an opening, then the other would cut straight into his body. They stood, both sweating, maintaining their guard, each looking for a weakness in the other man, a slight loss of balance, a momentary drifting of attention.

For several seconds they remained staring into one another's eyes, sword pressed against sword. Then, the pressure from Tsunogi increased, his body rock-solid as he slowly began to force Ryan's sword toward Ryan's right, inch by inch. When he had created the opening he wanted, he would then be in a position, having destroyed Ryan's guard, to thrust at his face, neck, or head.

Ryan was appalled by Tsunogi's strength. Matching power with him was like fighting a mechanical man, a creature of steel. Ryan felt his sword being forced farther and farther to the side. True, only two or three inches so far, but another inch and Tsunogi would have all the opening he needed.

Ryan fought back with all his strength. But he knew that he could not win ... until Tsunogi made his second mistake. Once again, with his eyes. A gloating look, the anticipation of the pleasure of cutting Ryan's body open. A sadist's anticipation ... and a momentary loss of concentration.

Ryan suddenly relaxed, letting his sword slide down and to the right. Caught off guard, Tsunogi lost his balance for just an instant, his own sword pointing off a little to his left, as he leaned slightly forward, fighting to regain equilibrium.

Ryan's sword lay directly across the line of Tsunogi's lower abdomen. Pivoting to his left, he drew the blade hard across Tsunogi's belly, felt the razor edge catch, then drag, as it sliced through flesh, sliced deep, past skin and muscle, deep into the guts beneath. Ryan used the weight of his body to gouge the tip deep, finally ripping it past Tsunogi's body. He was vaguely aware of the awful grunt of pain and shock Tsunogi uttered as he felt his guts sliced open.

Tsunogi bent slowly forward; his intestines were spilling out of his belly. Ryan was now to Tsunogi's right, slightly behind him. His sword rose; Tsunogi's blood was a red smear across the bright metal. Then Ryan struck, a downward blow, arcing to the right, his hands still light against the hilt, but with all his body behind the stroke, his weight settling down, body erect as the blade struck the back of Tsunogi's neck, severed the spinal column, then passed on through, cutting Tsunogi's head cleanly from his body.

A moment's shocked silence. Then, as Tsunogi was still falling, his head arcing away, Ryan was in movement again. He had to get away; there would be no winner's trophy today. Only a quick bullet.

He threw his sword toward the clump of shocked men who had been holding him. They shouted, dodged out of the way, one of them receiving a bad cut on his arm. By the time they had recovered from their surprise, Ryan was past them, running down the passageway. No shots yet, they were still too surprised. A bend in the corridor a few yards ahead. Then Ryan was around the bend, temporarily out of view.

Where to go? He could already hear them pounding along after him. Perhaps he could duck into one of the many openings running off the main tunnel. But they would only follow him, and most of those tunnels petered out into dead ends.

His calculations came to an immediate halt. Rounding another corner, he ran head on into one of the Arabs. Perhaps the man had heard the shouting and had come running. He was probably a guard; he was holding a Kalashnikov. Which was to Ryan's advantage, because the man wasted time trying to bring the weapon around. Ryan grabbed the rifle, tried to twist it away, but the guard held on tightly, suddenly shoving hard against Ryan.

People coming. A shout from just behind. Ryan knew he wasn't going to make it. He tried for the rifle again, when the guard suddenly lost his balance, falling to one side. Since they were both locked together, Ryan felt his balance begin to go along with the guard's. And then Ryan's right foot met empty space. He glanced to his right. He and the guard were half inside one of the larger openings in the cave wall. And beginning to fall through it. To his horror, Ryan recognized the opening. It was the one into which they threw the bodies of radiation victims.

24

Tetsuo and her men, rounding the corner, were just in time to see Ryan and the guard disappear into the opening in the cave wall. Just in time to hear the guard's horrified scream and Ryan's surprised bellow. The yells cut off with a loud grunt as the falling bodies hit an obstruction. Finally, a distant splash.

Tetsuo herself ran right up to the opening. She could see nothing. "Bring lights!" she shouted. To her surprise, no one moved. She turned, angry. "Why is no one . . . ?"

And then she understood. . . . Tsunogi was not here to enforce the order. Would never be here again. Only now was she beginning to realize how much she had depended on Tsunogi . . . to put into effect her slightest wish. To drive the others on. Whatever fear they had of her was partially fear of Tsunogi.

She spun back toward the black maw of the opening. "You bastard!" she screamed down the shaft. "You bastard . . . I'll kill you, make you scream. . . ."

Her voice died away as she realized that it was already too late for personal vengeance. Or was it? Had Ryan survived again? She turned away from the opening, her face ugly. "Light!" she screamed. "I said bring lights!"

They moved, then, two of the men racing away down the main corridor. They returned in less than a minute with powerful electric torches. Tetsuo took one, leaned into the opening, switched on the light. Its bright beam cut down through the darkness, past sharp outcroppings of rock. Far below, she could make out the gleam of water. Surging water, sucking in and out of some hidden underground opening that led to the sea.

She played the light over the jagged stone outcroppings, saw blood on one, a scrap of clothing on another. They had definitely fallen, then. She played the light all around, searching every niche that might hide a body that had not fallen all the way to the bottom. But, although the outcroppings were sharp deadly fangs of rock, they were not very large. A body should bounce all the way down to that watery pit, far below. Tetsuo could not imagine anyone surviving.

There! At the bottom! The shape of a body, maybe two bodies, half submerged. No way to tell who it was, not from this distance. Lately, they had been throwing quite a few bodies down the shaft.

She turned toward her men again. "Get a rope. A long rope. We will have to lower someone . . . to make sure that American bastard is really dead."

Once again, no one moved. "Well?" Tetsuo shouted.

It was one of her Japanese who answered. "But . . . there is radiation down there."

Tetsuo stared at the man. Saw the wooden look of stubbornness on his face. Oh, if Tsunogi were only here! But he was not, and without his presence Tetsuo sensed her authority eroding minute by minute. Too many men had been killed. There had been too many bodies. Most of them because of that man, Ryan.

She would have to assume that he was dead. No one could have survived that fall. On a sudden instinct, she flashed the torch to the sides. She saw mostly bare rock, no ledges wider than a few inches. No sign of Ryan at all, no place to hide, just the torchlight fading away into blackness. "Dead. He has to be dead," she muttered. But a doubt lingered in her mind. The bastard should have been dead so many times. And he had always come back. Like a nemesis. And all because of that boy ... what was his name? Yoshiro. She shivered. Had the boy put some kind of curse on her? Sent a devil to exact revenge? Sent this man, Ryan? This man who always came back from the dead?

Tetsuo pulled away from the opening. "We sail tomorrow," she said curtly. "The bomb will have been completed by then."

The men nodded, relieved. There still remained, deep inside them, traces of the habit of obedience to Tetsuo. Not so deep a habit, however, that any of them were willing to climb down into that black pit, alive with radiation. It was a relief to go back to their regular duties.

The men hurried off. Ryan heard them go. He was crouched not ten feet away, hidden behind an outcropping of rock. When he and the guard had started to fall, the guard, in his terror, had let go of Ryan, snatching wildly at the edges of the opening. In vain. An instant later he was gone, his scream fading away down the shaft.

Ryan, taller than the other man, had reached up instead of down. His hands had met the top of the opening while one foot was still planted against the bottom. For a moment he hung half in space, knowing he could not hold this position for more than another second or two. Then the fingers of his right hand felt a crack in the rock. He dug in with his fingers ... just as his foot slipped. He was then hanging by one hand over blackness.

He thrust the fingers of his other hand into the crack. The strain was terrible. He groped blindly to the right, now hanging by his left hand. A ledge. A small ledge, perhaps four inches wide. The fingers of his right hand clutched desperately.

He never knew, later, how he did it, but he scrambled

along to his right, hanging from his fingers, driven on by
an agility born of fear. Suddenly his feet met a lower
ledge, once again a very narrow ledge, but wide enough
for him to get a toehold. A moment later he was scram-
bling around a small outcropping of stone. Behind it was
a narrow platform. He crouched low. There were silhou-
ettes at the opening now, the murmur of voices. He heard
Tetsuo call out for lights. He shrank back into his hiding
place. Would it be wide enough to shelter him? Would
they send someone into the shaft to investigate every
niche, every hidden crevice?

To his surprise, it took a long time for the lights to arrive. Tetsuo was shouting again. Finally, bright beams
lanced down into the shaft. He heard Tetsuo order someone to climb down. Heard, to his disbelief, a refusal. Silence, until he heard Tetsuo muttering and cursing, then
her decision that they would sail the next day.

The sound of footsteps moving away. Followed by silence. Ryan's legs were cramping; he was crouched on his
heels, barely hanging on. He was about to move, to look
for a more comfortable position, when once again a light
flared on, shining down into the shaft. Ryan froze. He
could see Tetsuo framed in the opening. "You bastard,"
she was muttering. "You'll come back for me, won't you?
You'll live again."

Using the reflected light of Tetsuo's electric torch, Ryan
looked around him. To his left there was a sheer drop, but
behind him he saw a narrow ledge, disappearing into
blackness. Was it his imagination, or did that ledge, bending around to the side, widen?

The light flicked off. Ryan thought he heard Tetsuo
walking away, but he remained unmoving. He heard her
call out then, "Get that girl's body out of here. Throw her
down the shaft. The two of them can be together again."

Ryan remained crouched, his thigh muscles screaming
with pain. He gritted his teeth as he heard something being
dragged close to the shaft opening. Then a bulky dark ob-
ject was shoved through. Petra. He heard her body strike

stone farther down. Then, finally, the splash. Bastards, he thought, his mind seething with rage. Bastards. I'll kill every one of you.

If he managed to survive. As footsteps faded away, he slowly turned. His thigh muscles were cramping badly. If they cramped enough, he would fall. As Tetsuo had said, he would join Petra.

It was easier than he'd expected. The ledge did widen out, and within minutes he was able to stand erect, groping along a damp wall, in inky blackness, feeling carefully with his feet before each movement, making sure he did not step off into space.

So damned dark. But there! A glimmer of light ahead. He moved on. The light grew stronger. It was coming from a ragged opening about a yard across, bright enough now so that Ryan could see where he was stepping.

Reaching the opening, Ryan looked inside. A room. A glimpse of a heavy bench, just a corner of it. And then he knew where he was. He was looking right into the room where they were assembling the bomb.

Yes, when he'd been in the room earlier with Tetsuo, he'd noticed a ragged opening toward the back wall, an obviously unfinished area. The room was not neatly plastered like Fuad's lab. No doubt they'd been forced to abandon Fuad's lab after the radiation leaks and do their final assembly in makeshift quarters. Ryan was right outside those quarters.

He could not see much of the room; the opening was too deep, almost a horizontal shaft, running from where he was crouched right on through the wall. He caught glimpses of people moving around. At least two of them. Heard tools being used. Finally, a man said, in accented English, "You better get out of here. I'm going to start with the plastique now. If there's an accident . . ."

The sound of the door opening, then closing. The slow breathing of a man, growing more forced. Then the sound of the door opening again. Tetsuo's voice, saying, "When will you be finished?"

A muttered curse from the man. Then a grudging reply, "It's going slowly. I'm tired; I haven't slept for two days. See? My hands are shaking. I should rest. I should get some sleep."

"But ... we sail in the morning!"

Tetsuo's voice was querulous; she sounded as if she was beginning to lose her usual icy control. The man's voice, when he answered, was just as querulous. "And what happens?" he demanded, "if, when I start rigging the blasting caps, I'm so tired that I make a mistake? What if the whole thing goes off? Will that speed up our sailing?"

Silence. Then Tetsuo's grudging reply. "You're right. Get some rest. I'll have someone wake you in a few hours. Can you still finish by late morning?"

"I think so," the man said, obviously relieved. "Wake me around three or four."

The shuffle of feet, followed by the sound of the door opening again, then closing. The sound of that heavy padlock outside being slammed through the hasp. A click as it was locked. Even so, Ryan waited for another fifteen minutes before he finally started to work his way through the narrow opening. In a little more than a minute he was standing inside the workroom. Now ... if no one made periodic checks ... But why should they? The room was locked from the outside.

The bomb sat on the tabletop. The stainless steel hemispheres had been joined together. The whole bottom half of the resulting sphere already wore a thick coating of plastic explosive.

Ryan sat down on a chair, facing the bomb. The rest of it would eventually be covered with plastique, then they would place detonators all over it, evenly spaced, wired in parallel, so that they would go off simultaneously. That much he understood. The plutonium inside the sphere would be compressed by the inward pressure of the explosion. An implosion. Already at almost critical mass—mass, not weight, that was what counted—the compression would complete that critical mass. Then, boom! A very big boom.

Plutonium was an unstable element. Ryan had learned that much in school, years before. There was always some kind of reaction going on, protons, neutrons, electrons, flying around, knocking apart an occasional atom. Most of those wandering particles get lose in the vast spaces between the atoms. But, when there are enough of those atoms packed together in a close enough space, then more and more particles start hitting targets, smashing apart atoms, creating new particles, which in turn blast away at other atoms. Instead of slow atomic decay, the entire process mushrooms at the speed of light, all that energy being released in an instant. An atomic explosion. Heat. Light. Blast. Death. Tetsuo's dream of mass terror.

But here Ryan was, with her bomb. He thought of stealing it, of spiriting it away, maybe dropping it down that damned shaft. But then they'd only find it, follow it by the radiation it gave off.

No ... stealing it would gain nothing. Sabotaging it would only slow them down. Unless ... unless they were not able to detect the sabotage.

Ryan leaned forward, studying the bomb. With the outside only half coated with plastique, he could see where the two halves of the sphere had been joined. By a steel band that was bolted together.

And what could be bolted together could be taken apart. Particularly with so many tools lying around. Ryan set to work immediately. He worked clumsily at first; his fingertips were bloody from hanging on to the ledge, his nails were broken, but within ten minutes he had the band off. The hemispheres came apart stickily; he had to pry a little. Finally, as the two halves popped free, he could see the reason for that stickiness. The thick layer of paraffin lining the inside was clinging to the plutonium. There it was. A dull ball of metal, lying in its lethal nest, only inches away from Ryan's fingers.

He jerked his hands away, then controlled himself. What

had Tetsuo said? That metallic plutonium was relatively safe to handle?

That lead foil he'd seen during his previous visit, where the hell was it? He got up, began searching the room. He found a large quantity of it lying half hidden in a dimly lit corner. He picked up several sheets, laid them on the tabletop. He started to pick up the bottom hemisphere, in which the ball of plutonium nestled. Heavy. Very heavy. But then, wasn't plutonium the heaviest, or one of the heaviest, of all the elements? Heavier than lead, or even gold?

Tipping the hemisphere, careful not to damage the layer of plastique too much, Ryan finally managed to roll the plutonium out onto the sheets of lead foil. He had to use one hand to pry the plutonium loose from its bed of paraffin. His skin crawled at the slick feel of the deadly metal.

He quickly rolled the plutonium up in the lead foil. Now, perhaps it would really be safe to handle. One last step remained . . . to close up the sphere again. They'd never know. . . .

Stupid thinking. The weight. They'd be able to tell by the weight, or lack of it. Ryan got up, went over to the corner where he'd found the lead foil. There were stacks of it. He picked up several sheets, began to ball them together, then added more sheets, wrapping them around and around his ever-growing ball of foil. Finally, he had enough to jam inside the hemisphere, packed tightly into the space the plutonium had previously occupied.

He quickly put the sphere back together, tightening down the bolts snugly. Now the bomb looked just like it had when he'd come through the wall. The weight would be a little less, of course, since lead weighed less than plutonium. He could only hope they would not notice.

The plutonium. He would have to get it out of here. There was a pile of junk way back in a corner; it looked as if this area had been some kind of storeroom before being pressed into action as an atomic bomb factory. Among the junk he found a wicker basket, a *cesta,* the kind the islanders used to do their shopping, a deep wicker pocket with carrying ropes to loop over your shoulder.

He rolled the plutonium into the basket, then hefted the carrying ropes onto his shoulder. It was a heavy load, with all that lead wrapped around the plutonium, but manageable.

Before he headed back toward the narrow opening in the wall, Ryan checked the area to make certain he had left no sign of his activities. He had, of course; there was a lot of lead foil missing. He put down the *cesta,* then went back to the workbench, where he smoothed out, as best he could, the plastique that coated the lower half of the sphere. Then he backed away, looking at the bomb. As Kranek had said, it was a rather crude, simple design. Would it actually have worked? Ryan had his doubts. But one thing was certain . . . with its plutonium core missing, it definitely would not work now.

It was a struggle getting the *cesta* through the opening without dumping out the plutonium, but eventually Ryan managed. He slipped through into the darkness beyond, wondering if he'd really pulled it off. If they'd fail to discover that their bomb no longer had its plutonium heart.

He could only hope. Hope and wait.

25

Once Ryan's eyes had grown accustomed to the dark, he discovered a flat, open area near the fissure that led into the bomb room. Here he could rest. And observe. From time to time he crawled close to the fissure, to peer inside. He could see only part of the room, but that part contained most of the bench on which the bomb rested.

He fell asleep. Later, he was not sure at first how much later, noises woke him ... the banging open of a door, loud conversation. Giving his head a moment to clear, he crawled toward his vantage point. The man who had been working on the bomb earlier, the one who had demanded rest, was back, with his assistant. Over the next hour Ryan watched them pack more plastique onto the stainless steel sphere. Ryan held his breath, wondering if they would detect his tampering, become aware of the sphere's lighter weight.

They did not. He let out a soft sigh of relief when the steel was completely covered. Then the two men began inserting the detonators, one by one, until the sphere, now a muddy brown color, was covered with a hedgehog of detonators.

The men slowly, carefully began wiring the detonators

together, so that they would all receive the same electrical charge at the same instant. Ryan crawled back out of sight; he preferred keeping his distance. One mistake and the detonators might go off. It would take only one of them to set off the plastique. Of course, that would not result in an atomic explosion, not with the plutonium now in his possession, but it would nevertheless be a very big bang. Enough to wreck the workshop and blow debris in through his spy hole. The two men doing the delicate work must be sweating a great deal more than he was, knowing that death was one slight fumble away. No wonder the man building the bomb had wanted to rest.

Hours later, Ryan, napping, heard the door opening again, then the sound of many voices. He crawled back to the spy hole. A large metal box, trailing electrical cables, was being wheeled into the room. He watched as the bomb was lowered into a cradle inside the box. Then the same two men began connecting the wires leading from the detonators to the electrical cables.

Ryan knew he was looking at the bomb's control box. It undoubtedly contained some kind of timing device to detonate the bomb when it had reached its target. Perhaps it also contained hidden booby traps, to set the bomb off if anyone tried to disarm it once the timing device was set. It was still a somewhat crude device, but one that might have worked.

He crawled back to his hiding place. He did not intend to fall asleep, but he did. When he finally awoke, he realized that something had made him wake up. Perhaps a sound. No, just the opposite. Lack of sound. He crawled back to his spy hole, peered cautiously into the room.

It was empty. No technicians, no bomb. The lights were still on, but they seemed dimmer than before, then they suddenly went out. Ryan was aware that a background noise, one that he had barely noticed before, the steady sound of the electrical generating system, had ceased.

They must be getting ready to pull out. They were finished with this cave complex. They had their bomb . . . so they thought.

Ryan let an hour pass. The darkness inside the room was total, but a little light filtered into his hiding place from outside, through small fissures in the cliff face. It must be daylight. Finally, after hearing nothing at all moving, Ryan slipped through the crack in the cave wall into the bomb room. He always carried a small lighter in his pocket, one of the disposable kind. He flicked it on. Using its dim light, he began to search the room. While he'd been sabotaging the bomb, he'd noticed a flashlight sitting on a rough shelf back in a corner. It was still there. And it worked. The batteries were not strong, but they gave enough light so that he could see where he was going.

To his relief, the door into the main passageway had not been locked. He turned off the flashlight, then stepped out cautiously into total blackness, total lack of sound. They must have pulled out completely.

He hesitated, wondering if he should go back for the plutonium; it was still inside the *cesta,* lying deep within the cave complex. He decided to leave it there, hidden as well as it could ever be hidden.

Turning the flashlight back on, he walked quickly down the passageway. When he passed the gaping hole in the cave wall, the opening of the shaft where they'd thrown Petra's body, he forced himself to look away, blanking out his mind, trying not to think of her somewhere down there, submerged in dark water, sharing that darkness with radioactive bodies. Sea creatures must already be feeding off her. If only . . .

Ryan shook his head angrily, walking on. The passageway grew narrower. Suddenly, there was a door ahead. A large metal door. He turned off the light, pressed down on the large lever that latched the door. It swung open quietly on well-oiled hinges. To his surprise, light lay ahead. He was looking into a room dimly lit by natural light. He stepped through the doorway, closing it silently behind him. Crossing the room, he found himself looking into another room. A shaft of sunlight was flooding in through a window. Moving to the window, he looked out. A quick study of the terrain convinced him that he was in the house at the base of the hill, where he'd seen the guard on his first search of the area. The house where they'd captured Petra.

No sign of any guards now. Ryan headed toward a door, stepped outside, kept moving quickly, until he was in the cover of some large boulders. Still no sign of anyone. They definitely were gone.

He immediately set out for the cove sheltering his boat. When he reached the bluff above the cove, he saw, far out at sea, almost lost in a light haze, the sails of a large schooner. Tetsuo's boat. They were already under way. He had to get moving. But it took Ryan longer than he had expected to work his way down the cliff trail to his boat. He nearly fell into the water when he jumped aboard from the big rock. Tired. So damned tired.

Going below was painful. Too many reminders of Petra. A piece of her clothing. The remains of her dinner. Her last dinner. "I'll get them for you, Petra," he murmured. "I'll get every last one of them."

He fell onto the bunk, tried to think what he must do next. Tired. Too damned tired. He was asleep within seconds.

It was late afternoon when Ryan awakened. He quickly took off his filthy, tattered clothing, then, going on deck, he dove into the water. He wanted to be clean, wanted to wash away from his body the foul, radioactive atmosphere of the caves. He shuddered when he thought of Fuad. Wondered if Tetsuo had thrown his body down the shaft before she abandoned the cave complex. Shuddered, also, as he remembered the greasy feel of the plutonium against his skin. He scrubbed himself with salt water until his skin hurt.

Climbing back aboard, hopeful that he'd washed any clinging bits of plutonium from his body and hair, Ryan let the sun dry him. Then he went below again, to rub antiseptics and antibiotic cream into every cut that he could find, no matter how small.

Time for action. He dressed quickly. Moving into the

cockpit, he started the auxiliary, then pulled up his mooring lines. Within minutes he was heading out of the cove, into the open sea. As soon as he had passed the headland, he became aware of a light breeze, so he set the sails. Once they were drawing well, he steered onto the course that would take him toward the rendezvous.

During the night he set the automatic pilot, a rather simple device that he did not completely trust. He catnapped for several hours, waking up from time to time to scan the horizon ahead for the lights of passing traffic. The wind died away before dawn. When the sun rose, he started the auxiliary again.

Too slow. He would not make the rendezvous in time. He went below, then coded and sent another message, asking for a closer rendezvous.

The day dragged on. Would Tetsuo and her crew have reached some kind of landfall by now? Hidden the bomb somewhere? But that made no sense. From what Ryan had overheard, they planned to take the boat into an American harbor, with the bomb aboard, set the timer, and then abandon the boat. He could imagine Tetsuo and her crew tying up at a Potomac dock within killing distance of the White House, of Congress. Tetsuo sitting miles away, watching the mushroom cloud rise over Washington.

It was late afternoon when Ryan saw the distant outline of ships on the horizon. He had wondered what kind of backup Central planned to provide, but his wondering had not prepared him for the reality. An entire damned attack carrier squadron was bearing down on him.

He got onto the radio, this time broadcasting in the clear. A crisp military voice responded. Ryan lowered his sails, watching as the carrier altered course, heading straight toward him. An attack carrier is smaller than a regular carrier, but it still towered over his little boat like a metal mountain. He cringed as the carrier's massive gray steel side came nearer and nearer. The huge ship was almost dead in the water now. Ryan started up his auxiliary, then nudged his boat closer. A large rectangular port opened in the steel cliff above him. He saw sailors peering down at him, with an officer off to one side. "Are you Mr. Ryan?" the officer called down.

"Yeah. Hey, can you hoist my boat aboard?"

The officer stepped back, began speaking into a telephone. A few minutes later Ryan saw movement on deck, far above. The gantry of a small crane came into sight, hanging over the drop. A boat was lowered bearing several men. They swarmed aboard Ryan's little boat. With calm efficiency, barely paying attention to Ryan, they passed broad straps beneath the hull, finally fastening them to a cable. By then Ryan had transferred to the other boat. He watched as the cable tightened. His boat rose up out of the sea, dripping water. He noticed that the bottom was quite clean. Then his boat disappeared over the edge of the carrier's flight deck.

A small port opened up lower in the carrier's side, closer to the water. A ladder was lowered, and a moment later Ryan was aboard. This was not his first time aboard an attack carrier, but he was still impressed as he was led through huge steel compartments designed to hold hundreds of marines, armed, ready to land. For the moment there were just a few marines in sight, playing basketball. They glanced curiously at Ryan and his escorts.

A young lieutenant was Ryan's guide. He ushered him into an elevator. They shot upward, coming out, finally, onto a passageway near the bridge. Ryan took a moment to look out over the broad flat expanse of the flight deck. It was packed with helicopters, the carrier's main reason for existence. There were large troop-carrying helicopters capable of landing, from the air, a marine attack force, and smaller, leaner attack helicopters, with their deadly loads of missiles and bombs. Ryan was aware that he was standing above the decks of a war machine of the most amazing destructive power. Power enough to destroy a small city. Power to land large bodies of infantry, complete with air support. Thinking of Tetsuo Hidaka's wooden schooner, he decided Central's response was definitely overkill. Not that he was complaining.

"This way, sir," the lieutenant said. He led Ryan onto the bridge. From here, he had an even better view out over the flight deck. Now he noticed his boat being lowered into a large metal cradle. He turned away from the view, looked around him. The bridge's interior was painted the usual navy gray. There was nothing luxurious inside, just lots of heavy steel plates, angular instruments, sharp edges. Hell, the bridge was actually a little cramped. There were quite a few people present, probably more than usual. Ryan's eyes immediately went to the captain. He was a full captain, the eagles easy to spot on the collar of his neatly pressed khaki uniform. "Mr. Ryan?" the captain asked, holding out his hand.

Ryan extended his own hand. The captain's handshake was firm, warm. "I've been waiting days for this meeting," the captain said.

"Days?" Ryan asked, surprised. "You mean, this whole task force has been waiting just for me?"

"Well . . ." The captain looked nervously around him, then said, in a much lower voice, "Considering what we're dealing with. I mean, the ramifications, if that bunch of nuts is able to . . ."

Coded words. Apparently the captain was one of the few who knew what was actually at stake. Which was as it should be. The captain was turning now, looking toward another man. Ryan had already noticed him, and vaguely wondered what the hell he was doing here. A civilian. Actually wearing a suit. A small man, thin to the point of being scrawny, with a smooth, empty face. Nothing there at all. The original nerd. "Isn't that right, Mr. Francis?" the captain was saying to the little man.

The little man stepped forward. "That's correct, Captain. Considering what's at stake. . . ."

Ryan's mouth dropped open. No mistaking the odd,

grating quality of that voice. The coldness of it. Ryan suddenly laughed. "Well I'll be damned," he said when he'd finally gotten his voice back under control. "You took my advice. You finally left your hole."

26

Central's mouth formed into a small pout of distaste. "Games again, Ryan?"

Then, as if suddenly aware of the company around them, Central let his voice trail away. He drew himself up to his full height, which only made him appear all that much smaller next to Ryan. "I assume you found it," he said guardedly. He glanced around the bridge. Junior officers were looking out through the great windows, their expressions studiously neutral. A seaman was at the wheel. Of course, they all wondered what these two civilians were doing aboard their ship. Only the captain was looking directly at Ryan and Central, but Central's eyes still looked nervously around the bridge. "Found the . . ."

"Yes," Ryan replied laconically.

"And did they . . . ?" Central asked. "Were they successful?"

"Uh-huh. They made one. As far as I could determine, just one."

"And it's, uh . . . ?"

"Aboard a schooner. That sailed from Minorca yesterday morning. Probably heading toward the Atlantic."

"Damn!" Central said petulantly. "Why did it take you so long . . . ?"

His eyes narrowed. "I had reports of some strange happenings on Majorca. Something about a woman being involved. Were you up to your old tricks again, Ryan? Wasting time with some cunt?"

Petra. To hear her described in such a way. And by Central. . . .

Ryan felt something click inside him. He was uncertain whether it was something clicking on or clicking off. But a definite click. "Now you know the score," Ryan said coldly to Central. "What are you going to do about it?"

Central suddenly looked worried. "I . . . don't know." He looked sharply at Ryan. "You say it's aboard a boat?"

The captain moved closer. He appeared nervous. "I think we should go to my day cabin," he said, glancing at the officers and men half surrounding them. He led the way to a small cabin next to the bridge. When he'd closed the door there was barely enough room for the three of them. The captain sat on his own bunk. Central was seated opposite Ryan. "Now," Central said acidly. "I want you to tell me every damned thing that's happened."

So Ryan told him. About the schooner, the cave complex. He even described the bomb, and the large metal box that housed it. Central reached the same conclusion as Ryan . . . that the bomb was probably booby trapped. "We'll have to get them to surrender," Central said worriedly. "Or sink them far out at sea."

Ryan nodded. He had not mentioned that he had removed the plutonium from the bomb, nor did he intend to do so. At least, not yet. He did not know why he held back; it was probably all part of that soundless internal click. Sitting here, looking across at Central, looking at this slimy little man, he remembered the trail of blood that had characterized the mission: Cory, gutted; Kranek, shot to pieces; Petra, with Tsunogi's sword thrust through her chest; even Heller . . . no, he couldn't just turn the whole thing over to Central.

The captain left them alone; he was eager to get back to the bridge, to set in motion the hunt for Tetsuo Hidaka's schooner. Ryan and Central remained in the day cabin, looking steadily at one another. "Ryan," Central finally murmured. "I smell a rat. I know that look in your eye. . . ."

Ryan abruptly stood up, turned toward the doorway. "Fuck off, Central. I found what you were looking for. And it cost. Cost one hell of a lot more than someone like you could ever imagine."

Central smiled. "Oh, so that's it? The human cost. You always were a sucker for that kind of thing. You never could get it through your head that it's results that count. We're in a war, Ryan. A war against . . ."

But Ryan was already out the door, headed back toward the bridge. Central followed, eager to question Ryan further, but once again, with so many people present, they could not talk openly. Which was fine with Ryan. Every time he looked at Central, his flesh crawled.

The hunt for the schooner claimed everyone's attention. Not much could be done that night; it was already almost dark. Ryan was shown to a cabin, which he shared with a young lieutenant. He did not know where Central was staying. The lieutenant tried to engage Ryan in conversation. He was a good-natured young man, but Ryan, exhausted, wondering what game he was playing with Central, simply knowing that it was always necessary to play some kind of game with the bastard just to keep him away from your throat, turned over and went to sleep.

He was up on the bridge at dawn. The captain had arrived before him. "We're steaming toward Gibraltar," the captain said. "You mentioned that you thought they would head for the Atlantic. Surveillance aircraft are already airborne from Spanish bases. If that schooner's still at sea, we'll find it."

Ryan nodded. Well, maybe the schooner was at sea, maybe it wasn't. Maybe they'd offloaded their dud bomb already. Not that it would do them much good. But he

wanted them nailed. Now. Wanted *her* nailed. Tetsuo
Hidaka. Wanted her stepped on like a bug. Which should
be easy enough with all this military weight on her trail.

When Central finally walked onto the bridge, Ryan
sensed rather than saw him. He felt the hair rise at the
back of his neck. "You forgot to ask what they're going to
do with . . . what they made," Ryan said quietly.

Central was walking around in front of him. Both he
and the captain were looking intently at Ryan. "You
know?" Central finally asked.

Ryan, deadpan, answered with a single word. "Washington."

Both men paled. "Don't worry, Central," Ryan murmured. "That hole you live in will probably survive."

Now the stakes were clear to Central and the captain. Or
so they thought. The hunt continued. Except that the
weather wasn't cooperating. "Fog," the captain said to
Central. "The whole western end of the Med is socked in
with fog."

Indeed it was. The task force itself was now disappearing, ship by ship, into a thick white mist. Yet they plowed
on at undiminished speed, their navigational aids easily
seeing where a human eye could not.

It was night before the air search yielded results. An officer came up to the captain, showed him a map. The captain turned toward Ryan and Central. "We think we've
spotted him," he said. "Off the southern coast of Spain.
You were right, Mr. Ryan. He's heading for the Strait of
Gibraltar and the Atlantic."

"And Washington," Ryan added. "And it's a her, not a
him."

The captain looked at Ryan questioningly, but made no
comment other than, "We've told the planes to keep well
away, so that he . . . she isn't alerted. We should catch up
to them by morning."

Another night on board. Ryan had trouble sleeping. He
could sense the hull of the carrier knifing through the wa-

ter. Flank speed. The captain, knowing the stakes, was going full out. The next morning Ryan was on the bridge again at dawn. This time, so was Central. The captain was unexpectedly grim. "We think the boat's spotted one of our planes," he said. "They've suddenly changed course. They're heading toward the Spanish coast."

"My God!" Central burst out. "They have to be stopped before they get anywhere near a populated area. Can't you have your planes ... sink them? If they know they've been spotted, they may decide to set off the ... well, they might do it out of spite."

The captain looked slightly embarrassed. "Well ... we might have been able to do that a few hours ago. But it would be a little tricky right now." He cleared his throat. "You see, we came up on them during the night. We're only about a mile and a half away from the schooner. If they set off the ... Well, we'll go with them."

Ryan watched Central turn pale. Safe here on board, with all this military might wrapped around him like a huge suit of armor, he'd never had to consider personal danger. Now he was definitely considering it. Ryan watched him swallow nervously. "Well, my God, I don't see them," Central burst out.

But then he did. The carrier had been traveling through more fog. Now a patch cleared, giving them a glimpse of the schooner, indeed, just a mile and a half away. "Back off!" Central half screamed. "Back off!"

The captain immediately gave an order. Ryan could feel the heavy throbbing of the engines diminish. But it was too late. A signals officer walked onto the bridge. "Captain," he said. "We've started intercepting some pretty wild radio traffic. It's real close. We think it's coming from that schooner over there."

The captain nodded. "Put it on the bridge speaker."

A moment later they all heard it, a wild voice, ranting, shouting. Ryan immediately recognized it as Tetsuo Hidaka's voice. "The planes!" she was screaming. "Those boats! Take them away, or we'll blow you to pieces!"

"Is that . . . ?" Central started to ask.

"Yeah," Ryan replied laconically. "And she'll do it. She's a real nut case."

He meant it. He'd detected a note of wild strain in Tetsuo's voice. What a blow it must be for her to have come so far, and now to be cornered.

"What the hell?" Central muttered. "Captain . . . fall back a few miles. Then sink her."

The captain shook his head. "I know the authority you carry, Mr. Francis. I was fully informed. But this is still my ship, and we're just off the Spanish coast. By the time we drop back out of . . . lethal range, that schooner should be about half a mile off the city of Marbella. That's a tourist city, Mr. Francis. There are thousands, maybe hundreds of thousands of people in and around Marbella, from all over, even from the United States. I won't be responsible for incinerating them. It looks like . . . whoever that woman is, she has us in check."

"Captain," Central half shouted, his voice almost as shrill as Tetsuo Hidaka's, "I order you to . . ."

Ryan had been wondering what kind of clout Central carried. Obviously, considerable. Ryan was only half aware of the little man's words. He was listening to the radio again. To Tetsuo Hidaka. Her voice had lowered in pitch. Now she was talking in Japanese, half muttering, making hardly any sense at all. Obviously ready to slip right around the bend.

"Does anyone here speak Japanese?" Ryan suddenly asked.

There was a moment of surprised silence, then head-shakes.

"Well, I do," Ryan said. "And I think it might help if I talk to her in her own language. Listen to her. She's talking in Japanese now. Can it be arranged?"

Since no one had any better ideas, both Central and the captain nodded. A few seconds later, Ryan was speaking into a mike. "Hidaka," he said, his voice steady. "Tetsuo Hidaka. It's me. I've come back for you."

Dead silence from the speaker. Ryan wondered if he'd lost her. "Tsunogi sent me," he added.

"What?" Tetsuo blurted. The question came as a shocked gasp. "Who ... who are you?"

"It's me. Peters. Come back from the dead again, just as you said. When you were looking at my body, down at the bottom of the shaft."

"No!"

"Yes, Tetsuo. I've come to take you back with me. Into the shaft. To join Fuad. I've come to kill you. Come to eat your soul."

If she had screamed then, if she had begun to shout insults and threats, it might not have worked for Ryan, but instead Tetsuo began to mumble in a dead, expressionless voice. Ryan was unable to understand everything she said; a lot of it was gibberish, most of it having to do with hushed references to ghosts. Evil spirits. Ryan continued speaking during gaps in her ramblings, but she didn't seem to hear him. Of course, the others on the bridge, not speaking Japanese, had no way of telling that this was not a true dialogue.

Ryan turned to face Central and the captain. "She says she'll deal with me," he said. "And only me. Face-to-face. Which means this task force has to back off."

"But how can you ... ?" Central started to ask.

"A small boat," the captain said. "Will she accept a small boat? Like a motor torpedo boat?"

Ryan was relieved that the captain had suggested it himself, because it was just what he wanted. He definitely did not want Central to know what he planned to do. "Sure," he replied. "I think that's more or less what she had in mind. You see ... we've met. You might say that we've crossed swords. There's kind of ... a bond between us. An adversarial bond."

Ryan was wondering if he'd overdone it. No one said anything. By now, to placate Tetsuo Hidaka, the carrier had been turned around and was steaming away from the schooner. The captain gave an order. Five minutes later a young lieutenant came onto the bridge. "This is Lieutenant Davidson," the captain said to Ryan. "He's the commander of one of our MTBs."

The captain turned to Davidson. "Lieutenant, you'll be taking Mr. Ryan aboard your boat. I want you to obey any order he gives as if it came from me. As if it came from God Himself."

"Yes, sir," Davidson said. He glanced curiously at Ryan.

"Well," the captain said, turning to look out the bridge window again. "Get on with it."

Davidson started to turn. "If you'll come with me, sir," he said to Ryan.

"Wait a minute!"

Central had hold of Ryan's arm. "I don't think I like this. I don't trust you, Ryan. I think you have something up your sleeve. . . ."

Ryan looked down at Central's hand. Central hastily withdrew it. "If you're so fucking worried," Ryan said coldly, "why don't you come along? Just to make sure. Just to keep an eye on me."

Central paled. Everyone on the bridge saw his face blanch. Only Ryan and the captain knew what Central was actually thinking. Head straight toward a possible atomic explosion? Not likely. "But then," Ryan said mockingly, "you never were one to risk your skin, were you, Central? Even for a payoff as big as this one."

Central glared at Ryan. Looked around the bridge, watching as the others turned away from him. He spun back to face Ryan. "I'm going to call you on this one," Central hissed. "I'm coming with you. I'm going to watch every move you make. And so help me, if you screw up even a little bit . . ."

"Then get your ass in gear," Ryan snapped. He was already turning away to follow Lieutenant Davidson. He skipped down the ladder after the lieutenant, not bothering to check if Central was following.

Davidson took Ryan below, to the well deck. The captain must have called ahead; the deck was already being flooded. The long racy hull of a motor torpedo boat was beginning to float out of its cradle. "If you'll come aboard, sir," Davidson said.

The MTB was free of the cradle now. Crewmen were drawing it over toward a landing stage. The lieutenant jumped aboard. Ryan followed. "Wait! Wait for me!" he heard from behind him. He turned. It was Central, hesitating, until one of the crewmen offered him a hand, helped pull him aboard.

Lieutenant Davidson was already moving around the boat, checking that everything was in order. Ryan watched, assessing. He immediately noticed the atmosphere between Davidson and his men. Close. Fond respect from the men, fond leadership from Davidson. The proverbial tight little ship.

The water level inside the well deck now matched the outside water level. The great doors at the stern of the carrier began to open. Ryan heard the torpedo boat's huge diesels roar into life. Men rushed to their stations. Mooring lines were cast off. The doors were barely open when the boat shot forward, out into the open sea. Ryan saw Central stagger, almost lose his balance. Davidson, at the wheel, turned to face Ryan questioningly. "Head toward the schooner we've been shadowing," Ryan said to Davidson. He had to shout to be heard over the roar of the engines.

Davidson nodded, turned the boat in a tight arc, heading one hundred eighty degrees away from the carrier's course. Except for this one small boat, the entire task force was heading at flank speed away from the schooner, away from the Spanish coast. In the captain's mind, away from certain destruction.

The torpedo boat was skimming along over the water at a high rate of speed. Ryan felt good. It was exhilarating, feeling the wind against his face, the salt spray. He studied Davidson, saw that he felt good, too. Felt obvious pride in his little command. Ryan looked around the boat, noticed the gun mount forward. Twin fifty-caliber machine guns. He also noticed sailors loading ammunition belts into the breach of each gun. He glanced at Central. He hadn't noticed; he was staring down at the deck, his face rigid.

It was a while before the schooner came into view. The carrier squadron was well back on the horizon, pretty much out of range of any atomic explosion. The torpedo boat reached a fog bank. Davidson immediately cut his speed. The sound of the diesels diminished to a low growl. Davidson stared intently into the fog. A crewman was studying a radar screen. "There she is, sir," the crewman said quietly. "A blip about a mile away."

That had to be the schooner. Another five minutes, and suddenly they were out of the fog. Ryan tensed. Yes, there it was, less than a mile away now, Tetsuo Hidaka's schooner. A beautiful vessel . . . if you knew nothing of its intended mission, of the hatred and violence aboard it.

By now, they'd been spotted. Suddenly the radio burst into life. Tetsuo Hidaka's voice screaming, "Go back! Get that boat away from me!"

Ryan saw the look of surprise on Central's face. "But she . . . You said . . ."

Ryan had already picked up the mike, said in Japanese, "I'm coming for you, Tetsuo Hidaka. We're all coming for you. Me. Kranek. The Spanish girl. Yoshiro, the boy who died for you all those years ago. We're coming to kill you."

Ryan turned toward Davidson. "Full speed ahead, or however you say it. Straight toward the schooner."

Davidson nodded. The diesels began to roar again. The boat seemed to leap half out of the water. A huge white rooster tail rose up behind, with the stern sinking lower, the bow rising.

Tetsuo was screaming something over the radio, part in Japanese, part in English. It was hard to make out her meaning, although there was mention of bombs, of death.

Central could not help but be aware of Hidaka's tone of desperation. "Ryan!" he screamed. "What the hell do you think you're doing? My God, she'll set off the bomb! She'll kill us all!"

Ryan looked coldly at Central. "Shut the fuck up, little man."

Central turned toward Davidson. "Turn this boat around!" he screamed. "I order you to turn this boat around!"

Davidson continued to look straight ahead. "The captain told me to take my orders from Mr. Ryan. That's what I'm doing."

He turned toward Ryan, questioningly. Ryan nodded toward the schooner. "Carry on, Lieutenant," he said, wondering if he sounded sufficiently nautical.

They were less than half a mile from the schooner now. Ryan could see the Spanish mainland beyond it, only a mile away. See the garish smear of high-rise hotels along the waterfront. He could imagine the hordes of tourists. Imagine Tetsuo Hidaka willing to incinerate them all.

She was still ranting over the radio. "This is my last warning!" she screamed in English. "Turn around, or you're all dead! Everyone will be dead. I have a weapon with me, a power, that will kill even ghosts!"

"She's right!" Central screamed back, shoving his face close to Ryan's. "My God, what are you doing? You'll kill everybody!"

One of the sailors was standing on a small bridge, studying the schooner through binoculars. "Hey, Lieutenant!" he bawled out. "It looks to me like they're mounting some kind of gun amidships."

A short silence. "Looks like a light machine gun," the sailor continued. "Maybe thirty-caliber. They—"

Suddenly, the ping of bullets striking all around the bridge. The sailor cried out, staggered backward, fell onto the deck, his shoulder and chest spouting blood. Other sailors ducked for cover. Davidson stayed put at the wheel. He pointed toward a sailor, then toward the twin fifty gun mount. "No!" Ryan shouted. "I'll take the guns!"

Davidson started to say something, but Ryan was already sprinting forward. A sailor was there before him, slamming the bolts back, loading each gun. Ryan pushed him aside. He began to track the guns toward the schooner, then felt someone tugging at his arm. He turned. It was Central. The little man's face was wild with fear and anger. "Ryan!" he screamed. "You can't continue with this insanity! You know what you're forcing her to do!"

Ryan shoved Central away, and when the little man started to lurch back toward him, the sailor stepped in the way. The sailor's face showed anger. He looked back toward where his shipmates were working over the wounded sailor. "Give 'em hell, sir!" he shouted to Ryan.

Of course, the sailor knew nothing about the supposed bomb aboard the schooner. What he did know was that one of his shipmates had been wounded and machine gun fire was still coming from the schooner. Like Ryan, he was out for revenge.

The schooner was only three hundred yards away now. Thirty-caliber machine gun bullets were slamming against the steel guard that sheltered Ryan's position. He settled his hands onto the central bar that linked the triggers of the two guns. He pressed. The guns bucked and roared. Lines of tracers began to streak toward the schooner.

It was no contest ... twin fifties against a single thirty-caliber. Ryan's first burst was a little short. He adjusted his aim, and now his bullets began to strike the schooner. The torpedo boat was close enough for Ryan to see splinters flying aboard the schooner, whole chunks of wood tearing loose. He scythed the gunner away from the thirty-caliber gun, saw the man slammed backward, could even see the blood fly. He hosed the big fifty-caliber bullets all around the deck. He must have hit a stay. One of the huge sails began to fall.

Tetsuo Hidaka. Where the hell was she? He saw her, then, running along the deck. He traversed the gun after her, saw his bullets hitting right behind Tetsuo. She was running faster than he could traverse. He was shooting the schooner apart behind her. A deckhouse scattered into pieces.

Someone was firing the thirty again; bullets were slamming into the torpedo boat. Ryan corrected his aim, opened up on the gunner, this time a long burst. He saw the gunner killed, more importantly, saw the thirty-caliber gun knocked off its base, out of action.

Back to Hidaka. Yeah, there she was, halted now, right above an open vertical hatchway. The two vessels were now less than a hundred yards apart. Ryan could see Tetsuo's mouth moving, knew she was screaming something toward the torpedo boat. Central saw her, too. "For God's sake, Ryan!" he screamed. "She's warning you for the last time! Stop this madness!"

Ryan traversed the fifties back toward Tetsuo, pressed the trigger bar. Huge chunks of the schooner began to fill the air as he zeroed in on her. Yet, Tetsuo stayed on her feet; he was missing. Then, with one last scream, one last shake of her fist toward the torpedo boat, Tetsuo disappeared down into the hatchway.

Ryan fired a final burst. The schooner was half wrecked by now. "My God!" he heard Central scream. "She's going to do it! She's going to set off the bomb!"

Ryan spun toward Davidson, shouted over his shoulder. "Get us the hell out of here, Lieutenant!"

The boat turned in a tight circle that took it to within thirty yards of the schooner. "It's no use!" Central screamed. "We'll never get far enough away! We'll be vaporized!"

Ryan grinned at Central. "Well, we all gotta go sometime."

"You son of a bitch!" Central screamed, his face a mask of terror. "You did this to us!"

Ryan looked back over the torpedo boat's stern. They were almost a hundred yards away now. Suddenly, the schooner seemed to erupt. Flame and debris shot into the air as the plastic explosive coating the bomb ignited. Ryan heard Central's despairing scream. Ryan continued to watch, saw that the schooner, what was left of it, had split in half. "Die, you fucking bitch," he murmured. Finally, he had to duck under cover. Debris was raining down. Small chunks banged against the torpedo boat's deck.

Then, comparative silence, only the roar of the torpedo boat's diesels, which quickly diminished as Lieutenant Davidson cut back on the throttles. "Jesus H. Christ," the lieutenant burst out, staring back at the schooner. The two halves were settling quickly, about to take their final dive. "What the hell did they have aboard that tub anyhow?"

"You don't want to know, Lieutenant," Ryan replied. He turned, wondering where the hell Central had disappeared to. Then he saw him. The little man was lying on the deck behind the gun mount, curled into a tight ball, his face screwed up into a mask of terror.

Then Central realized that he was still alive. His eyes slowly opened. He saw Ryan grinning down at him, obviously also alive. He glanced around, saw that he was still aboard the torpedo boat, and that it was still in one piece. He staggered to his feet, looked over the stern, saw the bow of the schooner slide beneath the water. He spun around to face Ryan. "What?" he stammered. "What . . . ?"

"Well gosh, Central," Ryan replied, as deadpan as possible, hardly able to keep the amusement out of his voice. "There may have been, just *may* have been, one or two little things I kinda forgot to tell you."

27

They stood together in uneasy silence halfway up the carrier's island, the big man and the small man, watching as the little sailboat was lowered over the side into the water. It was Ryan who finally broke the silence. "I keep the boat, then. Free and clear."

Central nodded, just a brief jerk of his head. Kept looking ahead, rather than at Ryan.

"And the money. Don't fuck with my money, Central. The original fifty thousand in my Swiss bank account. Another fifty as a bonus. For all my good work."

"You'll have your money, Ryan. And your toy boat."

Central muttered something under his breath. Ryan looked at him sharply. "What?" he demanded.

Central turned, glared at him. "I said, 'And your lousy life, too.' "

Ryan looked the little man straight in the eye. "Right, Central. You don't want to fuck with me. You don't ever want to fuck with me."

They both looked forward again. Ryan's boat was now in the water. Sailors, working from a launch alongside, were removing canvas slings from the hull. "I'd better get below," Ryan said.

He turned to face Central. "What the hell are you bitching about?" he asked in a slightly bantering tone. "You're a hero, Central . . . the man who put his own neck on the line, the man who blew Tetsuo Hidaka and her homicidal crazies right out of the water. Literally out of the water. The man who will personally recover the stolen plutonium. Be grateful, Central. That ought to be worth one hell of a budget increase."

"You tricked me, Ryan." But this time Central's tone was somewhat lighter. Ryan could tell that the little man did indeed enjoy his new role as a physical hero. Of course, if Ryan ever told anyone back in Washington how the rotten little bastard had cowered on the deck of the torpedo boat, whimpering and howling in terror during the final charge toward Tetsuo Hidaka's schooner, that image might change. No reason for that to happen, though. Hell, in time Central would probably even forget all about that part of it and totally accept himself as a hero.

What the hell did it matter? Ryan, with that much of a club to hold over Central, had gotten what he wanted . . . title to the boat, plus an extra fifty thousand dollars. And his freedom from Central. No more working for the little creep.

Ryan led the way down through the interior of the ship. The lower port had been opened. Ryan could see his boat bobbing gently in the water a few feet below. *His* boat. Lieutenant Davidson stood to one side of the port, smiling. "Nice little sloop," he said to Ryan.

Ryan nodded, smiling back. "Thanks. I think so, too."

"My crewman's going to be all right," Davidson said. "He'll be in the hospital for a while, but all right."

"Glad to hear it."

"Good work with the guns," Davidson continued. "Chewed the hell out of that schooner. A shame it had to be done. A beautiful boat."

"Yeah." Ryan held out his hand, shook Davidson's, then

stepped out onto the ladder and jumped down onto the deck of his boat.

He was busy for the next few minutes, unshipping the tiller, then starting the auxiliary. When he looked back toward the port, Davidson was smiling down at him. And damned if Central wasn't smiling, too. But, while Davidson's smile cheered Ryan, Central's did not. It was a cold, gloating smile. "You'll be back, Ryan," Central said in that creepy voice. "The money won't last forever. You'll be back, begging."

"Don't count on it, Central."

The sailors on the staging had already untied the mooring lines. Ryan caught them as they were tossed aboard, then quickly secured them in place. He slipped the engine into gear, and a moment later his boat was moving away from the carrier, away from the vast gray steel cliff that towered above. One last glance at Davidson, waving cheerfully. And at Central, standing unmoving, a puny figure, unless you were aware of the power he represented. "Good-bye, you little shit," Ryan murmured. He turned his eyes away from the carrier, preferring to look out over the blue vastness of the Mediterranean.

Once Ryan's boat was out of the carrier's lee, a wind sprang up. He cut the auxiliary, set the sails. By the time he had everything arranged to his satisfaction, and was once again seated in the cockpit, hand on the tiller, he was far from the warships. The task force had gotten under way. The port where Davidson and Central had been standing was closed, the two men out of sight.

Ryan leaned back against the hull. God, this felt good. Out on his own, free. Finally, genuinely free. No mission hanging over his head. No financial worries. Well, not for a while. Nothing to do but . . . just sit here on his ass and sail.

An hour later, a thought occurred to Ryan. Just where the hell was he headed? What did he intend to do? What plans should he be making? Hell, did he even *need* any plans?

There was Inge, of course. Maybe he should send for Inge. No ... she was married to her job, could never get away for long enough to make it worthwhile. Besides, it was too soon after ...

Petra. Thinking about her hurt. Hurt a lot. All that ... new joy in her life. Lost. Taken from her. How much better he'd feel if she were here with him now, on his little boat. No, *their* little boat.

But she wasn't here. Could never be here. Time to shut off that line of thinking; it could only cause pain. At least she'd be taken care of. When he'd told Central where the plutonium was hidden, he'd also told him about the place where Petra's body lay. Made Central promise that Petra would be found and buried wherever Son Feliu buried its people.

The sea stretched on ahead. He checked the compass. He was heading east. Toward Majorca. A beautiful place. Perhaps someday he would go there again, get to know it in a different way. But not now. Majorca was way too hot for him, would be for a long time.

Ibiza. He wondered how Glen was doing, what hustle he was into now. No, Ibiza, or any part of Spain, was out of the question. What the hell. There were plenty of other places. Italy lay ahead. Far ahead, past the Balearic Islands. And to the north, southern France.

Maybe he'd head north, then coast along the French and Italian rivieras. He had an image of lovely little Mediterranean harbors with castle-crowned hills rising inland. Small cafés, down by the water, only yards from his boat. Old cities, seeping history, with no one there for him to kill. Without his having to worry if anyone was there to kill him. No moral dirt to deal with. Free at last. Lord God Almighty, free at last!

So why, then, he wondered, as his lovely little boat sailed over this beautiful sea, headed toward marvelous treasures, did he feel so damned empty?